Teen
Killers
Club

Teen
Killers
Club

A Novel

LILY SPARKS

**CROOKED
LANE**

NEW YORK

Published in the United States by Crooked Lane Books, an imprint of The Quick Brown Fox & Company LLC.

Crooked Lane Books and its logo are trademarks of The Quick Brown Fox & Company LLC.

Library of Congress Catalog-in-Publication data available upon request.

ISBN (hardcover): 978-1-64385-229-4
ISBN (ebook): 978-1-64385-230-0

Cover illustration by Adams Carvalho

Printed in the United States.

www.crookedlanebooks.com

Crooked Lane Books
34 West 27th St., 10th Floor
New York, NY 10001

First Edition: November 2020

10 9 8 7 6 5 4 3 2 1

Dedicated to my sister Allison,
who said this was her favorite book
from the first draft,
&
every high schooler who has ever spent lunch
hiding in the library

Chapter One
The Girl from Hell

~

Prison is a lot like high school. The same institutional beige hallways, the same long hours of sitting in forced silence, and the same rigid social pyramid of cliques upon which your life depends. In both prison and high school, I've been a total loner.

Boarding the prison bus this morning feels uncannily like getting on my school bus almost two years before. There's the same sudden silence from the girls already cuffed in, and their eyes follow me in the same sidelong glances as I shuffle down the aisle to the same place I sat on my old route: the way, way back.

Of course, we're all in orange and beige jumpsuits, but you wear uniforms in high school too. I wore black jeans with the same thrift store leather jacket every day back then, layered my neck with thin black chokers and cheap silver chains, circled my eyes all the way around with black lines like they were key words in a poem, and kept my hair a violent blue. It's now faded to the color of old jeans, with my roots grown out almost to my eyebrows.

What's missing is the laughter. Starting freshman year, whenever I'd pass by a knot of people, there would be a sickening three-count of mounting tension and then the snickers would burst out behind me. Even Rose, when she was with her other friends, would laugh.

Now no one laughs. They're too scared.

It turns out being feared is lonelier than being ignored. It's ironic, all the effort I spent trying to look "scary" in high school when now I'd give anything to sit across from someone whose skin didn't crawl at the sight of me, Signal Deere, "The Girl From Hell."

"Assistance up front! We need an escort!" the driver calls to Officer Heather, who's clipping my handcuffs to the latch on my seat belt. She swears softly under her breath and cinches my restraints with a final tug before turning down the aisle.

Correctional officers are, by the way, worse than even the worst high school teacher. Imagine the bossiest, pettiest kid in your class being put in charge for a day. That's a correctional officer. Or at least that's how they are at Bellwood Oregon State Juvenile Penitentiary, the beige and concrete labyrinth I finally got out from under this morning.

When Officer Heather lands at the bus door, her expression sours, her voice rising loud enough for me to catch ". . . *not* in my job description!" about her latest charge, a figure hidden from my view by four massive male security guards.

"Is that NOBODY?!" one of the girls whispers a few rows ahead.

"What? Nobody's not real, she's like the bogeyman."

"Yuh huh, look at her! With the ski mask and everything!"

"I'm not riding on a bus with Nobody! They can't just stick her in with Gen Pop, that freak is *dangerous*—"

Silence falls abruptly as Officer Heather leads Nobody, who is maybe six feet tall, down the aisle by her cuffs. Like the rest of them, I've heard the stories, and they're all looking true: she is unnervingly gaunt and lanky, and her long pale arms are crisscrossed with ugly, shiny red burn scars.

"I'll put you with Blue," Heather says for the benefit of the whole bus, which is on the edge of mutiny at this apparition from prison folklore. "You two *Class As* can chat."

The completely silent bus erupts into hissed whispers at this:

"Class A?!!"

"Blue hair is a Class A?!"

"They can't be in here with us!"

Correctional officers are *never* supposed to reveal our Wylie-Stanton Index Classification. If other inmates find out you're a Class A, it's a death sentence. Though I've been "lucky" enough to spend most of my incarceration in a single concrete cell in Diagnostics, in my few brushes with General Pop I've kept my head diligently down. But with these words, my cover is blown.

Although where we're going, I guess it won't matter.

Nobody folds her tall frame into the brown vinyl bench beside me, her broad shoulders pressed against mine, so close I can see the loose threads blown by the slow, ragged breath through the hole cut in her ski mask. Officer Heather's hands shake as she fastens her in.

And then, in a sly gesture as she turns to go, Officer Heather plucks off Nobody's ski mask.

Nobody rockets forward, howling, shaking her bleached blonde hair over her face, which is a blur of hot pink in my peripheral vision, and the entire bus gasps as one.

"What are you doing?! Give it back!!" I yell.

"No nonregulation clothing during transfer!" Officer Heather barks, fleeing up front.

Nobody whimpers like a kicked dog as she strains to cover whatever is left of her face with her scarred hands, but her cuffs are too short and she can't reach. I look away and see the man who's just boarded the bus, the same man who met me in a holding cell in the bowels of Bellwood this morning. *"DAVE!"* I scream to be heard over the wild girl beside me. "Dave, can't she keep her hat?!"

Dave frowns under his unmarked baseball cap. He looks from Nobody to Officer Heather and leans toward her, consulting.

The girls in front of us take advantage of the moment, twisting around in their seats to gawk.

I lean forward and hiss: *"Turn back around. Right. Now."*

And here is the real difference between prison and high school, here is the difference between being Signal Deere, loner goth, and Signal Deere, the Girl From Hell: the second I say turn around, *they do.* They whip around in their seats and hunch, frozen in fear like startled rabbits.

Like I could somehow break loose from my cuffs and claw their shocked faces right off their skulls. Because I'm a Class A, and who knows what I can do.

The brakes shriek and sigh as the bus rumbles into gear and I turn toward the window as much as my restraints allow, to give Nobody some privacy. Still, her pain is inescapable—as is her harsh, chemical smell, which gets stronger as she rocks back and forth, back and forth. They must hose her down with antiseptic instead of letting her shower. Might as well get used to it, though, because if Nobody is the other Class A, then we're headed for the same place.

* * *

Dave described it as a brand new "program" for young Class As when I met him this morning. My first impression of him was that despite lacking any official insignia, he was more in uniform than the prison guards who herded me into the room. He was calmly cycling through calls on something like an Apple Watch as they cuffed me to the table and withdrew. I could hear him say "affirmative" before he pulled his sleeve over the gadget and fixed me with an appraising stare.

When I'd asked if he was there for my appeal, he threw back his head and laughed.

"You tested Class A on the Wylie-Stanton, and *you plan to appeal?!*"

In case you haven't been in prison recently, the Wylie-Stanton is a profiling algorithm run on everyone convicted of a felony now, sort of like a personality quiz ("Which Kind of Criminal Are You?"), except you don't have to answer any questions. No, the Wylie-Stanton just takes all your available data—and there's a lot: they have your emails, your grades, your medical records, your internet browsing history, your purchases, your texts and tweets, and whatever other binary trail your ISP has made through digital space—and runs it through an algorithm.

It's like the algorithms Amazon uses, except instead of using your search history to predict if you're in the market for frilly tops and laundry detergent, Wylie-Stanton will predict if you're up for some murder and arson.

If you're a sweet little old lady who'd never so much as jaywalk, you'll be ranked as the lowest class, Class D. If you're capable of killing another person, you'll get moved a couple rungs up the ladder to Class B. The very top of the classification system, the Class As, are the .001 percentile, human-shark, super-manipulative, criminal genius maniacs. Charles Manson, for example.

And me.

"I didn't kill Rose. I was framed," I told Dave. I'd said those words so many times, to so many people who didn't believe me, they'd begun to feel like lies.

"Well, what your file says," Dave indicated the manila file in front of him, "is that you were found in a woodshed with Rose Rowan's body in your lap, her murder weapon in your hand, and no evidence of a third party in the shed. And your only defense is you have no memory of the night she died." He studied my face carefully. "And worse than any of that, on conviction you tested Class A."

"I plan on appealing."

"Let me save you some time with that one." Dave gave me a tight-lipped smile. "I guess you don't get newspapers in Diagnostics, but it passed the Senate last month: appeals from Class As will no longer be heard in court. Class As are no longer eligible for parole."

I curled forward a little, as though I could brace myself after impact.

"Class As can't be fixed. Can't be rehabilitated. Heck, you don't even feel remorse, do you?" He opened my folder, and rifled through evidence photos from my trial until he found my official Wylie-Stanton classification paper, tilting the large glossy crime scene prints toward me as though trying to shove them in my face.

I looked away fast, but not fast enough. A flash of Rose's red mouth and strands of her dark hair floating in a halo of blood burned into my brain even after I squeezed my eyes closed.

"That's what the public thinks, anyway. So I can *promise* you will serve every last minute of your eighty-year sentence." He rapped on the desk between us and I opened my eyes to see he'd swept away the photos and placed a contract in front of me. "Or you can join this little program we're starting."

"What kind of program?"

* * *

Click click, click click.

Nobody's cuffs rattle as she rocks. The bus creaks and sways. We're pulling into another prison yard, the facility the Gen Pop girls are going to. It seems huge from the outside, a vast concrete warehouse for bodies; but I'm sure that, like Bellwood, inside it's as cramped and airless as a submarine. My gray cell was barely wide enough for me to stretch both arms out. I had no window, just a strip of fluorescent light they kept on twenty-four hours a day. I got good at sleeping with a blanket over my head.

Officer Heather is on her feet, rapping out directives before we've come to a complete stop. As she's unbuckling the girls closest to us I call, "How much longer?" but she doesn't respond. I doubt she knows anything about the program we're going to anyway, given what Dave said about it.

"We want to use Class As' skills in a . . . productive way. For the last two months, I've been going to major juvenile institutions like Bellwood around the country and collecting all the Class As under eighteen."

"There are other Class As?" Part of me had wondered, deep down, if Charles Manson and I were the only ones.

"Of course. There's another Class A at Bellwood. She's already signed on."

He slid a pen toward me.

"This is your last chance to leave this place outside of a body bag, Miss Deere."

I stared down at all the lines of fine print, trying to make sense of the legalese. My pen tip hovered over the signature line as I read.

"We'll be leaving within the hour," Dave pushed. A glance at the clock told me the hour would be up in fifteen minutes. Not enough time to read before I signed.

"What do you want us for?"

"That's classified."

"How am I supposed to agree to it if I don't know what it is?" I set the pen down. "What, you want to run tests on us, is that it?"

Dave stood up, then went to the two-way mirror, cupped one hand against the glass and tilted his head back. Satisfied no one was looking in on us, he turned back around and said with a shrug:

"We'll be training you to kill people."

* * *

Click click, click click.

Nobody's cuffs again. I glance over at her scarred wrists and see what's really been making that piercing click: a straightened paper clip. Just like the one that had been on the copy of Dave's contract I'd signed.

Click click.

She digs it into the lock of her handcuffs, one hand already free, one long arm she can swing out to do anything she pleases with.

Click click.

Her cuffs spring open and fall to the floor.

Nobody's cold blue eyes lock with mine through the strands of her white blonde hair for just a nanosecond. Then she springs into the aisle.

"Behind you!" I yell, but she's already shot past Dave and Officer Heather and pounced on the driver, her long scarred arm swinging back wide before driving the straightened paper clip into the side of his neck. Jagged screams tear from his throat as we go flying into the oncoming lane.

Chapter Two

Welcome to Camp

～

My head cracks against the window as an electric sputter echoes through the bus and Nobody springs backward, her long body rippling with convulsions from Officer Heather's taser. Dave catches Nobody before she hits the floor, yelling at Officer Heather to stop, all of them bobbing and swaying as the panicked driver wildly overcorrects, sending the back of the bus fishtailing out in front of an oncoming eighteen-wheeler.

As the tall chrome grill of the truck's cab plows toward my window, time stops. I understand with perfect clarity that I am shackled to my seat by my cuffs as several tons of metal fly toward me and there is no escape, though I saw the cuffs back and forth with all my strength. The gaping mouth of the bellowing truck driver racing toward me will be the last thing I ever see. Will I feel it when the speeding metal meets with my body in between, will I hear my bones popping, will my brain be able to register my skull collapsing in around it, or will I get lucky and die instantly?

Still better than what Rose got.

"Hold on hold on hold on!" the driver screams.

The brakes shriek and I tumble across my seat, the truck's horn chasing us off the highway and onto the soft shoulder of the road as the bus careens to a stop. I lean against the seat in front of me, forehead slick with sweat, my heart pounding so hard my vision pulses.

The bus door swings open with a sigh and the driver flees, his blue collared shirt purple with blood.

"Okay. I'm calling a van to take them back to Bellwood right now," Officer Heather gasps at Dave, who still holds Nobody in his arms.

"Don't." Dave wearily lays the limp, unconscious Nobody across the first bus bench. "Call for a medic, have the ambulance take you and the driver to a local hospital."

Heather is already dialing her phone. "I need to report this incident immediately—"

Dave calmly takes the phone out of her hand. "No, you don't."

"One of these little *freaks* just tried to kill us! This incident must be investigated and reported in their case files and—"

"They don't *have* case files. The moment we crossed the Washington state line these girls *ceased to exist*," Dave says. "So if you want to sit through a year's worth of disciplinary proceedings for impeding a federal officer, keep arguing with me. If you want to help someone, go help the driver."

Three cars pass as they hold each other's gaze. Then with a small wobble she backs down, her shoulders bowing. She pulls the first aid kit off the wall, and stumbles down the bus stairs. Dave climbs behind the wheel, pulls the doors closed, and turns in the tall driver's seat.

"We've got about three more hours of driving ahead of us," he calls to me. "How we doing back there?"

I give him the most sarcastic thumbs-up I can manage.

"Hey, Dave?" I call. "What do you mean we 'ceased to exist'?"

The only answer I get is the squeal of the brakes releasing as Dave eases back onto the freeway.

* * *

The landscape goes from industrial to rural, and then to something like primordial forest. Dark pines taller than most buildings in my hometown line the roads. There's no towns or farms or even buildings, until we finally pass the world's smallest gas station, with a hand-lettered sign out front reading: "LAST GAS 50 MILES."

For a long time after that, the view remains the same: trunks and branches and forest floor, except for one moment of blue, when we pass a field of lupin reaching up to the sun, and then the trees close in again. But the moment is dazzling.

It takes me back to the field of wildflowers the day Rose's mom married her stepdad, Tom. After the ceremony, we sat in the shade and watched Rose's new dad wrap his arms around her mom, Janeane, while the photographer clicked away. The only time Rose smiled that day was when someone with a camera reminded her to.

"They got me a bed," Rose said, watching them. "It's a four-poster. It has a canopy and everything. I got to pick it out."

"That's so cool."

"And he's getting my mom a car, but he said she doesn't have to work anymore, so it's mostly just to pick me up from school and for shopping and stuff."

"It's like a fairy tale or something."

"And you'll be sleeping over like, all the time. Right?" She turned to me then, and I stuck out my pinkie.

"Whenever you want," I promised, and we linked our fingers together to make it official.

But after she moved across town to the nice neighborhood and joined her stepdad's church, things changed.

Everyone who went to Rose's church hung out together, and when they got to high school their youth group became its own little world. They went on group outings instead of dates, they drank root beer instead of Rainier, and they gave each other promise rings junior year. By ninth grade it was very clear there was no place for me in their world of two-story houses, church lock-ins, and wilderness retreats. Rose joined their lunch table while I ate PB&Js in the library and read creepypasta off my phone.

I still followed all Rose's social media accounts. Her life was like a high school soap opera I couldn't stop watching. Every moment seemed to take place during golden hour at the center of a circle of beaming friends. That's what made it so weird when Rose reached out to me again, junior year. When she needed to keep a secret from her "real" friends. When she started seeing a guy whose name she wouldn't tell me.

She just called him "Mr. Moody."

* * *

The bus jounces me back to the present as we trade the freeway for a narrow dirt access road that sends vibrations up my cramped legs. The trees close in tight around us. I'd love to pull down my window and breathe the forest air, but my hands are still cuffed.

"We're getting close!" Dave announces cheerily.

I glance up front and my eyes immediately lock with Nobody's. She's sitting straight up in her seat and staring at me through the frayed eyeholes of her mask. How long has she been awake?

How long has she been *staring at me*?

She rises slowly from her seat, the way a snake rises out of a coil. Squaring her broad shoulders, Nobody lurches down the long narrow aisle toward me. Her orange jumpsuit is dark with rusty arcs of blood. One of her long hands, clenched into a fist, is gloved with arterial spray.

Even if I call out for Dave, he won't make it to me before she does. I'm cornered and pinned in place. I clench my jaw and desperately hold her stare as she lands beside me, looming over me, her eyes just visible through her mask.

Then her arms shoot out over my head and she unlatches my window. It falls open, cool forest air rolling in with a smell like Christmas trees and sunshine.

"Thanks?" I mutter.

Nobody nods, crosses the aisle and lowers the parallel window, then crosses again to the window in front of me. Soon a cross-breeze is sending my hair flying around my face.

"Almost there!" Dave announces. "Here's the sign for the entrance to camp!"

I twist in my seat and crane my neck as we pass beneath two tall wood posts bracing a weathered wood sign that reads:

WELCOME TO CAMP NARAMAUKE.

Where's the chain link? The barbed wire? The prison guards?

The walls, for crying out loud? All I see between the trees are blackberry bushes and butterflies.

I scan for a guardhouse or gun tower as we pass under the gate, but instead, as the trees clear, I'm greeted by the most beautiful field I've ever seen, which dissolves into sand ringing a lake of shimmering blue water with a weathered dock.

Through the windows on the other side of the bus I clock a low log cabin with a stone chimney, its front steps almost buried in banks of lavender, its roof thick with velvety moss. Next to the cabin is a covered patio, and beyond that I glimpse what must be a fire pit, ringed by sun-bleached logs.

Straight ahead four little cabins peer through the trees, red with faded white trim, their sides spotted with fallen shingles.

We're going to live in an abandoned sleep-away camp?

Dave parks, then strolls to my seat and unfastens me from my cuffs completely. Confused, I stand and put my hands up for him to cuff again, but he just goes back down to the driver's seat and throws open the bus doors.

"Come on, you two, time to meet the others," Dave says, and jogs down the bus steps.

Nobody and I look at each other in surprise and then, warily, follow him outside. The cool wind rushes to meet us with the smell of pine and lavender, sunlight bathing us from the top of a limitless blue sky. I stagger down the gravel path, lovestruck by the world.

As we pass by the log cabin, a curvy woman pops out of a side door with a giant tray of crayons in her arms. She's mid-thirties, like Dave.

"The new recruits!" She smiles and two symmetrical dimples appear in her plump cheeks, which bolster a pair of red cat-eye glasses. "I'm Kate, and you must be Signal and—"

"Nobody," Dave interrupts. "She prefers Nobody."

Kate nods quickly. "Okay, Nobody it is! Everybody's down at Arts and Crafts."

Kate doesn't have a holster or taser or nightstick, or any of the usual fun accessories correctional officers carry. Just a silver whistle around her neck, like a gym teacher's, and a small key fob dangling from her wrist. In her sweatshirt, jeans, and worn-in hiking boots, she could pass for a real camp counselor. She and Dave speak companionably. I can't make out what they say, but they walk with their backs to us. Like they're not afraid of us at all.

"Okay. After dinner, then." Dave breaks off their conversation and announces, "Kate will take it from here. See you guys in a few!" as he jogs back up the path.

"You guys had a long drive, huh?" Kate peers at Nobody's blood-stained jumpsuit.

"Yeah," I answer after a long cold silence from Nobody. The lake fills the horizon completely, a golden haze coming off the water and silhou-etting a graceful sycamore in the middle of the field below. Under its branches is a picnic table.

Around the table four kids sit, lazily coloring with markers on yel-lowed construction paper. Their voices float up to us, laughing and teas-ing, three guys and one girl. As we get closer the voices drop away, and all four faces turn to stare.

I would never have guessed they were Class As, not in a million years. They look totally normal, except their clothes are weirdly out of style and a bit too bright, like the kids in a foreign language textbook, the ones who are endlessly talking about who will bring cassettes to the party.

The shortest of the guys, a scrawny black kid with huge aviator glasses, wears a bright green T-shirt with a giant yellow smiley face on it. Next to him are two twins, one in red and one in baby blue, who're almost as tall as Nobody. Both have dark crew cuts and big, toothy smiles that flash at the same time as we approach.

"Oooh, more ladies!" one of the twins says approvingly, and the only girl at the table rolls her large dark eyes. She has short curly black hair framing a heart-shaped face. Her T-shirt, neon pink, reads in lavender glitter letters: *Secretly a Mermaid.*

"Where's Javier? And Erik?" Kate frowns.

"Kitchen. Tree." The boy with glasses answers, staring straight down and continuing to color.

Kate smiles. "Oh, that's right! I told Javier to get dinner started."

She let a Class A into a kitchen? With all the knives and things? Alone?

And then she forgot?

"How you doing up there, Erik?" Kate calls skyward, to a guy in the tree. His face is hidden by floppy, dark-blond hair, but his rolled-up shirt sleeves reveal alarmingly defined muscles. His shoulders bow slightly forward, tensed in a posture that makes me expect a sulky reply, but instead he calls down, "I'm *exploring nature.*"

His voice is deep and confident, and dripping with sarcasm.

"All right! Well. I should head to the kitchen, then. Signal, Nobody, this is the rest of Camp Naramauke: Erik's up there—" she points to the tree. "This is Dennis in the smiley face shirt, Kurt and Troy are our twins, and last but not least we have Jada. Grab a crayon and jump right in!" She throws us a cheery wave and sallies right back up the hill.

I haven't even been able to go to the bathroom without a guard watching me for the last twelve months. Now here we are, in the middle of a field ringed by forest, under the open sky, seven verified Class As . . . *coloring?*

I follow Nobody to the table, and we both awkwardly take sheets of the yellowed construction paper and sit at the empty spots left at the picnic table benches, directly across from each other. Her hands are still stained with dried blood, but no one remarks on it. There's just the gentle squeak of markers.

I look back at the lake. Kate's out of sight. The water is so close. I could run to the edge, kick off my shoes, dive in, and be halfway to the far shore before she comes back. We all could. I glance around the table: so why don't they?

Just because I can't see a fence doesn't mean there isn't something keeping us here. Maybe there's an electric current in the water. Or drone surveillance, or snipers on the far shore.

I don't want to find out the hard way.

"So like . . . are there cameras all around the camp or something?" I whisper to the table.

The scrawny black guy with the giant glasses continues to stare straight down as he talks: "No cameras. No electricity, either, except in the main cabin." His voice is a complete monotone. "No internet, no Wi-Fi, no cell phones . . ."

"We find *other* ways to stay busy." One twin grins suggestively, revealing a small overlap between his two front teeth.

"Troy, you are *so gross*," Jada groans. "But hey, new girls: how many, huh?"

"Getting straight to it I see," Dennis says, still not looking up from his paper.

"Dennis's number, obviously, is zero." Jada looks from me to Nobody again. "Come on, ladies. We all know each other's numbers already. How many?"

"How many *what?*" I stall.

"She's asking how many people you've killed," the deep voice from the tree says. Only it's not in the tree anymore, it's right behind me. He's crept down so silently I didn't hear him over the wind rustling the leaves.

There's a throb in my chest as my heart rate surges. I can feel him hovering so I don't turn around. I pick up a yellow crayon and start drawing a line of stars across my paper, using all my focus to keep my hand from shaking. Of course. Of course that's the first question here. They're killers. Underneath the bright shirts and construction paper, that's all we have in common. We're convicted murderers.

Nobody uncaps a green scented marker and holds the tip in front of where her nose must be, sniffing like it's perfume. Then she says in a rusty voice, "Six."

One of the twins laughs, impressed. "Whoa, for serious? Second only to Erik!" His thick black eyebrows jump up as he continues chummily, "Me and Kurt got three between us—"

The prolonged scream of an air horn tears across the field. Everyone at the table freezes. Then the twins leap up and start *running*. The guy from the tree—Erik, I guess—climbs up, onto, and over the table, his long sneaker landing right on my paper as he launches himself off and runs up the hill. My stars are torn in half.

"What's that sound?" I ask Dennis, who is lining up his paper carefully, matching the corners exactly before folding it in fourths.

"It's the air horn. It means we're going to have a drill." The same monotone, though his expression seems annoyed. "We've got to drop whatever we're doing and run to the east lawn." He heads toward the hill the other boys have just disappeared over, and Nobody rises to her feet and walks after him without a backward glance.

Jada, however, waits a few feet from the table, her forearm shielding her face from the sun and me. Is this some overture of friendship? Jada *has* been the only girl here for a while, and of the two girls that have just arrived I am, for the first time in my life, the normal one. As I approach she reaches a small hand out to me, and smiles.

But when we connect her grip is vicelike, her little pink-polished nails biting into my arm. She twists my skin, hard, and her smile deepens as I wince.

"Just so you know, Erik likes me." Her eyes narrow, her voice strong and clear. "And if you make a play for him, or if you tell him we had this talk? *I'll cut you.*" She releases me, still smiling, then jogs up the hill ahead of me, revealing a glittery turquoise seashell on the back of her shirt.

Like, what?

I stumble up the incline, flabbergasted. Jada is beautiful. Prettier than most of the popular girls at my high school. How could she possibly be threatened by me? Maybe this Erik is a player.

In addition to being a killer.

I run, full speed, face flushing, eyes tearing. At Bellwood, the few times they allowed me to exercise, I was only allowed to shuffle in ankle chains. Now I sprint wildly through the high green grass, birds shooting low over my head across the blue sky, calling out like they're cheering me on.

Way, way across the field, there's a guy running against the dark wall of pines that surround the little cabins, parallel from me. The moment I notice him he smiles and speeds up. Okay. You want to race? *Let's race!*

Down at the end of the field, on the lawn across from the main cabin, Dave stands with the rest of the campers beside an orange cone, a square blue tarp behind him and an air horn in his hand. He waves his arms over his head as the others clap and cheer, watching to see who will get to the cone first.

My atrophied legs are almost at their breaking point, but I tilt forward and gain speed, lungs burning, keeping just ahead of the guy from across the field, until he makes a final surge before I get to the cone and we knock into each other, hard.

Up close he's way taller than I thought, and apparently made of iron. When I slam into his chest I actually bounce back.

"Whoa, easy!" he laughs, grabbing my arms to keep me from falling, and my forehead almost knocks into his chin. "You okay?"

I'm too winded to answer, he's knocked the breath out of me, and then our eyes lock—his huge and dark and melancholy. Though maybe that's just the tattoo at the edge of his left eye, a tiny blue tear poised to slide down the long, narrow line of his cheek.

"Earth to Signal! Get in line and listen up!" Dave claps his hands, and I break off our stare and take my place in between Dennis and Nobody.

"All right, guys, now that Javier and Signal have finally joined us, it's drill time!" Dave announces to the group as I struggle to control my panting. "What better way to welcome the new recruits than a drill, am I right?"

There is scattered applause, not from me. I'm bent over at the waist as a cramp stitches up my side. If we're going to do sprints or push-ups for this drill I might as well give up now. The blue tarp I noticed from the field is draped over a pile of something, a tall pile, almost as high as Dave's waist. With my luck, it's probably medicine balls.

"This is a timed drill. You have three hours, from now until dinner. It's real simple, though I wouldn't call it easy." Dave leans down, grabs a corner of the plastic sheet, and with a flourish pulls it back. "All you have to do is hide a body."

Eight limp bodies lie stacked on top of each other, their limbs tangled together, gazing up at the sky with unblinking eyes.

Chapter Three

The Bleeder

≁

I'm going to faint. Right here, right now.

All the others lunge forward. There's a loud rattle as Dave throws down what sounds like a drawer of cutlery. A box of knives, cleavers, and small saws spill out in the grass in front of us.

"Hey." The guy with the tear, Javier, has hung back while the others bicker over the knives. "They're not real." He whispers.

"What?" I force myself to look at the pile of bodies, where one of the twins is working a busty woman loose from the arms of the other cadavers, and see the fingers of her hands are molded together. They're . . . plastic? But they aren't just mannequins—there's no seams in their flesh, their hair catches the wind, and their bland faces are uncanny and individual.

"They get them different places—special effects houses, old medical mannequins, and some are uh . . ." His tone gets embarrassed. "Like, sex dolls we think."

"Oh."

"Freaked me out too, the first time," he says, and then he lopes ahead of me and plucks a short male mannequin off the pile.

He saw. *He saw me freak out.* Did anyone else see?

Nobody hoists up the last mannequin. The tarp is empty, but Dave turns to me.

"Don't worry, I saved one for you!" he moves aside the corner of the tarp to reveal a young female figure with long brown hair, lying face down in the grass.

"How thoughtful," I mutter. She's surprisingly heavy when I pick her up, and taller than me. I awkwardly cradle her in my arms. There's two knives left so I grab one, struggling to carry it all.

"Don't forget this!" Dave tucks a trash bag under my elbow, and I mutter a thank you.

I get about ten steps away from the tarp before I sink to my knees under the weight of my "victim," a knot forming in my stomach that rises slowly toward my throat.

Around me buttons are popping off shirts as the others set to work, the flailing limbs of the mannequins rising over the grass as clothes are ripped clear of torsos so saws can ravage plastic flesh. One of the twins has a stockinged foot on his shoulder and is bending the leg sharply backward at the knee. Jada cuts four fingers off her mannequin with one knife stroke, her expression eerily remote. I see Erik's head bowed over the grass and quickly look away.

"Now remember," Dave lectures, circling us, "this is not about dismemberment skills, it's about concealment. This is an *evidence drill*. If I find any evidence, even so much as a button, that's a fail."

"But we don't have tarps to use!" one of the twins protests.

"Oh? I see two tarps on this field," Dave chides, sounding exactly like my old AP Biology teacher during a lab. As the twins race for them I turn over my mannequin, smoothing the long dark hair out of her glass eyes. Someone has gone to the trouble of molding her face into a smile, and her skin is a horribly lifelike type of silicone. I look around, stalling, and my eyes land on Nobody sitting with a headless torso in her lap.

The remembered smell of blood, like a hot handful of pennies, burns at the back of my throat.

When I woke up in the shed that morning, I was sitting upright on the floor beside the scarred card table. Rose was curled up in my lap, facing away from me, her back against my stomach.

I could feel a pool of cooling warmth below us, and realized she'd drunk too much and wet herself in her sleep. I debated how to wake her up, if I should play it off with a laugh and make a joke out of it, or if that would hurt her feelings. At last I softly shook her shoulder, a smile in my voice, though my head throbbed and my throat was painfully dry.

"Hey, Rose? Rose, you got to wake up . . ."

I shook her harder then, and her head turned. But it turned the wrong way. The back of her head moved impossibly forward, dropping at an angle her neck could not allow. Her body was still in place, shoulders hunched, not moving, a thing separate from the head that was making a slow, long roll across the floor. The face slowly turned up and regarded me, red streaked across her cheek, eyes wide open and blank.

"You're white as a sheet." The hushed voice jerks me back to the field. Javier has dragged his mannequin close to mine. "This is a timed drill. They don't mess around about that here." Javier glances meaningfully across the field at Dave, whose back is turned as he discusses something with the twins.

"I—I can't . . ." I choke off the words. He can't know, none of them can know, that unlike them I'm *not* a homicidal maniac and I don't want to kill anyone.

Javier leans forward.

"You ever play with Barbies? These are just giant Barbies. He doesn't care how you carve them up. Start with her arm. Right above the elbow. That's the weakest part."

He hands me his knife, and I clumsily roll up the sleeve of the mannequin's knit shirt, already soaked with dew.

Just a Barbie. *She's just a Barbie.*

The knife sinks into her soft pale silicone arm and blood weeps from the wound. Vomit rises in my throat.

"Oh dang, you got a bleeder!" Javier sounds genuinely surprised. "Some of the more expensive ones have fake blood inside, but they're usually drained already. I've never seen one with the blood still in."

I can't speak. I just stare at the thick red liquid pooling inside my mannequin's elbow. She's still smiling up at me.

"How about we trade?" Javier offers, moving in front of me, taking my place over the mannequin. "I've never gotten a bleeder before. I want to try one. Cool?"

"Yeah, cool." I nod, numb, and crawl toward the fake body he's been working on. The head and one arm are already off, and the mannequin is much more Barbie-like than mine, with hard plastic skin all hollowed out inside like a chocolate Easter bunny. I can pretend I'm just packing up a store mannequin. Okay. I can handle this.

But I cannot freak out like that ever again.

I am surrounded by murderers more ruthless than anyone from Bellwood. The girl who gets through this program and gets out into the world again is the Girl From Hell. The girl who doesn't make it through this program is the innocent loner who's so pathetically awkward her whole town believes she killed her best friend.

"We're forty-five minutes in! You should be past dismemberment and into clean-up," Dave calls out, then pauses beside me and Javier, back to back in the grass, and watches us work for a moment.

"Javier, you took the bleeder I saved for Signal," he says, annoyed.

"We wanted to trade," I explain. Dave cocks his head.

"You were okay with that, Javier?"

"Yup, it's fine," Javier mutters, still carving away.

"Even though the bleeders are much more difficult to conceal?"

"Better practice," Javier says gruffly.

"Great attitude!" Dave grins. "Javier's got the right idea, campers. Because when you're in the field, this is going to be a million times messier. You guys have it easy with this drill! Or then again, maybe you don't . . ."

Everybody groans in anticipation of what he's going to say next.

"Because guess what, campers, each of these mannequins has been marked with a specific smell and we *will* have a canine in. So when you go into conceal phase, remember to account for smell! Because what did we come to camp to learn, everybody?"

He pauses, and everyone but me and Nobody says, in unison: "How to not get caught!"

"That's exactly right! Also, Javier," his voice drops and he leans over us, his face stern. "I already marked Signal down as having the bleeder, so I'm going to need you to trade with her again. Good attitude, though. Points for effort. But Signal gets the bleeder."

Under Dave's watchful eye Javier and I trade places again.

"Okay, guys, you should all be in conceal phase in the next fifteen minutes, so I'm going to the kitchen to get some dinner. Meet me over there when your body is *well* and *truly* hidden!"

Javier has stacked the bleeder up like a pile of firewood inside the trash bag. Meanwhile, I haven't even finished dismembering his mannequin. I hear him frantically sawing away and mumble an apology I'm not sure he even hears. Embarrassed, I gather up the bits of torn clothing and bundle them up with the limbs as the quiet grows deeper around us, the other campers moving on to the next phase. When I look back again Javier is gone.

I'm the last one left on a field much colder and bluer than when we started. Shivering, I rise from the ground and try to haul the bag up with me. No chance. It's far too heavy.

Okay. I'll drag it, then.

The trash bag glides easily over the damp grass behind me, but I'm tired and moving slow. The horizon behind the lake goes from neon orange to cool blue by the time I get to its short dock, and then the rack of canoes on the encircling sand makes me stop short.

I can go now. I'll grab one of the canoes and strike out for the far shore, it'll be night soon, I can run into the woods, they'll never find me. I drop the bag just as a distant whistle sounds: Kate is standing in the door of the main cabin, just across the field. She gives me a wave, then disappears inside.

They're not completely oblivious then.

I hoist my bag again and haul it all the way to the edge of the dock, then swing it out into the water. I pretend to wait to see if it'll come up, but I'm actually staring at the far shore, gauging the distance.

I can cross the lake before dawn, while it's still dark. The security is ridiculous here because the rest of these psychopaths don't want to leave. They were *loving* that ghoulish pop quiz. *This* is where they belong.

But I'm not like them.

Decision made, I turn my back on the water and climb up through the long grass toward the glowing orange windows of the main cabin.

"Last, but not least!" Kate greets me with a paper plate inside the knotty pine dining room. The four round tables that fill the room are empty, chairs pushed back, and the enormous foil trays on the counter between the dining area and kitchen are almost scraped clean. What remains smells amazing, though, and I hurl myself toward the leftovers as Kate frets behind me.

"They just about finished everything. There's some chicken left in the kitchen, though."

"I'm vegetarian." I slap a good spoonful of green bean casserole on my plate.

"Oh. Well, that's nice. After you've eaten, we need to get your clothes together."

After I've emptied my plate twice, Kate takes me down a narrow hall to a closet lined floor to ceiling with shelves, all bursting with old clothes. They're all out of style and just a little too bright. I realize, when I pull a T-shirt loose and see a name written on the tag, that they're about thirty years' worth of lost-and-found items. Kate hands me a giant fabric shopping bag, the handle badly frayed.

"Grab anything you want and come back if you need something. Socks and underwear"—she pulls out a giant Tupperware bin stuffed with generic white Hanes—"are in here, all brand new. Toiletries—" she taps another plastic bin with generic deodorant, soaps, shampoos, tampons, and even *Bic razors*. "Anything else you need, jot it down on the notepad for the next time Dave or I go to town." She taps a composition notebook wedged between two stacks of sweatshirts, then bustles away.

Civilian clothes are exactly what I need most for tomorrow's escape. By the time I've winnowed out the few items that are warm, dark, and my size, Kate returns with a glowering Jada and Nobody, who has ketchup smears around the mouth hole of her balaclava and clutches an overstuffed clothes bag of her own.

"I thought you could show Nobody and Signal to the girls' cabin, so they can get changed and wash up before fire circle." Kate holds out two coarse towels for Jada to carry for us.

"*Fine*," Jada sighs, snatching them. "Follow me."

We follow her down the pale gravel path to the small red cabin set farthest back in the woods, our steps somehow much louder in the dark.

"So much for my days of having a private cabin!" Jada pushes open a rickety screen door that swings shut behind us with a scream, and clicks on a large halogen lantern hanging off a top bunk. A few blinks and it washes the small space with sickly green light, revealing bunk beds in each corner of the square room, each with a camping lantern hung on one bedpost and a laundry bag on the other. Since there's only three of us, we can all have a top bunk.

The floors and walls are thin wood paneling, and despite an astringent cleanser smell mildew creeps in green waves from the floor to the windows, their torn screens fluttering in the chilly night air.

"Bathroom's in there." Jada points to a green door opposite the front one. "But if you were looking forward to a hot shower you can forget it. None of the cabins have heated water." Jada holds the towels out to me, but when I reach she lets them fall to the ground.

Nobody tenses, waiting for my reaction. I can't let this slide.

"Are you *that* scared I'm going to steal your boyfriend?" I look Jada in the eye. "Calm down, he's not my type."

Jada sneers. "Just remember. Sluts get cut." She pivots away and stalks to the door, and as I finally bend down to pick the towels up she shouts: "*Enjoy my cabin, skank!*" and slams the door so hard it bounces twice against the doorframe.

Nobody finishes making up her bunk without a word to me, then follows Jada out. And then it's just me, the silence, and a lonely little moth who's fallen in love with my lantern.

I shrug on a hoodie, wrestle sheets onto my thin mattress, then climb down from my perch and walk straight into Erik.

He's standing in the middle of the cabin. How long has he been there, staring? How'd he even come in without me hearing the door?!

"I climbed in through the window." Erik jerks his thumb toward the torn screen, but aside from this motion he's eerily still. He's so tall, his shoulders so broad, it's unsettling to imagine him twisting through the small window while my back was turned. "Kate wanted someone to check in on you, make sure you hadn't gotten lost. So I volunteered."

Jada must have loved that.

"Yeah, well, I might actually just go to bed." I shrug. "I'm pretty exhausted."

"Are you?"

"Yup." The hair on my arms is rising. Maybe just from him being so close. I haven't stood face to face with a guy for this long in . . . well, maybe never.

Erik has the strikingly handsome features of a teen idol, slightly skewed by a square, heavy jaw. It's almost indecently muscular, disconcertingly well engineered to tear flesh from bone.

"You don't have to come hang out. But you should, because they're not going to stop asking about your number until you tell them."

"Yeah? And what's yours?" I say, stepping back toward my bunk bed, though he hasn't come any closer.

"Ten," he says. I recoil and dimples appear on either side of a broad smile. "Yours?"

"Eleven," I say, lifting my chin.

"You're a terrible liar," Erik says. "You're the Girl From Hell, aren't you?"

The blood drains from my face and his smile goes even wider.

"I thought I recognized you, Signal Deere. I followed your case and I have to say, I went back and forth on you. The evidence was overwhelming. But seeing you in person, it's obvious." He pauses for just a moment then says, "You're innocent."

This is all I've wanted to hear someone say for the last year. But not him, and not here. In a camp full of homicidal Class As, being innocent makes me prey.

But I still can't bring myself to say I did it.

"What the hell are you talking about?" I bluster.

"Your face is incredible." He squints at me, drawing closer. "Every thought just bleeds right through." I don't know what my face gave away, but I try to wipe it clean now. He just keeps staring, then finally says: "You're *sure* you're a Class A?"

"They didn't keep me in solitary for fun," I say through clenched teeth.

He steps closer. If he weren't a Class A predator, I'd think he was about to kiss me. And that's when I notice his eye. It's torn. Or at least, the pupil is, the pupil of his right eye isn't a circle, it's an irregular oval, like the slit of a cat's eye.

"It's called coloboma," he snaps, a nanosecond after I've noticed it. "It's a congenital eye defect. Generally, there's two kinds of people: the ones who look away when they see it and the ones who make it a point to keep looking. You're a looker." Erik talks so fast it takes me a moment to catch up to what he's saying, then he steps back, shoulders bowing a little, and viciously bites at his nails. "You *really* shouldn't be here. You want to escape? Go. Right now."

He nods to the back door, like he wants me to break into a run. He's trying to scare me. Trying to get me to admit what I really am. I can't let him.

"Thanks for the pep talk," I say with all the bravado I can muster. "But you don't know me and you have no idea what I'm capable of."

"I know you're not capable of killing." His deep voice is so certain, his cat's eye not blinking as it locks with mine. "And I know you won't survive this place."

Hinges behind us shriek: Nobody stands in the doorway, holding a flashlight. She looks from me to Erik, then walks quickly over and throws her long arm around my shoulders.

"Hey, hot stuff," she says in her creaky voice. "I've been waiting on you." The lips behind the wool ski mask quickly brush my hair, and then she turns and fixes her gaze on Erik. "Everything okay in here?"

"Yeah," I say gratefully, catching on. "Thanks for checking in, baby."

Erik's eyebrows fly up. "I'm sorry . . . are you two . . . together?"

"She's mine." Nobody's stance is relaxed, but there's a quiet challenge in her voice.

"Oh please. No way," he scoffs. "You're in a relationship with a girl who's been in solitary the last year?"

"We wrote a lot of letters," I answer for her, and take the rough hand on my shoulder, pushing away the memory of it gloved in the bus driver's blood.

Erik rolls his eyes. "If you say so, sure. Whatever."

"Jada was wondering what was taking you so long," Nobody says, but Erik doesn't respond. He just walks out, letting the door bang shut behind him. We stand together for another moment and then Nobody swiftly withdraws her arm, ducking down to look out the window before turning to announce: "All clear."

"Thanks," I exhale.

"Yeah, well, you told Jada he wasn't your type, so . . ." She shrugs. "He marked you out as his. When we were under the tree. Jada saw it too."

It's the longest speech I've heard her make. Her voice is rough, but the unbalanced girl beside me on the bus from this afternoon is way more articulate than I'd assumed. Was that just an act she put on? To freak out Officer Heather?

"But I've got the second highest body count, so if you're with me he'll back off." Nobody clears her throat, and there's a brief embarrassed silence before she says, "To be clear, I have an actual girlfriend. Who I love very much. So nothing is going to happen between you and me." She takes a beat. "No offense."

"Cool, no problem." I nod quickly, hoping I don't look surprised, but now I've got so many new questions. Like, does she kiss her girlfriend through the ski mask? Or does she feel okay taking it off with her? Am I literally the only person in the world who's never dated before?

A short knock derails my train of thought, Kate's silhouette visible through the screen.

"Guys, there's one last thing we have to do tonight." She comes in and quickly turns to fasten the front door. Nobody and I spin around to see Dave come in from the other direction, through the bathroom door, carrying a black case. He sets it down and fastens the only other way out, then says:

"Put your hands over your head."

Nobody takes a step back but Dave is faster. He grabs her elbow and spins her into the bunk.

"What are you doing?!" I yell as Kate grips my arm.

Nobody thrashes around, Dave goes red-faced trying to pin her arms behind her back. She's taller than him but he outweighs and outmaneuvers her, twisting her arms together and knotting her wrists with a cable tie, wrenching it so tight her fingers start to go dark red.

"The more you relax, the less painful it will be," Kate says. "It's the last step."

"Hands," Dave barks at me. "Now."

"WHAT'S the last step?! What are you *doing?*"

Dave yanks my wrists together, ties them, and then uses another cable tie to attach me to the bunk bed post across the room from Nobody. I'm not resisting, but he still slams me into the bunk, cracking my head against the wood frame. There's a snapping behind me, I twist my head enough to get Kate in my peripheral vision, pulling on thick rubber gloves as Dave hands her a nightmare object of surgical steel and plastic tubing out of the black case.

An injection gun? What are they injecting us with?

Nobody kicks out, she howls, but Dave is too strong. Kate jerks up the back of Nobody's mask as Dave holds her scarred, twitching shoulders in place, and she sobs uncontrollably. I never imagined she could cry.

"You have to hold still," Kate is so calm. "It won't damage you if you hold still."

"*Please*," I plead. "Why don't you just tell us what this is first?! We have rights, YOU CAN'T JUST—"

Before I finish the sentence, Kate presses the surgical gun to the back of Nobody's neck and pulls the trigger.

Chapter Four
The Teen Killers Club

∽

Nobody falls in a pile on the floor.

"You're all right." Kate's voice is directly behind me, Dave's hands wrenching my shoulders, my own voice screaming in my ears:

"Just tell me what it is first! I won't struggle if I just know! Just tell me what it is!"

"Stop talking." Dave flattens me against the bunk like he wants to leave bruises. Gloved hands scrape my hair from the back of my neck and a cold circle presses above where my shoulder blades meet, and then comes the unreal sound of metal punching through my skin.

Hot, mindless pain radiates up my neck and through my jaw and all the way down my spine, snowballing larger and larger as it spreads until it's the only thing that exists. My teeth grind, my jaw locks, my vision blurs, my body bucks, wanting free of itself. And then I go limp, hanging from my wrists, and then I'm somehow face down on the floor, curled up beside Nobody. I try to get up and the floor dips and rolls below me and the green bean casserole comes up, sour with stomach acid.

Kate's voice breaks through: "Girls? Girls? See this, girls?"

In sharp focus: an oblong chrome pill, right above my face.

"This is what I just injected you with. It's in your neck right now, along with a mild disinfectant and muscle stimulant to keep your body from rejecting it. It's a kill switch. There are three ways to set it off."

I'm going to be sick again. I'm going to be sick.

"We have an electronic perimeter around camp that's programmed to trigger your kill switch if you're on the wrong side of it. Think of it as an invisible fence. The fence extends a mile out from the far shore, across the sign road, and up the far side of the east creek. If you cross the fence, your kill switch will go off instantly.

"Once it's armed, the kill switch has an internal sensor that will self-activate if the blood around it suddenly oxygenates: in other words, if you try to cut it out, it will go off."

"Also, try not to get stabbed in the neck," Dave adds.

Kate clears her throat. "Finally, Dave and I have these clickers. They work kind of like remote controls." She extends her arm, so the pill is hovering well away from her, and nods to Dave.

He holds up his fob and clicks, and the air fills with the smell of melting rubber as whatever chemical is inside the chrome pill releases and starts melting Kate's gloves.

"Your switch has been placed between several rather crucial arteries," Kate says, ripping off her gloves as they start dribbling from her fingers. "If we see you threaten another camper, or act out in a harmful way, or you attempt to escape, we will click our remotes, and your kill switch will release this substance into your bloodstream."

And turn us off. Like we're a TV.

Kate's gloves are now a puddle on the floor. "Any questions? Concerns?"

"You can't just kill us." My voice comes out broken.

"Believe me, we don't want to," Kate says gently. "We are trying to give you as much freedom as we can."

I should have gotten in the stupid canoe. I should have bolted when Erik jeered at me to run. Now it's too late.

Kate wipes up the melted latex and, matter-of-factly, my vomit, as Nobody and I lie clammy and shivering on the ground.

"When you two are feeling better you can go ahead and shower up, and go meet the others 'round the fire," Dave says as they duck out the door. "Congratulations. You're officially campers now."

The idea of getting up off the floor is unimaginable. It's not until several long cold minutes pass that the haze of pain starts narrowing to a small persistent burning at the base of my neck, like a venomous spider bite.

Nobody and I silently pull ourselves to our feet and retreat to the bathroom, showering in opposite end stalls under ice-cold water. I hear her crying, a soft, hoarse sound, and wish I could cry too, but it's like everything inside me has been wrung out.

We dress in silence and walk side by side through the dark toward the main cabin. There's a glow around the side porch and the sharp smell of campfire smoke.

"There they are!" a male voice calls, and Jada yells: "We're making s'mores!"

Four long logs circle the wide iron fire pit, which breathes plumes of white sparks and radiates crackling red heat. I drop onto the opposite end of the log Javier sits on. Nobody settles between us, leaning back from the fire.

One of the twins strums a guitar on the log across from us. He looks up and says,

"'Yo quiero Taco Bell!'"

". . . What?"

"Your sweatshirt."

I look down and see the phrase emblazoned on my chest in bright purple letters.

"Oh I . . . didn't see it before."

He nods. Then: "Did you puke?"

I'm unsure how to answer him.

"'Cause if you haven't yet you probably will. I puked when they put mine in," he adds. "Troy did too."

"Troy did too *what?* What are you saying about me to the new girls?" The other twin walks into the shifting circle of firelight from the main cabin with a paper plate stacked with graham crackers and broken chocolate bars.

"That you were sick after kill switches."

"Nah, I was fine."

"Dude, you puked!"

I quickly wipe the corners of my mouth.

"It hollows you out." The hushed, low voice comes from Javier. The firelight brushes the long line of his cheek with amber and sets tiny gold sparks in the center of his eyes.

"I was wondering why you were all so well behaved." My voice is still scratchy. "Now I know."

"Yeah, but don't stress about it too much," Kurt, the twin with the guitar, says. "As long as you don't try to escape or kill another camper, you're perfectly safe."

"Safe? The way they manhandled us back there, no guard would've gotten away with that at my prison—"

"It's strategic. Not personal. They need to establish physical authority up front," Erik's voice cuts in. There's a crazy elevator sensation low in my stomach as he emerges from the dark and sits heavily beside Kurt. I don't make eye contact but am all too aware of him as he snatches a bag of marshmallows from beside the log and spears one on a stripped branch. "They're two middle-aged weirdos in charge of the first-ever elite force of teenaged assassins. How did you *think* they were keeping us in line? Merit badges?"

I can feel him staring me down, so I force myself to meet his gaze through the leaping fire, and he laughs. "Awww, someone doesn't like getting treated like one of the bad kids!" I turn my head, bracing myself for when he starts taunting me about being innocent in front of the others.

But instead he says, sarcastically: "Guess you should've thought about that before you tested as a Class A."

"But why use Class As?!" I ask wearily. "Aren't there special forces and spies and stuff who *volunteer* and *train professionally* for this kind of thing?"

"The people we're going to be killing are U.S. citizens." Kurt places his fingers along the frets in a series of chords without strumming. "So they need a crime scene that's, uh, unprofessional."

"And then if we get caught they can be like 'More senseless Class A violence!'" Troy does a voice like a stern newscaster: "'How fast can we round these monsters up and shoot them directly into the sun? NASA experts weigh in!'"

"So what, they *expect* us to get caught?"

"Hopefully not. That's what our training is for."

"But why not train older Class A types and give us a chance to . . ." I'm about to say appeal when I remember that's not an option anymore.

"Um, have you *met* an older Class A?" Jada shudders theatrically. "I had two locked up on my block. They could barely get through a room inspection with three bosses and a taser."

"Yeah, most Class As are a little too far gone down the bones-as-wind-chimes road after twenty-five." I can hear the smile in Erik's voice, though I don't look over at him.

"It's really not a bad deal, considering," Troy says cheerfully. "In ancient times they would have just strapped us to stakes and burned us for demons or something,"

"They're trying to do basically that now," Kurt sighs. "Congress is majority Protectionist."

"Majority what?" I ask.

"Protectionist? Hello?" Jada snaps. "Protectionists, the people who think everyone should be forced to take the Wylie-Stanton? And anyone who tests as Class A should be like, killed or something? 'Prevention Is the Best Protection,' those people?"

"Oh, they would never kill us," Erik says. "That would be *inhumane*. They'll just drug us to the point where all we can do is watch TV and piss our pants."

"Luckily we don't have to worry about that," Javier says quietly. "Since we're in the Teen Killers Club."

"Yeah. Now you've gotten your kill switch, you're officially a member!" Troy says, with *ta-da* jazz hands.

"*Is* she, though?" Jada picks at a graham cracker, her almond-shaped nails glinting in the firelight. "She hasn't even told anyone her number yet. She could be a zero like Dennis, for all we—"

"One." Nobody's gravelly voice startles me. Jada sucks her teeth and Troy stifles a laugh, but then Nobody adds, "A decapitation." And there's a small, appreciative silence.

I don't *want* their approval, but I need it. For this crowd, scary is good, crazy even better.

"So not eleven?" Erik blinks at me innocently, and I bite my lip.

So he's decided to play dumb about my case with the group. But the cost of that might be endless teasing. Which, fine. Teasing I can handle.

Javier leans forward past Nobody so his eyes connect with mine.

"One way to look at camp is, like, as a chance to do good," he begins.

"*Good?*" Erik's laugh cuts across the fire. "'A chance to do good'? Did you actually just say that?"

Kurt's strumming slows.

"Did I stutter?" Javier keeps his tone light, but the rebuke is there. "Yeah, that's what I said. Our targets are *seriously bad people*. Domestic terrorists. Cult leaders. Corrupt politicians—"

"Putting aside your naive acceptance that Kate and Dave would only have us kill 'bad people,'" Erik interrupts, "you know there's no such thing as good and bad, right? There's strong and weak. That's it. That's the only binary that exists. When the strong kill each other in the name of the weak they call it being good. When the strong kill in their own name, it's called evil."

"There's also the view that killing *anyone* is evil," Dennis says. I'd almost forgotten he was here, he's been sitting so quietly on the log to my left this whole time.

"That's *classic*, coming from a zero!" Troy laughs, and everyone else joins in.

"FROM ZERO TO HERO!"

"Dennis the Non-Menace!"

"How are you a zero?" I ask him as the others continue laughing. "How did you end up here if you never killed anyone?"

"Dennis kept having murder fantasies," Erik answers for him. I didn't realize he was listening. "He was afraid he'd act on them, so he asked his computer teacher to give him the Wylie-Stanton and tested off the charts. He also ran a little dark net site called . . . what was it called again?"

"Skullsex dot com," Dennis says flatly.

"How could I forget!" Erik laughs.

"We didn't have any actual threads on copulating with skulls." Dennis adjusts his oversized glasses. "Cannibalism, torture, decapitation—" He gives me a gentlemanly nod. "But no skull fetishists. Still, it got the tone across."

My stomach turns over as everybody else chuckles.

"Dennis is the highest Class A out of all of us," Erik adds, "despite being a zero."

"I'm more of a programmer than a killer, per se," Dennis says modestly. "But of course, everybody here has their own method."

The rest of the group has gone back to talking amongst themselves. Dennis's even voice is so low I have to lean in to hear him.

"What methods?" I ask, unsure I even want to know.

"Jada draws victims in and strikes when they least expect it. The twins are hedonistic process killers. Erik is an apex manipulator—"

"He's a what now?"

"He kills people by getting in their heads. He doesn't need to touch you, though he's happy to do it that way too. But most of his victims he broke down psychologically."

"Right." I roll my eyes, and Dennis turns from the fire and looks at me.

"I'm perfectly serious," he says. "And Javier—"

"You telling her all our numbers?" Javier leans in.

"Dennis, please!" Troy interrupts, "I'd prefer to go through my kills myself, in *detail*."

"No, thanks," I shake my head, unable to handle any more, "I don't want to know."

The entire circle goes quiet, staring at me. Everyone is bewildered, because obviously, what could be more exciting to a bunch of killers than reliving their crimes! Erik looks like he's about to burst out laughing. I take a deep breath and try to cover.

"I mean, sorry, I just don't want to compare report cards, okay? All the posturing and 'I'm harder than you' stuff. We're not fighting for cafeteria tables in Gen Pop." I try to sound casually tough. The hoarseness helps. So does the idea I've decapitated someone, probably. "Like, everybody here already got accepted into murder Harvard or whatever. So can't we get to know each other as people instead of rap sheets? Can't we just . . . hang out?"

Jada lets out an uncertain, mocking giggle, but Javier nods emphatically, and there's a note of real emotion in his voice as he says, "Yeah. Yeah, I'd like that a lot."

"I know *I'd* appreciate moving the emphasis off our body counts," Dennis says, and Troy shrugs.

"I can *hang out*, like bros, like brosefs, just chilling and stuff." There's a slight edge in his voice, but he's smiling.

Erik stares right at me with that awful wolfish smile. Like he's *so* onto me.

Then Nobody asks Kurt if he knows any Dolly Parton, and he starts strumming and the atmosphere relaxes.

"Ooooh, we should play truth or dare!" Jada claps her hands delightedly. She's moved next to Erik. She puts her hand on Erik's shoulder, but he leans forward to throw little bits of grass into the fire and it slips away.

Troy chimes in:

"Hell yeah! Truth or dare! I dare you to take your top off," Troy bellows.

"Ew, nasty!" Jada reaches behind Erik to shove Troy, hard. "Kill him, Erik!"

"I thought we were all pretending to be normal, like Signal wanted?" Erik addresses me then: "Truth or dare, Signal?"

I consider the choice, the only sounds the crackle of the fire and distant roll of the lake.

". . . Truth."

"Okay." Erik's eyes flit to Javier and then back to me. "Are you in a relationship?"

There's a flurry of comically dramatic gasps. My adrenaline spikes, but I know exactly what to say.

"If you must know, *nobody* is my girlfriend." Emphasis on the small n.

Erik immediately catches it, blurting: "Wait, wait let me rephrase!" But everyone drowns him out clapping and making catcalls. Nobody does a collar pop, and Troy loses it. I look to Javier, but his head is down, he's stripping bark from a stick.

And now it's my turn to ask.

I look around the circle, then turn to Javier with the biggest smile I can muster.

"Javier, truth or dare?"

He smiles, a small smile, but it changes his face, makes him go from manly to boyish.

"Dare."

Now I really have no idea what to say.

"But I'm not taking off my shirt," he adds.

"I dare you . . ." I swallow, a little overcome by my new power. "To . . . sing along with the next song Kurt plays."

Kurt does a drum roll on his guitar and launches into an opening chord, but when it gets to the point Javier should sing he doesn't. His shy smile becomes a nervous cringe, and I realize I've hit a nerve. Big muscly Javier is afraid of singing in public?! Well . . . that's actually kind of adorable.

"Wait, what song is this?" I ask with my best confused expression.

"It's 'Redemption Song.' By Bob Marley."

"Ah ha! So you *do* know it! Get singing, then!" I reach out as if to poke him in the arm but draw back before I connect, and just like that, his smile is back.

He clears his throat, waits for Kurt to get through the intro again, and then comes in, clear and soft and on key. One after the other we join in with him, until we're all singing, except Erik. He just stares at me through the fire, but I don't care. I'd forgotten how good it feels to sing. Like the opposite of crying.

Chapter Five

On Your Mark

～

"RISE AND SHINE!" Kate's voice cuts through my sleep as she snaps on the halogen light right by my face.

"It's still dark,"

"It's still morning. How's the neck?" she asks chummily.

"Awful." I'm unable to look her in the eye; her friendliness is so galling after yesterday. I instead shimmy down the ladder and start to follow Nobody toward the bathroom, but Jada stops us, pulling jeans over her pajama leggings.

"Don't bother with the shower," she mutters, sleep in the corners of her eyes. "Until after the obstacle course."

* * *

What I can make out in the shivery light of morning doesn't look fun.

After we hike up to the overgrown soccer field, Dave has us line up with the boys along a fat stripe of white spray paint. Across from us wait three chain-link fences, each about ten feet apart, and a grid of rope staked to the ground that leads up to a super tall sheet of plywood. Like, tall-as-a-house tall, with a square hole punched in it the size of a picture window. And that's just what I can see from starting line.

"Campers!" Dave's breath condenses in the freezing air. "Time for our morning obstacle course run! For our newcomers"—his eyes catch mine before he sips from a steel thermos—"we run the obstacle course every day. We run it because it will save your lives. Your activities cannot be linked back to any official channels—"

"CIA," coughs Troy, earning a swift glare from Dave.

"Which means: when the time comes, and you go into the field to take your target out and you mess up, no one is coming to save you. No agency will claim you. You get caught, your prisons will report you as fugitives. To every authority outside this camp, you are just a Class A, doing what Class As do best. And the sentences on Class As are getting tougher every day."

He points up to the obstacle course.

"That's why all our lessons are based on learning general skills you can improvise with out in the field. We are training you to take care of yourselves. Because out in the real world, much like out on that obstacle course, there is no safety net."

Wait, what? No safety net?!

"What did we come to camp to learn?" he yells.

"How to not get caught!" they yell back.

"What did we come to camp to learn?" he hollers right at me.

"How to not get caught!" I join in.

"All right! So! Pretty simple!" Dave continues briskly. "You're gonna go straight through the course, one obstacle after the next, fast as you can. When the first person gets all the way through, they turn around and chase the person who finishes after them. You catch the person behind you, you're done! Sit down and relax. But if they make it past you to the tree line, you have to go through again. Easy, right?"

The way the others laugh at this chills me. I never played a sport in school. I ditched gym whenever possible. Apparently, I chose wrong.

"What about the last person?" I ask.

"Last one automatically has to go again," Dennis tells me, with a look on his face that speaks of bitter experience.

"On your mark!" Dave yells. "Get set. *Go!*"

We sprint forward and I learn how to climb chain link by watching Erik and Javier shoot ahead. (Throw your hands up as far as you can, hitch your foot up high, keep your knees locked at the top, and throw yourself down.) I'm winded by the third fence, and when I jump down I land in knee-deep, ice-cold mud.

"Effing GROSS!" Jada groans, landing with a squelch behind me. Nobody slogs past us and grapples up the grid of rope ladders toward the big square hole in the plywood wall. I chase after her, but when I scramble through there's *another* plywood wall beyond it, with its own square window, placed *even higher*.

It has to be twenty feet off the ground.

Connecting the two windows is a narrow rope ladder that looks like a faulty bridge from an Indiana Jones movie. Below, just like Dave warned, is nothing but the ground, a plot of cold mud. The rope ladder creaks back and forth in the morning breeze.

"You have got to be kidding me," I mutter, climbing out onto the first few rungs.

"Yo! Passing from behind!" someone calls.

And whoever is behind me proceeds to *flip the ladder over.* The black earth and white sky trade places as a roller-coaster scream tears out of me and suddenly I'm hanging upside down, the weight of my entire body pulling at my slippery hands and feet, as Kurt literally climbs over me. Once his weight shifts off the ladder, sky and earth blur as the ladder spins, then swings sickeningly back and forth, left and right, again and again, my cold clenched hands going needles-and-pins numb before it finally settles.

Head down, I creep across the ladder to the second square window and get a leg through, clutching the wall so hard the plywood buckles in time with me. A length of rope hangs down below the second window and I watch as Kurt finishes rappelling down to the ground, with no harness.

"You can do this. You can do this. Get your feet flat on the wall," I tell myself out loud, as if I'm some reality show contestant on TV. I grab the rope and back out over an almost two-story drop.

But this isn't TV. This is me, a bag of meat, and gravity. I immediately slide down the rope. I have to clench my fists so hard the skin flays off my palms to grind to a halt, five feet from impact. When my raw fingers release the coarse rope, I drop hard into cold thick mud.

Three lanes of the same freezing wet dirt zigzag under a low grid of barbed wire. Getting on my hands and knees isn't low enough, I have to sink to my belly, head down, face practically in the muck, to keep the wire from snagging my hair. At least there's no way to fall. When I finally slog through to the end of the barbed wire run and heave myself back to standing, I'm soaked through and shivering hard.

And what's waiting in front of me is . . . an apartment building? No. What?

I stagger closer. It's yet another climbing wall, but dressed like a building: the detailed façade includes vinyl siding, a door, and three pairs of window frames nailed to the plywood. There's muddy tracks, but no rope or ladder. How are we supposed to get up there?

Dennis shoots in front of me and throws himself at the door, grabbing the white lintel of the doorframe, one of his sneakers landing on the doorknob.

We're supposed to free-climb up a thirty-foot tall fake building?

"MOVE, SIGNAL! YOU'RE IN LAST PLACE!!" Dave shrieks right in my ear, and I turn on him, wet, freezing, and as angry as I've ever been in my life.

"I can't!" I blurt and Dave's whistle drops from his mouth. "I'll fall, okay? I can't climb anymore. I am physically exhausted."

Behind Dave, from the campers who've finished, I hear a low: *"Ooooooh."*

"And how," Dave says after a long silence, "do you think you're going to feel after you murder and dispose of an adult body, Signal?!" He pushes his face close to mine, eyes unnaturally wide. "You think you're going to be *refreshed*, Signal? No. You're going to be 'physically exhausted.' You can't clear a scene, you get caught. You get caught, *you fry*. Or hang. Or get a lethal injection. Or you learn how to MOVE YOUR ASS AND CLEAR THE COURSE."

There's a faint giggle from behind him and my face burns.

"Get back on your mark. You're running again. All the way this time."

No.

"Erik! Jada! Kurt! On your mark!" Dave snarls, and blows on his whistle, high and shrill.

"Last place, huh?" Erik calls, beating me to the starting line, his hair and the whole side of his head (including one of his dimples) plastered with mud. "I was first, you know. But Javier was second and got past me."

"Yeah? Cool story. Hey—" I tap my cheek. "You got a little something on your face."

Javier jogs toward us, and lands on the other side of me.

"Why are you running again?" Erik calls over to him.

"Extra credit," Javier shrugs. "What, you nervous I'll outrun you again? Because you should be."

"On your mark!" Dave yells. "Get set! GO!"

The first run of the obstacle course was the most grueling physical ordeal of my life. The second time is infinitely worse. Because now I know what's waiting at the end.

When I get to the fake apartment building, Jada's still rappelling down the wall and Erik is halfway up the apartment façade, climbing up the drainpipe. I guess Javier got through first. Kurt flies past me and I lurch after him, trembling with exhaustion.

I leap for the lintel and hoist one foot up onto the doorknob, throw my arms up for the windowsill and dig my fluttering fingertips into its ledge. My vision narrows as I try to pull myself up. I can't, my arms won't respond, I can't—

A flash of muddy pink flannel in my peripheral as Jada passes me.

No. I *cannot* do this again. I've got to move.

I haul myself up so my hips are level with the windowsill and bring one foot up on the ledge, then reach up and grope above my head as I push myself upward, until I can grip the top of the window frame and pull myself up. So now I'm standing on tiptoe, on a thin wood windowsill, two stories off the ground.

I just need to get over to the drainpipe. It's on the other side of the window next to the one I'm clinging to. I just have to take one big step from my window ledge to the next one. So easy. Don't think about how far it is down. Two stories, but don't think about it.

I turn my head slightly and glance down at the next windowsill. The muddy ground between swims up like a rising tide of dark water and my pulse throbs in my ears and I cannot move.

"SIGNAL!!!!" Dave screams from far below, "I COUNT TO THREE AND YOU ARE DOING THIS AGAIN, LAST OR NOT, I SWEAR—"

It feels like I'm moving in slow motion, as I swing my leg out over the churning ground, and rest my foot on the far ledge. I take a breath, shift my weight, and my muddy sneaker instantly slips.

The world leaps to the side, the ground racing to claim me.

And then it goes still again.

Someone has caught the back of my shirt. An iron arm winds around my waist, and as I'm pulled back to safety two dark eyes meet mine with a small cartoon tear beside them.

"I got you." Javier's voice is calm and unhurried as I wrap my shaking arms around his neck. "It's okay, I got you."

"LET'S MOVE IT, LADIES!" Dave bellows idiotically below us.

I cling to Javier as he expertly crosses the gap between the two windows, so we're beside the drainpipe.

"NO HELPING!!!" Dave shrieks.

"It's easy from here," Javier says. "I'm right behind you. Okay? I'm not going to let you fall."

"Okay." But it takes a few moments before I can let go of him and reach for the drainpipe. From there it's a short distance to the small platform of the fake roof. I climb out onto the roof the way a kid gets out of a pool, flopping onto my stomach, kicking my legs and rolling onto my back. Dave's whistle blows distantly, but I'm too relieved to care.

There's three tiers of fire escapes down the back of the fake apartment building. My legs wobble under me as I trot down them, ready to collapse. But just as I'm back on solid ground and turning away from the whole hateful course, I see Erik. Crouching down low. Ready to chase me.

Jada and Kurt passed him? Did he *let them*?!

So he could chase me?

The teen idol dimples deepen as he grins. I feint left, then jog right, but it doesn't fool him. He leaps, long arms going wide, and then he's on top of me, the hinge of his jaw digging into the top of my head, my face so tight against his neck I can feel his pulse drumming fast against my cheek.

We hit the ground together, hard, his sharp hip bones digging into me, his arms bound around my shoulders, my face against his throat. His muscular weight crushes down on me one moment, then pulls me under the next, again and again, as we roll over and over the crisp cold grass until we sprawl to a stop, me on top of him, his cat eye locked on mine with some expression I don't understand. For a moment I can't move. Then he smiles and whispers,

"Weakling."

Dave's whistling is hysterical as we untangle from each other. I've never been so dizzy. The ground bobs up and down, up and down, like I'm on a swing. Black magnetic filings eat through reality and knit into darkness, and all I know is I'm on the ground again.

* * *

"Here she comes." Dave's voice, annoyed. A few blinks bring full consciousness back, along with the mortifying realization that all the campers are crowded around watching me come to. Nobody kneels at my side, holding my hand awkwardly.

"You blacked out," she explains. "For like, five minutes."

"Someone needs to work on her stamina, huh?" Dave laughs to the group.

"No kidding, Dave," I mutter.

"Javier and Kurt, you two run the course one last time. Then we'll break for lunch. Signal, since I don't especially feel like slapping a cast together today, how about you jog the field three times and join us once you've finished. Who wants to count her off?"

"I will," Nobody volunteers.

"How about someone who isn't dating her?" Dave snaps, eliciting a delighted *"Daaaamn, Dave!"* from Troy. Jada volunteers.

"Okay! Jada, you count her off. Javier, Kurt, let's hustle . . ."

My head is still swimming as I get to my feet, I'm more hobbling than jogging my first lap. I watch the final run on the obstacle course: Javier moves through it so quickly. How was he behind me when I fell?

Did he purposefully lag behind to help me?

Jada, sitting on an ancient hay bale with a faded archery target clinging to it, holds up two fingers as I pass by.

"I'm starting my third lap," I gasp.

"I'm the one counting."

"Yeah, well, it's my third lap," I insist, and stagger on, quietly furious, as Dave leads the others off the field. My head is getting light again and it's an effort just to stay upright. Maybe Jada will let me just call it a day so we can go eat.

I turn back to the hay bale, and she's standing. Something about the way she stands, shoulders back, arms at her sides, makes me stop. And that's when she runs toward me.

I try to run but my side seizes, and she overtakes me, yanking my hair, pulling my head back and pressing something hard and sharp to my cheek.

An arrowhead. From the hay bale.

"I told you," Jada snarls in my ear. "Be a slut, get cut."

Chapter Six
Crown of Weeds

～

The sharpened arrowhead presses into the thin skin over my cheekbone, the white clouds above us the only witnesses to whatever comes next.

"This is pathetic," I sputter, bluffing wildly. "You know I've got a girlfriend. Who'll be *pissed* if you hurt me."

"You didn't look like you had a girlfriend when you were rolling around with Erik."

"*He* grabbed *me*."

Wrong answer.

The arrowhead cuts a stripe below my eye as I step hard on her foot. I twist away but she pounces and I'm sprawled out in the grass with her crouching over me, forearm pinning down my neck, the arrowhead jerking the corner of my mouth into a perverse half-smile. A single hot tear of blood winds down the side of my face.

And then a voice rings out across the field:

"Jada?" Erik's voice is infuriatingly calm, almost laughing. "Why is Signal on the ground?"

She just stares through me, hand tensed, until footsteps land in the grass just above my head.

"Girl stuff," Jada says darkly. "We'll just be a minute."

"Yeah, well, Dave wants to see her." Erik yawns. "And he's going to notice if parts are missing."

"Wow." Jada glares up at him. "You're as bad as Javier. Maybe let Signal fight her own battles?"

"Not much of a battle." Erik's voice shifts from calm to cool. "She fainted ten minutes ago and she's unarmed."

"I just want to make her face match her girlfriend's." My stomach lurches as Jada goes on. "Or would that bother you? Is that why you came racing up here to check on precious princess Signal?"

"Jada," Erik sighs. "Why did you lie to me?"

She's thrown. "What?"

"When you said you'd never be with a guy who only cared about looks. That was a lie."

"No, it wasn't."

"So why mess up how *she* looks? Why ask if that would bother me? Kind of seems like you think I only care about looks."

"*Of course* you only care about looks," Jada laughs angrily. "Are you kidding me? That's *how you work, how every guy works!*"

"So all guys are like your stepbrother." Erik must be crouching down because his voice moves closer, like he's just beside me. "They see a stack of parts instead of a person, and they're constantly on the lookout for a better stack of parts?"

"Damn it, Erik." Her arm on my neck shifts, just for an instant. I'd jerk away but the arrowhead is still in my mouth, the point rattling between my teeth. "You think I'm blind?! Ever since she got here you keep staring at her, you're obsessed with her—"

"Jada," Erik says. "Look at me."

And then she does. Up close, the transformation is remarkable: her eyes had been remote before, but when they lock with Erik's her face softens. She looks younger, and desperate from pain.

"If you think I see you the way your stepbrother did, but you still want to be with me, then on some level you're accepting your stepbrother's view of you," Erik's deep voice continues.

"Shut up!" Jada snarls. A tear flashes down her face and hits my neck, warm as a summer raindrop.

"I know you gave up everything to get away from him," Erik goes on. "But he's hiding in every guy you meet. You still see the world through his eyes, whether you're looking at Signal or at me. Is that why you're angry?"

Jada's lip jerks, her chin dimples. She sits back on her heels, and I immediately roll to my side and wobble to my feet, expecting any minute for her to pounce on me again. But when I look back Jada is rocking back and forth, head hanging between her knees, sobbing. When my eyes meet Erik's he mouths, *Go.*

So I run to the lower field as fast as I can.

* * *

When I get there, the Teen Killers Club is sitting on a patchwork of old blankets and faded quilts, puffed up by the uncut grass underneath so it looks like they're picnicking on top of a giant down comforter. They're all eating from lunch bags Kate brought up from the kitchen. Nobody waves me over, holding up a bag with my name on it. Kate squints beyond me.

"Where's Erik and Jada? Why didn't they come back with you?"

"They're . . . talking."

Kate's smile drops and she shoots to her feet. She breaks into a run as she nears the tree line.

"They're just talking!" I call after her.

"Talking with Erik can be life-threatening," Dennis reminds me between bites of a PB&J.

"Here," Nobody says gruffly, swatting my leg with the lunch bag. "Eat."

I peer inside: a sandwich, banana, and *Sour Cream & Onion Ruffles?!* A lesser fake girlfriend might have eaten them herself, but Nobody has my back.

"Oh man, I haven't had these in forever," I gush, popping open the bag and shoving the shards into my mouth with shaking fingers.

"You're bleeding," Nobody says matter-of-factly.

"Huh . . . how did that happen?" I drag the least muddy bit of my sleeve across my cheek. It's not a good look that I got rolled by Jada after fainting on the obstacle course, and everyone hates a snitch. Nobody doesn't press, so I cram my food down, hunched over so no one notices how much my hands are shaking.

When Kate returns with Jada and Erik, his hands are in his pockets and her face is a blank. They go to sit at opposite ends of the quilt, though. Troy leans over and says something that makes Jada give him a tight smile.

I dare a glance at Javier, who is stretched out on his back across a yellow blanket nearby, hands clasped behind his head as though sleeping. It's like he's activated by the sunlight: his skin glows, a small unconscious smile warming his handsome features.

I know I should thank him for saving me, but the idea of starting a conversation is terrifying. Which is ridiculous. He saved my life! It's actually weirder if I don't thank him!

I summon all my courage, lean forward, and tap him on his shoulder.

"Hey." I take a deep breath, "Javier?"

SMACK. A sopping wet trash bag flops onto the ground in front of me, hurled with enough force to scatter its muddy contents across the picnic quilts.

"Signal, you just failed your first test here," Dave announces, and everyone turns to stare.

"Didn't even need the dogs to find it," Dave continues, his voice rising. "Your body just *found itself*, Signal. Just washed up on shore while you were busy fainting up at the obstacle course."

The mannequin has landed face up, and memory of Rose's face after she wasn't Rose anymore comes back with searing clarity. Her blue eyes staring into eternity, her lips slack over red teeth. It is always there, in the back of my mind, under everything I see.

"You're getting *one last chance* with this body, Signal." Dave sounds far away, and I try to hold onto the anger in his reddening face, to connect to any kind of embarrassment that will pull me out of the flashback, but it's like the present is a dim film playing on the wall of the shed where I'm still trapped, Rose's body in my lap forever.

"Signal!!" Dave's hand grabs my collar, jolting me back to reality. "Did you hear me?"

I blink at him, relieved.

"What did you come to camp to learn?"

I honestly don't remember the phrase.

"*How not to get caught.*" Dave blows his whistle, still glaring at me. "Campers! Everyone else can return to their cabins to clean up. Everyone except for Signal, who is falling behind *yet again.*"

I get on my knees and start picking her up as everyone leaves. My arms jerk, my fingers spasm as I try to pile the fake girl back together.

And then I realize someone is staring.

"Okay, seriously, what now?" I say, looking up in the direction they've all left, expecting to see Jada again.

But there's no one.

I rise to my feet and turn in a slow circle, trying to hear past the rush of wind through the leaves. Behind me the first dark pines at the edge of the forest stand waiting. Their deep shadows could hide anything.

"Signal!" A voice from the opposite direction. Javier lopes toward me through the tall grass and I swallow a cry of relief.

"Look, I know we're not supposed to help each other." He looks over his shoulder, then drops his voice confidentially. "But there's kind of a trick to getting rid of the bodies. If you want, I could show you."

"Yes. *Please.*"

He catches up the stack of limbs, I grab the head.

"Okay then," he says. "Follow me."

*   *   *

Javier drops the mannequin parts. Here, in the heart of a scruffy little clearing almost retaken by the forest, is a rusted-out playground. It's impossible to imagine children playing here, but they must have once. What a magical place this camp must have seemed like then.

"We're really far from the group now," I point out uneasily.

"Yeah, we need to be. Can't let Dave smell the smoke," Javier explains. "The burn barrel's this way," he calls over his shoulder, hurrying toward a break in the trees.

"The what?"

I chase him down a narrow path to a grouping of tall, mossy boulders. The shortest one is at least seven feet tall, with dark streaks pressed into its green moss that make sense when Javier carefully climbs up its side.

He slips into the space between the boulders, there's muffled clanging, and then a large rusted trashcan appears above me.

"I'm letting go on three," he calls. "Ready?"

"Okay!" I reach up as the massive metal can rattles down and manage to slow its landing. Javier climbs carefully back down beside me, the lid under his arm, and lifts up the bottom of the can. I hoist up the top and see the inside is encrusted with something like black lava.

"We all melted our bodies down during the drill so they'd be easier to hide," Javier explains. We lug it back to the playground and stand it right in the middle of the sandpit. I dump the mannequin's head and a couple of limbs inside as Javier produces a small bottle of lighter fluid from his pocket.

"Where did you get that?"

"We keep it with the barrel, along with some matches and whatever else we can sneak out of the kitchen."

"But I thought we were only allowed to use what we were given?"

"The point of the test is not to fail." Javier gives me a sad smile. "'Allowed' doesn't get you much out here. Now back up."

He squirts lighter fluid around the inside of the can, lights up half a book of matches, then steps back as he throws it in.

A WHOOSH of angry orange flame shoots out and the birds hurl themselves shrieking from the branches overhead. Javier clamps the lid on and black smoke trails out of the vents bored into the lid.

"We can only do a couple pieces at a time. So it takes a while," Javier says, retreating toward the swings. I follow him to a patch of grass upwind from the blue smoke now winding toward the trees. The smell is sharp and caustic, even though we're a dozen yards away.

Javier yawns and lies back in the grass, throwing his forearm across his face, and the line of a tattoo peeks from his sleeve. To keep from staring, I turn away to see a patch of exceptionally hardy dandelions, so yellow they glow even in the shadow of the woods. I pick one, enjoying the peppery smell, the feel of the cool feathery petals against my cheek. I pick a couple more, and then, just like Rose used to, I begin to loop them together.

"How're you doing that?" Javier's got one eye open under the shadow of his forearm. I give him a big inviting smile.

"This? It's just a daisy chain. But with dandelions."

"I thought that only worked in cartoons."

"You've never made a daisy chain?" My voice comes out just a little too high. "If you want, I could show you."

"Okay." He sits up and his eyes meet mine directly and it's so intense I stare at the flowers again, picking two, splitting the stems and talking way too fast as I explain how to link them. I'm semi-coherent but he listens patiently. After a few moments of rambling instructions, I hear myself ask, "So, uh, what's your tattoo of?"

Javier pulls up his sleeve to reveal an outline of a little boy holding a radio controller and staring up at the sky. Above him is a small remote-control plane. The boy is drawn in one continuous line, but somehow that single line captures a dozen telling details.

"Wow, that's *amazing!* It must have cost a fortune."

"I did it myself." Javier smiles sheepishly. "Bic and needle."

"WHAT?!" I grab his arm before I really think that through. I stare down at the lines but all I'm conscious of is the sculpted arm they're etched into, and the heat creeping up my neck.

"Amazing." I retract my hands, embarrassed. "Who is it?"

"It's just from an old photo." He stares at the dandelions in his lap. I can tell there's more, but I don't want to pry.

"Would you draw me something like that? You're very talented."

"Tell that to this daisy chain!" He holds up a broken tangle of stems, and I laugh too hard, but he laughs too, so it's okay.

"Oh, see, you have to bring in the third one now . . . like that, and then . . . we bring the two ends together and . . . ta-da, it's a crown!" I start to set it on his head, but he shies away.

"You should wear it. The yellow will look nice against the blue."

When I plop it on my head he leans forward, his knees knocking into mine, and carefully adjusts it, his face so close I can count his eyelashes. He sits back and smiles at me.

"Now, that's really something. A real live flower crown."

"Well, not really." I look down, overcome. "I mean, dandelions aren't actual flowers, right? They're like, weeds, technically?"

"No way. Who even gets to decide that? They're definitely flowers. Don't believe anyone who tells you otherwise," Javier says, and he reaches up to gently move a strand of my hair in place under the crown.

"Hey there, you two." Erik's deep voice rings through the trees, and I turn to see him all cleaned up, his long hair damp, holding half a bag of marshmallows.

"Hey, Erik." Javier smiles, but it's a different smile. Tenser.

"Helping Signal with her homework?" Erik pushes a marshmallow into his mouth and chews it while staring him down. "Kate needs you for Arts and Crafts, she said."

Javier stands, runs his hand over his close-cropped head, his expression sweetly confused as he looks down at me. I stand too, knocking the broken dandelions from my hands.

"Thanks again, Javier."

"No problem. Keep with it. Shouldn't take more than a couple hours." He holds out the lighter fluid. I take the flat tin can and watch him disappear through the trees, leaving me all alone with Erik.

"Sorry if I *interrupted something*."

"We were just talking."

"No fair. Javier never plays with my hair when he talks to me," Erik says drily, and I quickly pull the dandelion crown off.

"I have a girlfriend, remember?" I walk past him to the old swing set behind us and perch on one of the rusty swings, the cold sand spilling into my shoes. Erik fishes another marshmallow out of his bag and walks slowly toward me.

"You should remind Javier next time you see him." Erik settles into the swing next to mine, his heavily muscled shoulders slightly bowed between the chains. "Marshmallow?"

I shake my head. "I'm a vegetarian."

"Of course you are," he says almost to himself. Erik bites the last piece of marshmallow off his long finger. He'd have beautiful hands, except all his nails are bitten down to the quick. It hurts to look at.

"First Javier saves you on the obstacle course," Erik continues, "now he's hiding your body? I don't want to get your hopes up, Signal, but he might have a crush on you."

"Doubtful," I mutter, mortified.

"It's either that or he thinks you're a complete idiot." Erik shrugs. "Or maybe he likes you *because* he thinks you're a complete idiot? Though personally, you strike me as the type who spends her weekends in the library."

Ouch.

"*Thanks*, but you can save the condescending psychobabble for your girlfriend."

"Jada's not my girlfriend, since you're dying to know," he says. "And since my 'condescending psychobabble' kept her from extending your smile to both ears, *you're welcome.*"

He catches my expression and recoils, laughing.

"What a face! Signal, you're awfully squeamish for a girl who *supposedly* decapitated someone and *allegedly* dates a burn victim."

"Yeah, well, I don't believe you have super psychic powers, so I guess we're even."

"'Super psychic powers'?!"

"That's what you've been telling everyone, right? That you kill people *with your mind.*"

"Oh, sure, yeah, that." Erik nods. "That's not superpowers. That's just having a knack for psychology." He turns his full gaze on me, eyes wide and earnest. Coupled with his long, expressive eyebrows and cat's-eye pupil, it's kind of overwhelming.

"You find a person's weakness, right? That's easy, people tell you their weaknesses all the time. Then you get friendly and slowly make them believe that weakness is gone. Once they believe that, boom." He jabs his thumb in the air. "You break right through it, right into their heads."

"How specific and rational that sounds." I roll my eyes, but it doesn't faze him.

"Eh, it's hard to describe something so . . . intuitive." His dimples are back. "What did Michelangelo say about sculpting? That he saw the angel in the marble and carved until he set him free? Not very helpful to every guy with a chisel. But that's the process."

"I'm surprised Dave and Kate don't let you teach a class."

"I wish they would. I'm starting to get seriously bored." Erik bites at his nails. "That's why I was hoping you'd let me help."

"Help with what?" I'm already bristling.

"Help figure out who killed your best friend."

Best friend. No one in the media coverage described Rose as my best friend. Rose herself laughed the title off after middle school. But it's how I've always thought of her, how I'll always think of her. I stare at the blue plume of smoke rising from the burn barrel and clutch the cold swing chains.

". . . How did you know Rose was my best friend?"

"Your face." Erik shrugs. "When Dave was reaming you out back there. You weren't listening to him. You were thinking of her. My guess is you loved her with all your heart." He gets up from his swing. "I better put another forearm on the fire."

He walks away, his swing rocking back and forth, the chains making a high seagull cry overhead, and my vision blurs. Because he's right. I loved Rose like a sister. Which is what no one, not her family or her friends or the world, seems to understand.

"Signal?" Erik's voice makes me drop my hands from my face, but he's not looking at me. He's lifted the lid with a stick and is staring into the barrel. "What was your body made out of?"

"Some sort of silicone. Why?"

"Silicone as in silicone bakeware? As in, highly heat and fire resistant?"

I hurry to the edge of burn barrel and peer in. My mannequin's head smiles up at me. Her glass eyes are blackened by smoke and her hair is gone but otherwise she's completely intact, and looking more than a little smug at her own resilience.

"You've *got* to be kidding me!"

I'm dizzy with exhaustion, my "99% Angel" sweatshirt is soaked through with cold mud from the obstacle course, and I'm back at square one. I seriously might collapse. Again.

"We'll stash her in the burn barrel and hide it in the woods." Erik's tone is decisive.

"It's too hot to touch."

Erik reaches for a large, faded pink plastic bucket at the edge of the sand box. "So we get some cold water from the stream."

"What stream?"

"The one that's closer than the lake, I'll show you. We can chat about Rose's case on the way. Or would you rather give me the bucket and have me get the water for you, Your Highness?"

I grab the bucket before he can make more comments about other people doing my homework.

"There's nothing to talk about."

"Really? Because I had a lot of thoughts about that senior she was dating." Erik walks past me toward the forest, adding: "Especially after his first alibi fell through."

"What?"

Erik turns back to me then, eyebrows raised. "You know. How Mike claimed he was at a party when she was killed. But when the police asked around no one had seen him, and then Mike confessed he'd left the party early to go smoke out with a friend." He watches me for a moment, then his tone softens. "Oh. You *didn't* know."

It's like being in freefall again.

"That can't be true." I clutch the bucket, my fingers going cold, the light-headedness from earlier washing over me. "Mike was a church kid, the pastor's son. He didn't even *drink*."

"Sounds like there's something to talk about, then." Erik shrugs, and disappears through the trees.

I hurry after him into the shadow of the forest, down a winding, narrow trail almost swallowed by banks of fern.

"How did you hear that?"

"It was covered in the news. How did you not? Your lawyer never brought it up?"

"My public defender wanted me to take a plea deal from the start." And I'd been so out of it during the trial, heavily sedated or manic with grief.

"So what, you never suspected Rose's *boyfriend*?" Erik pushes.

"Yes, but not Mike. The other one."

"Ha!" Erik laughs, eyebrows leaping, teeth flashing. "I *knew* you didn't kill anyone."

The air goes sour around us. My stomach fills with an acid tang.

I've just handed Erik my most damning secret.

Chapter Seven
Dog Mask

❧

"Is that what you wanted?" I choke the words out. "To get me to admit that?"

I can't believe I thought for even a moment that Erik understood me. He understands me the way a kid with a magnifying glass understands an anthill. I push past him, unable to bear his triumphant smile.

"Signal! Come on!" Erik calls after me. "I didn't *need* you to tell me. I knew the moment I saw you, I told you as much! That's why I want to help!"

No, he doesn't. He thinks Rose is just some weak spot in my head he can punch through. The trees blur into green and gold around me as I gain speed, the sound of water straight ahead.

"Signal, *stop*—" Erik's footsteps are heavy behind me before I'm pulled back from the edge of ravine, above a stream that slips and merges into a creek a few feet away. His hot hand clings to my shoulder, his voice just by my ear: "The perimeter of camp is the other side of that creek. You almost crossed the fence."

There's a feverish chill at the nape of my neck where his fingers brushed me.

"So what, was that part of your master plan?" I say when I find my voice again. "Get me out here, then push me over the creek once you were done chipping away at me, Michelangelo?"

"Very clever wordplay, Signal, very library of you," Erik sneers. "Maybe if you weren't so busy cooking up clever verbal jabs you could process the fact I have *no reason* to kill you. You're the first interesting thing that's happened at camp since I got here. All I want is to help solve your case."

"After you get done telling everybody else how innocent I am?" I turn to face him.

"I won't tell anyone you're innocent." His hand is on his heart like we're kids, but he looks completely serious. "I swear. Cross my heart and hope to die."

Part of me wants to give him the silent treatment for as long as we both shall live, but another part is deeply tempted. He can't exactly use the facts of my case to hurt me, the worst outcome has already happened.

"I don't know how you *could* help," I admit. "We're shut up in a camp hundreds of miles from where it happened. It's not like we can investigate for clues."

"Clues are the slow route," Erik says with utter conviction. "The fastest way to find a killer is to find the motive. Look at the crime. Look at the suspects. Make the connection."

I kneel down and dip the faded bucket in the creek, considering. "If you followed my case, then you know I don't remember what happened the night Rose died."

"I know," Erik says. "But you're still the best witness. Because you knew Rose, you know the suspects, and I promise you, *deep down*, you already know who the killer is."

I stare up at him as the statement hangs between us.

He wants this so badly. Why? He could just be bored. A guy as smart as Erik cut off from the world could just want a puzzle. Even one missing a lot of pieces.

I stand, hoisting up the full bucket, which he snatches away from me.

"Oh, so I'm too weak to carry a bucket now?"

"No, I'm too lazy to go back and fill it up again when you drop it."

"Ha ha ha," I say, but make no effort to take it back—it was ridiculously heavy. Instead, I walk by his side back up the trail.

"Why don't I tell you what I remember about the case, and you fill in what I've forgotten," Erik begins. "Rose was a popular junior with a senior boyfriend, Mike. There was a party in the woods the night she died. Her body was found the next morning, in a nearby shed. Correct?"

"Sort of. Ledmonton was a small town next to a big wilderness. The seniors would park by Lockwood Park, and walk through till they got to a wild part of the woods. Or you could cut into the wild part from the trailer park. But the wild part was big. The shed was almost a mile from where the party happened."

"Do you remember why you wanted to go to the shed?"

"I didn't," I tell him. "Rose did."

I always hated that old shed. The roof was rotted and went down at an angle; if it were an animal, you'd think someone had broken its back. Park kids used to make up stories about it. Claim they'd seen some bogeyman looking out its broken window. But no one ever went inside. Until that night.

"Rose called me and said she needed to get a picture there for her art project," I tell him. "I said it was late, but she said I would finally get to meet Mr. Moody, he was going to come and help too." I swallow. "She was alone when I got there, and her eyes were puffy, like she'd been crying. But she had all this makeup on, so I believed her when she said he was on his way."

"So she was depressed?"

"No. More like . . . she was jumpy. Talked a little fast, acted too cheerful. It was dark when I met her, and the shed was black inside. But she walked right in. So I followed."

"And then?"

"And then I don't know. My memory just jumps, like some kind of video glitch," I sigh. "The next thing I remember is waking up."

"What was this art project?"

"Her 'My Life' photo collage. It was this huge poster of cut-up photos of all her friends. Like, paper photos, the kind you have to get developed. I was flattered she wanted to include me. I mean, she wouldn't even talk to me at school." It's embarrassing to admit, but it's the truth. And if he's going to help me, I have to give him the facts, however ugly.

"Alright." Erik frowns. "So this Mr. Moody. What was his deal?"

"I don't know." I swallow. "That's the whole problem. She never told me his name."

"Why tell you about him at all?"

There it is, the familiar itch of guilt. "Because I covered for them."

After pointedly ignoring me for almost three years, Rose had come up to me one day and said, "I like your hair." It had been blue for months, but I was touched. A couple of days later she happened to be near where I caught my bus at the end of the day. We talked, and things felt almost normal, and then she offered me a ride home. When she dropped me off by the park, she asked if my number had changed, and I'd almost teared up when she texted me about sleeping over that weekend.

It was surreal being in Rose's room again. She still had the four-poster, but the shadow boxes of concert tickets and spent glow sticks were new. As was the slide bolt on the inside of her door, the kind of thing you install with six screws. I had plenty of time to look around, since Rose was busy frantically trying on different outfits.

"So here's the thing," Rose said, head emerging from a tight red sweater. "This guy is coming by and I'm going to like, go out and say hi for a little bit? I shouldn't be more than an hour. If my parents check in, could you just tell them I went to get like, my textbook from the car or something?"

". . . Oh, okay . . . Is it Mike?"

"Mike? No. You know the rules at Tom's church. You can't see someone you're dating alone. Only in a group."

"But Mike's okay with you seeing this guy?"

"Mike doesn't know. And it's going to stay that way," Rose said significantly. "That's why I asked you here. Because I can trust you to keep a secret."

She was right. Who did I have to tell?

She tiptoed out of her room at nine PM and left me watching Netflix with a knot in my stomach until midnight, when she came back starry-eyed and smelling like smoke.

"So what now?" I'd asked as Rose sat in front of her vanity and traced her poreless face with a makeover wipe. "Are you going to break up with Mike?"

"I can't break up with Mike. He'd kill himself."

"What?!" Then in a lower voice as she frantically shushed me: "Did he actually say that to you?! He can't threaten you like that!"

"It's not a *threat*. He just . . . needs me right now. But he's graduating in a year and then he'll be off at college. So why go through all the drama of a breakup and miss senior prom? It's not like my parents would let me see another guy anyway." She widened her eyes meaningfully. "You know how they are."

I nodded, getting it.

"So please, *please* come sleep over once in a while, please? Or else . . ." She held up my hand by the littlest finger. "I'm pretty sure I get to cut off your pinky."

* * *

"I slept over twice, three times a week after that," I tell Erik.

He absorbs it for a moment, then: "But there was no evidence anyone else had been in the shed the night she was killed. I remember the prosecution really hammering that home."

"Yes. *However*—" and this is the point I've been trying to make for the last year, "I've never lost time like that in my life. And I know this guy had serious drugs, because he started giving them to Rose. I think he gave me something that knocked me out. And something else happened. Something terrible." I take a deep breath to steady myself. "And afterwards, he staged the shed to frame me."

Erik bites his thumbnail thoughtfully. "This theory never came up during the trial."

"Because the police didn't find drugs in my bloodstream." I push my hair behind my ear. "But what if he used something they couldn't trace?

He was so careful. He had all these rules for Rose: no emails, no texts, no phone calls. She could only Snapchat him to plan a meetup, and they would only meet up when I was covering. So *I'm* the only evidence he exists. *That's* why he framed me."

"Can I see your hand?"

A little surprised, I hold it up. Erik holds his own up to it, our palms almost but not quite touching. His fingers pass mine by a good inch.

"Tiny and weak, surprise surprise," he murmurs. "She was strangled, if I remember, that was the official cause of death. Yes?"

". . . Yes."

"So if Mr. Moody wanted to frame you, he'd have to hide the markings made by his own, almost certainly larger, hands. Which would explain the mutilation."

I feel queasy as he goes on excitedly. "And if he decided to frame you after he'd just murdered someone, and then executed that plan so perfectly he actually *got away with it*, well, we're talking about a *pure psychopath*." His tone reminds me of guys from my high school talking about star football players. "The kind who can completely compartmentalize his kills from his personality. I call this type the 'Nice Guy' psychopath, like Ted Bundy. He's the *last* guy you'd suspect, a fine upstanding citizen, cool and calculating enough to present a perfect façade." He tilts his head and looks at me. "Almost the polar opposite of you."

"What's that supposed to mean?"

"Well, you're *obviously* pretending to be someone you're not." Erik shrugs. "The whole tough girl act you do, when you're the softest Class A in existence." He shakes his head as we return to the forgotten playground. "I told you last night I was worried about your odds here, and that was before you fell off the obstacle course and then *fainted*."

"Actually," I bristle, "when you're wrongfully convicted, it takes a certain inner strength—"

"Inner strength?" Erik laughs. "Okay, cool, but I'm talking about the kind that matters. Like when you're trying to survive camp. Or carry a bucket from point A to point B—"

"Wow, okay!" I snap. "You want proof I can be a hard ass? Keep threatening me!" I grab the bucket and splash the water into the burn barrel for emphasis. A wild, crackling hiss erupts as steam shoots up between us. Erik's too close—he catches it all in his face and folds over like he's been punched.

"Erik?! Are you okay?!"

He can't answer, he's coughing so hard, the cords of his muscular neck straining. I hurry to pat his back and offer the bucket, which still has a little water in it.

"I know its stream water, but it's better than nothing. Erik? Say something?"

He gives me a huge bleary smile, eyes streaming from his coughing fit.

"You can't help it, can you?" he laughs hoarsely, regaining his full height. "You're way too sweet to be here."

"I'm *not* sweet."

"You're sugar, cubed." He pulls the cuff of his sleeve over his palm and rubs at his eyes, clears his throat, then demands: "Also, when did I threaten you? I didn't threaten you."

"What you said last night! And again, just now! That I wouldn't survive here!"

"I'm not—I wasn't trying to *threaten you*, okay? It's just true. You shouldn't be here, because you're innocent." His eyes are shot through with red veins, making their sea-glass green color even more vivid. "Maybe last night I hoped to startle you into confessing, because it's, uh . . . not an easy thing to admit in this group."

It's such a candid statement I don't know what to say, other than "Whatever." And then, in as tough a voice as I can manage, "Sorry about the steam though."

"No big deal," he says, though there's a little rasp to his voice. And then we both gather the limbs of my mannequin and throw them in the burn barrel, the birds overhead filling the silence.

"So if Mr. Moody killed Rose"—Erik grabs the edge of the barrel—"we just have to figure out who he was."

I get the other end. "I feel like I'm talking your ear off about all this."

"I'm *riveted*," he promises. "And I want to go back to what you said before, that Mr. Moody had serious drugs. Where would he get heavy stuff in a small town like Ledmonton?"

There's only one answer to that. "Jaw Itznicki."

"What was he like?"

"Horny burn-out who smelled like he ate cigarettes?"

Erik's short, sharp laugh surprises me; I think it surprises him as well. "That's a *vivid* portrait," he says, grinning. "How would you sum up Dave?"

"Hmm." I tilt my head, "Quantico reject starts little league team?"

Erik almost drops the barrel, and that sets me off.

"Okay, okay," Erik smiles. "Back on track: tell me every detail you can think of."

"Let's see . . . Jaw was in our grade at school until he got expelled for hot boxing in the high school parking lot. He wore all black and bleached his hair white. He lived in the same trailer park I did—" I gaze directly into Erik's eyes when I say trailer park. He holds my gaze, unembarrassed: I guess he's a looker too. "But he did a lot of landscaping around Rose's neighborhood. And picked up money on the side, dealing drugs to the rich kids that lived around there."

"Did he strike you as mercurial in nature?" The side of Erik's mouth twitches. "Moody, even?"

"There's no way he was Mr. Moody." I shake my head. "Jaw sold drugs, but why would he want to keep Rose a secret? She would've been the best thing that ever happened to him."

"Maybe Rose was the one who wanted secrecy, if her parents were so strict."

"Well, yeah, Rose's stepdad would have freaked, but no one would have gone to jail. You have to understand, the way she guarded him . . . Like, it was a matter of life or death."

"Well, apparently it was," Erik says, then abruptly swings himself up the sheer face of the boulder Javier had carefully negotiated before. His agility is sort of unnerving. He's so normal, until he isn't.

"Hand me the barrel?" Erik looks down from the top of the boulder, through a cloud of shimmering green leaves. It takes all my strength to hoist the barrel high enough for him to reach. He pulls it up one-handed, the metal scraping against the rock before he throws it down with an almost musical clang.

"How would Mike have felt, I wonder," Erik says, "if he found out Rose had been cheating on him with Jaw?"

I fight not to look impressed as he skids gracefully down the sheer side of the rock and lands at my side.

"Mike certainly fits your 'Nice Guy' profile," I concede. "Finding out about Rose would've given him a motive. And he was in the woods that night. Do you remember who backed up his second alibi?"

"I want to say Van Gogh?"

"*Vaughn!*" Of course. I should've known.

I try to describe to Erik a fire drill at the start of our junior year. Everyone circled up in their friend molecules on the lawn, with those three at the center of our high school chemical structure: Mike in his varsity jacket, Rose's dark hair gilded by sunlight, dark and handsome Vaughn with an unlit cigarette behind his ear.

"My mom is such a psycho bitch. Truly," Rose sighed as Mike's arms wound around her and pulled her in against his chest. "Tom grounded me for a week because she snooped through my room and found her Chanel perfume in my drawer."

"You don't need perfume," Mike said, his face half-buried in her hair. "You smell good just the way you are."

"Vomit," Vaughn said.

"Awww. We need to find Vaughn a girlfriend." Rose tilted her head back, peering at Vaughn as Mike nuzzled her ear. "Who should we set him up with? What's his type? Blondes?"

"Brunettes," Mike said quickly.

"Brunettes! Really?" Rose burst out laughing. And then Vaughn reached out a long arm and flicked her forehead, hard.

"OW!" Rose yelped, hand flying up.

"Hey, not cool!" Mike was immediately out from behind Rose and throwing his best friend in a headlock. "Say 'I'm sorry, Rose!'"

A bright red, angry notch was blooming at the center of her forehead, but she laughed and pulled Mike off, and they helped Vaughn up, and the rest of us watched, wishing we could be one of those three.

"So," Erik says, "you think she was banging Vaughn too?"

"Whoa whoa whoa!" My face burns. "Rose wasn't—being intimate with anybody!"

"Sweet, innocent Signal," Erik sighs. "All those late-night Moody meet-ups. What do you *think* they were doing? Making daisy chains?"

"*Ha ha.*" I shoot him a look. "No way. She would've told me if they did it."

"She didn't even tell you his name."

That stings.

"*Still*," I insist. "She would've told me if she'd done it with him or anyone else. Because whenever she'd do stuff first she'd make a point of letting me know—"

Erik lets out a strangled laugh, and I realize what I've just told him. Absolute. Mortification. I cover my face with my hands and will myself to sink into the earth.

"*I hate you*," I say at last, and he breaks out into peals of bright laughter that echo through the pines.

"You *truly* forced that deduction on me."

"*Erik!*" I plead, embarrassed giggles bubbling up before I can help it.

"Hey, your sexual experience or lack thereof is your business, thanks for sharing but—"

"Signal!" Dave's voice rings through the trees, and Erik and I both turn to see him on the trail leading up from the cabins a few yards away, the rest of the campers in a line behind him. "Are you *still* hiding that body?" Dave snaps.

Jada is staring daggers at me, of course.

"I just finished."

"Then you can both join us on our wilderness survival basics lesson." Dave jerks his thumb behind his shoulder. "It's a silent hike. Mouths shut, ears alert!"

As I slink past Dave, I see Javier toward the back of the line, and I can't bring myself to make eye contact with him until just as I pass by. I make a point of turning my head and smiling at him, but he must not notice, because he doesn't smile back.

*   *   *

After an endless lecture on foraging and finding water in the woods, Dave tells us we're free to return to our cabins for some rack time. I fall in beside Nobody.

"So what do you think of camp?" I ask.

"Beats a cell."

"I'm still angry about how they handled the kill switches."

"I like that we can walk around."

"And the obstacle course was *brutal*."

"I came in third." She sounds proud.

"The campers here are all *insane*."

"Javier saved your life today."

"Yeah . . . he did," I admit sheepishly, "He seems really nice."

"Watch out for when guys are nice. They're usually pretending."

"Well, then I guess Erik gets points for openly being a jerk at least." I look over, hoping to get her impression of Erik, but she stares straight ahead. "So, uh, what did you mean yesterday?" I prod. "When you said he marked me?"

"You ever see a dog piss on a tree?" She looks at me. "Like that. But without him having to piss."

Okay. Time to change the subject, I guess. "Did I miss anything good?"

"Wound assessment. When to make a splint or walk it off. And I spoke with Jada." Nobody pauses. "She's . . ." Her gravelly voice breaks off.

"A raving psycho bitch?" I finish.

Nobody's sharp glare registers even through her mask's small eye-holes. There's a long pause before she goes on.

"Sometimes trees catch fire at the roots and burn up from the inside. You can't tell looking at them. You could walk through a forest with a hundred trees burning like that and there's not even smoke. But then, if you peel back the bark, you'd see the wood is glowing red, all burning up inside." She clears her throat after this rather surprising speech, then continues, "Jada's burning up on the inside. You want to call that being a psycho bitch, I can't stop you. Just try not to take her head off, I guess."

Oh, that's right. Nobody thinks I actually decapitated a friend of mine. No wonder she's playing peacemaker. And from her perspective, what an *absolute hypocritical brat* I must seem.

"I'm sorry," I say. "I shouldn't have talked behind her back like that. I promise I'm not a psycho bitch either, okay?"

"Maybe no one is a psycho bitch," Nobody grumbles. "Maybe psycho bitches are just people with problems you can't see."

Maybe she's right. Maybe we're all stuck in the details of our complicated, sordid, unseen worlds; maybe we're all papering over the surface of ourselves and everyone else with simpler explanations. But it's never enough to contain us. We break through or we shrink to fit.

"Signal." Nobody has stopped walking and I slow beside her. "Do you feel that?" She lays one of her long, scarred hands on my arm. Above us, the wind rushes through the leaves with a sound like the tide pulling away from the shore. And I feel it too. Again.

Someone's watching us.

Nobody turns her head just a fraction. "There," she whispers, her voice low in her throat. "By the pines."

Fifty yards ahead of us, framed against a knot of dark pines, is a man in a mask.

The mask is rubber, white with blue markings, and molded into the face of a smiling bulldog. His arms hang at his sides and he stares right back at us.

"Probably just another test. Probably just Dave," Nobody mutters.

"It's *not* Dave," I whisper back. "Dave's not that tall."

Chapter Eight
The Boys' Cabin

~

"Race you to him?" Nobody asks.

"Are you out of your mind?!" I hiss.

"It's chase or be chased," she says, matter of factly. "Together on three."

The man in the dog mask does not move at all. A dead thing could not be more still.

"One . . ."

Run toward a huge, hulking stranger!? *Who's been following us through the woods?!*

"Two . . ."

If she goes alone, it's one on one. If we turn and run, she's right, we're prey. Two of us, well, maybe it could scare him. Maybe he thought we were just normal girls.

"*Three!*" Nobody yells.

She sprints toward him and I race after her with an exasperated scream. Just as Nobody is close enough to reach for him, her red hand clawing through the air, the man in the dog mask turns and scrambles away. He's clumsy but surprisingly fast, with the careless hurry of an injured animal.

"Wait!" I yell, reaching for Nobody's sleeve. "Nobody, wait!"

But she's deaf to me. He's running for the ravine, slipping and sliding in the dark mud that surrounds the stream of water hidden by the trees, turning his head to glance back at us. I can feel Nobody's excitement as she flies away from me, her legs stretching endlessly forward, bounding toward the creek he's scampering through. Erik's words ring through my mind: *Watch your step or you'll cross the fence.*

He's leading her toward the creek. If she crosses that invisible line, she'll die.

I duck under a low-hanging oak branch as I race after her, shrieking at the top of my lungs: "NOBODY! THE CREEK! THE CREEK!!!"

She glances back, just enough to break her stride, and I leap and pounce on her, in a gesture that's pure Erik. Dog Mask, who'd disappeared through the trees, returns to the clearing. He stares back at us, cocking his head to one side, giving the rubber dog features a strangely disappointed cast.

"He's trying to get you to cross the fence," I gasp, hugging her tight. "He's trying to trigger your kill switch."

Nobody's pale blue eyes lock with mine. Then she picks up a massive rock and hurls it at him with startling accuracy. He disappears into the brush, but she doesn't follow this time.

"Well, *that's* a stupid test," she says, and we walk in silence through the deepening orange of dusk. And it's strange to know the sky would still glow and the birds would still sing if we were still back there lying dead in the creek.

* * *

"There you are." Kate is sitting on the low steps to the girls' cabin, stubbing out a cigarette as we approach. "Jada got here half an hour ago. Where've you two been?"

"Dave had us do some pop quiz," Nobody says.

Kate stands and puts her hands on her hips, her voice stern. "No, no he did not. Dave and the boys got back before Jada did. Don't lie to me."

"I'm not lying, okay, ask him! He had some guy follow us wearing a stupid dog mask."

Kate's mouth drops, then snaps closed. She stiffly turns and walks away without another word in response.

"That wasn't a test," I tell Nobody, but she just shrugs.

"Whatever. I'm starving."

* * *

I could cry at the smell of hot food when we go to the main cabin for dinner. I've never been so hungry in my life. There's a vegetarian entree too, macaroni and cheese, but before we can start shoveling it onto our plates Kate blows her whistle for our attention.

"Campers, listen up! After dinner and dish duty, we're going to combine cabins. The girls will be moving in with the boys!"

A hubbub breaks out across the room, but somehow my voice rises above it when I ask: "Is this because of the guy we saw?"

Everyone starts asking me questions at once. Kate has to blow her whistle again.

"Yes, okay! We had a trespasser at camp today. We found a boat pulled on shore. We believe he's a local fisherman or hiker. Dave is off investigating now. Until we've sorted it out, we're going to be using the buddy system: don't go anywhere alone, always travel with at least one buddy. And if you run into an adult who isn't me or Dave, don't engage. At all. We clear?"

"Can we hunt him too?" Troy grins.

Kate gives him an exasperated look. "Let's try not to crap where we sleep, guys."

* * *

I take a quick shower in the relative privacy of the girls' cabin before we pack up, and finally wash the obstacle course off me. The water is painfully cold, but nothing has ever felt as cozy as the giant turquoise fleece I bundle up in afterward.

After dressing I join Nobody and Jada in packing up our stuff, which takes a surprisingly long time considering how few things we have to gather—sheets, footlockers, bath supplies—and haul it all through the dark to the boys' cabin. We're significantly slowed by the fact Kate will not let us walk alone. She makes us all go together as a threesome as we drop our belongings off by the door to the boys' cabin. Only once all our things are in a big leaning pile on the shallow porch does she disappear into the trees, walkie-talkie crackling on her hip.

The boys' cabin is identical in layout to the girls: four unvarnished wood bunks in each corner and uninsulated knotty-pine walls awash in waves of mildew.

"I smell gym socks," I tell Nobody as we stagger into the cabin, comforters bundled in our arms. "And . . . flowers?"

"You're welcome. We cleaned up for you!" Troy grins, pushing a broom and chewing on the end of one of his blue hoodie strings.

"This is 'cleaned up'? Yikes," Nobody mutters.

"The top bunks are all taken, and Troy sleeps under me, but the other three bottom bunks are free," Kurt adds, leaning back in his own top bunk across from the door, then starts noodling out "More Than Words" on his guitar.

Javier is on the top bed of the back-left corner bunk, writing in a notebook, and he gives me a small wave. I'm about to walk straight to the bunk under his when Jada shoves past me and dumps all her bedding there, claiming it.

Okay, fine. I turn to the bunk bed behind me. Dennis is up top, reading a worn copy of *The Art of Intrusion*.

The door to the bathroom bangs open and I whip around to see Erik walk out, hair sopping wet from the shower, towel knotted around his waist, his chest clenched tight against the cold.

Jada drops what's in her hands and practically spins on her heel to get out of his path.

"Whoever has the gardenia soap in there, I just used it," Erik announces to the room. Muscles I didn't even know existed flash along his sides as he bends to pluck a white thermal off his bunk and pull it on.

"That'd be Troy!" Kurt throws a pillow down at his brother. "He specifically requested it from Kate when we first got here."

"I like a sumptuous scent, okay?" Troy fires back. "Most alpha males do. Floral smells boost testosterone. That's why in ancient times kings wore leis and corsages and flower crowns into battle."

"They did?"

"To be honest, no they did not."

"Stupid!" Kurt laughs.

BANG! Jada's footlocker slips from her hand in the middle of the room, hits the ground and hatches open, scattering a cosmetic portrait of her insecurities across the floor: concealer, zit cream, extra-strength deodorant.

"PARTY FOUL!" Troy shouts, and there's a high wolf whistle from Kurt and a tiny gasp above me from Dennis as Troy picks a red lacy bra up off the floor.

I duck down to snatch up the box of super-size tampons that are within reach and tuck them in the corner of the footlocker before anyone notices, and then, cursing inwardly, drop to my knees and help pick up the rest.

Kurt snatches the bra from Troy and fires it across the cabin like a slingshot. It hits the wall with a rattle and slides down under Erik's bunk as the guys burst out laughing.

"Wow, it's almost like you've never seen a bra before." Erik bounds up to Kurt's bunk and has him in a headlock. Kurt laughingly punches at Erik's arms, hard, as Troy attempts to wrench him off. I use the distraction to slip across the room, kick the bra from under Erik's bunk and pack it away with the rest.

Once we've gotten everything back in the footlocker, Jada latches it and slides it under her bunk with a shove, not acknowledging me. But Nobody shoots me a discreet thumbs-up, the masked person's version of a smile.

"Erik," Dennis calls from over my head as I tuck in the corners of my fitted sheet. "What do you think Dave took with him to go 'investigate' that hiker? Long-range rifle with a silencer?"

"Dave should be forced to use only the soup-can lid shivs he had us make our first day at camp."

"Oh man, dude, those were the dumbest!" Kurt pipes up. "What do you think the hiker has on him? A Swiss Army knife?"

"That guy was *not* a hiker." I turn around, my pillow hugged to my chest, midway through putting on a fresh case. "Nobody and I saw him, and he was wearing a big weird rubber mask. Who goes hiking in a mask?"

"Dog Mask. Old timey. Very creepy," Nobody agrees, the cabin going silent. The boys telegraph a glance around the room, and Erik's dark eyebrows fly up as he stares at me.

"Interesting!" Erik rubs his hair with his towel, peering at me through its folds. "Yeah, I don't imagine animal masks are a hot item at the old REI. What happened exactly?"

"He followed us through the woods after nature time with Dave or whatever."

"We tried to get him," Nobody adds defensively. "But he got away."

There's a shifting sound above me as Dennis sits up, and Javier's eyes search my face.

"Yeah, when we ran at him, he bolted straight for the creek. Like he was trying to get us to follow him across the fence." I sit down on my bunk, legs unsteady. "Like he was trying to set off our kill switches."

"How would he know where the fence is, though!?" Troy insists. "This camp is like, a top-secret program that got going, what, two weeks ago?"

"If that's what Signal says happened, that's what happened." Erik bites at his nails and stares at me, damp hair hanging in his alert face. "So how would he know about the fence?"

"I don't know, but Kate knows who he is, I think. When we described him to her, she got weird." But before I can say more, the door swings open and Kate strides in:

"Fifteen minutes till lights out, guys! Early to bed, early to rise!"

There's an uneasy silence as Kate watches us collect our toothbrushes and bathroom gear. How much did she overhear?

When I come back out of the bathroom the lanterns are all off, and while I'm burning to discuss Dog Mask with everyone, I can see the firefly glow of Kate's cigarette through the screen door.

There's a long silence, and then a very high fart.

"TROY!!!" Kurt yells, "Shut up your BUTT!"

"Who *was* that?!" Troy cries indignantly. "No, seriously, guys. Who would do such a thing?! Let's get to the bottom of this. Who's got a bubbly tummy in the house tonight?"

"*Troy,*" Erik growls, "one more noise out of either of your ends and I will climb over there and permanently connect your rectum to your esophagus."

I hear Dennis start laughing overhead, a string of hushed, uncontrollable giggles, and that does it, I crack up and now we're all laughing, so hard Kate calls "Go to sleep!" from the porch and we settle into cozy silence.

As I curl up on my side and slide my hand under my pillow, I feel a crisp sheet of folded paper. I carefully pull the note out and tilt it to catch a dim beam from the porch light.

It's a drawing of a dandelion, captured in one flowing, elegant line. And underneath in block letters is written:

"FLOWER FOR SURE."

* * *

"Rise and shine!" Dave claps his hands right in my face.

Pain rips through me when I try to sit up, muscles seizing in my arms and legs. I have to grip the ladder at the end of the bunk just to stand.

"Little sore there, huh?" Dave laughs.

"*Everything hurts.*"

Kate, by his side, frowns at me.

"Then you can take the morning to rest."

"Really?!"

"Yup. But you'll need a buddy."

My first thought is Nobody, but she seems to actually enjoy the obstacle course. The only person who dreads it as much as I do is, obviously . . .

"Hey, Dennis?"

Dennis, halfway down the ladder, has his glasses off. He looks too young without them.

"You want to be my buddy this morning? Skip obstacle course?"

"Yes, yup, okay." He nods quickly. For monotone Dennis, this is the equivalent of a "HELL YEAH, GIRL."

"That works for me." Kate smiles. "Dennis can get in some computer practice and your muscles can heal."

"Great! Now I just have to see if I can get my clothes on," I joke, and Erik, walking by, rolls his eyes at me.

"Weakling."

As everyone else departs for the field, Dennis and I follow Kate to the main cabin, to a small nurse's office down the hall from the dining room.

There's a sun-bleached CPR chart peeling off the wall next to a metal first aid kit hanging open, empty. What would Dave have done if I'd fallen and actually broken my leg? I don't want to know.

Kate unlocks the drawer of a dented metal desk and pulls out a stout chrome briefcase with a military laptop inside. She plugs it into a generator under the desk, then pulls out a blinking cordless Wi-Fi hot spot from her pocket. Once the laptop powers up, she types in several lines of code and only then is Dennis allowed to take his place at the keyboard.

"And this is for you." She hands me a door lock cut in half with a panel of clear Lucite so I can see the tumblers inside. She points to a pile of paperclips by an ancient office chair.

"You get this open while he works on the pacemaker." She pats a small lump in her pocket absently. "I'll be in the kitchen. Holler if you need anything!"

Dennis gives me a look as we take our respective seats across the room.

"Thanks for getting me out of obstacle course this morning," he says haltingly, his hands fluttering over the keys.

"No prob, bob," I say, straightening a paper clip. "I honestly don't know how I'm going to do that course every day. I almost passed away trying yesterday and I'm already dreading the thought of doing it tomorrow."

"The obstacle course is a waste of time." Dennis shakes his head. "They know I'm going to be taking all my targets down with a computer, yet they still insist on making me crawl up buildings like Spiderman. It's *ridiculous*."

"How do you kill someone with a computer?"

"I can hack the brake systems in most modern cars. Ditto navigational devices and landing gear on private and small commercial planes," he says with a sniff. "I'm almost there with hacking pacemakers, except I can barely get Kate to give me two hours in a row with the camp laptop, and she's built like a million stupid firewalls to keep me in the training program, which cause more bugs than I'd ever actually need to deal with." His tone is almost comically monotone when he adds, "It's truly infuriating."

Dennis, with his button nose and sprinkling of whiteheads across his chin, can make planes fall out of the skies. Okay.

"The reason I bring it up is, you helped Jada last night, and now you're helping me this morning." His large eyes fasten on my face. "Why?"

Because Nobody had made me think about what Jada might have been through. But I don't want to start spreading rumors, so I'm not sure how to answer this.

"Class As are deficient in empathy," Dennis goes on, his lenses opaque from the blue glow of the laptop screen. "Some can pretend to be empathetic. But it's always to shield a larger, self-serving agenda."

I blink at him. "What are you saying?"

"I'm saying that I'm not fooled by your nice-girl act." He drops his chin, peering over his glasses. "And I want to know what this favor is going to cost me."

"It's not an act!" But it is, just not the one he thinks; I'm trying to act like one of them and failing miserably. "You of all people should know being a Class A doesn't mean being a heartless psychopath. Didn't you turn yourself in before you could hurt someone? That's like, a noble thing to do."

"Turning myself in was ultimately self-serving," Dennis says. "I didn't want to be punished when I inevitably caved to my impulses."

"So you sent yourself *to jail*? Sorry, that doesn't seem self-serving to me. That seems kind and good."

Dennis's face tightens, but his voice doesn't change. "I know what I want, Signal. I want to cause someone pain."

"But you *don't*," I push, waving a straightened paper clip at him. "You don't cause anyone pain. Because something in you is stronger than that urge. Call it self-preservation or kindness, it amounts to the same thing. Strength of character."

He stares at the screen without answering, but his keyboard is silent.

"You're an awfully positive person," he says at last, in the same icy monotone.

"You're the first person who's ever gotten that impression of me."

"And you're the first person who's told me I was strong." He pauses. "But like I said, you don't fool me." And his keys clatter momentously.

You don't fool me.

Exactly what Janeane had said at my trial.

Rose's mom had loomed large in my childhood: long-limbed and beautiful like Rose, with an irreverent sense of humor and ever-present American Spirit cigarette. But when she started dating Tom, he made her drop the smoking, and my mom as a friend. After they married she became someone who frowned instead of laughed at off-color remarks; she kept her hair in an angled bob and diligently jogged. Still, you can't admire someone that much when you're that young, and then stop caring about them.

That's why I broke down when she took the stand as the last witness for the prosecution and testified against me. When she told the court I had always been a little off. And that I had been obsessed with Rose.

"The defense keeps saying, she's just a girl, whatever she did, she's just a girl. That's what I kept telling myself. What can she do? She's just a girl," Janeane told the court in a broken voice. And then she turned to me, and I made the mistake of looking in her eyes.

Janeane's face was not one I knew. The pain, the rage as raw as if her skin had been flayed off and every bloody nerve laid bare to the staid municipal courtroom.

"Well, you don't fool me anymore, Signal. *You don't fool me.*"

I curled up then, hands covering my face, and heard myself plead, "I'm sorry! *I'm sorry!*"

"I saw those photos! I saw what you did to my baby!" she wept. "You're sorry! You're just a girl, right? Just the girl from hell!"

Quick footsteps and Kate runs in beaming and holding up the pacemaker, which blinks red.

"I'd be dead on the floor if this was attached! Great job!" She throws her arms around Dennis. He looks embarrassed but pats her shoulder.

"Our goal for next time will be turning it off entirely." She shifts him out of the chair and Dennis sighs with exasperation.

"If you let me back on I could—"

"That's enough for today, Dennis. How's the lock coming, Signal?"

"Almost there," I lie, looking down at the lock in my lap with two straightened paperclips jammed into it.

"Well. You can finish up later, everybody's in the kitchen," she says. "Dennis, you go on ahead, and Signal if you could stop at the pantry on your way and grab a box of the latex gloves? It's right next to the lost-and-found closet. They're on the top of the right-hand shelf."

I make my way down the hall to the pantry, throw open the door, and pull the cord swinging from a bare lightbulb. The pantry is the size of large coatroom and crammed with aluminum shelves from floor to ceiling. Most of the food appears to be from the same era as the lost-and-found clothes: dusty vats of cling peaches, a laundry detergent-sized bottle of something called "Gravymaster." I suspect if I turned the light off again I'd hear the discreet chewing of mice.

I spot the latex gloves on the top shelf, but when I yank a step stool from behind the rack it dislodges something. There's a flutter of paper and I see a printed, black-and-white face for just an instant before the paper lands under the shelf.

Rose's face.

It's Rose's face or I'm losing my mind.

I crouch down and slide my hand under the bottom shelf, pushing past my repulsion at the grime, reaching until I touch smooth newsprint. I carefully slide the newspaper out and smooth the creased front page of the *Washington Times*.

The hideous bulk of the shed, with its one little window like a gouged-out eye, stares back at me in black and white. I lay my cheek against the gritty floor and look under the shelf to see a curve of folded newsprint. I reach again and pull out a stack of clippings: several from when the trial started, another with my own yearbook photo and the all-caps headline: "THE GIRL FROM HELL."

But what about Rose's face? I slide my hand behind the shelf, forcing it between the tightly packed broth boxes and rough unvarnished wall, the wood scraping my knuckles, and grab it just as the door creaks open.

"Signal? Signal, are you still in the pantry?"

Chapter Nine
Remembering Rose

❧

I drop the clippings back under the shelf just as Kate looks in, an edge to her voice: "Find those gloves alright?"

"Yeah, but I was looking for the step ladder and I knocked something down behind the shelf," I say, my tone bored. I don't know whether to be reassured or frightened at how well I've learned to compartmentalize.

"No worries," Kate says, the aluminum ladder shrieking in protest as she opens it up for me. I hop up, grab the box, and hand it down to her with a tight-lipped smile, my mind still reeling.

Kate nods for me to walk ahead of her into the kitchen for the next class, or lesson, or activity, or whatever you want to call these life hacks for assassins.

"Okay, campers." Kate claps for everyone's attention. The rest of the campers, cleaned up after the obstacle course, are ranged about the long wood laminate counter that runs along three walls of the narrow, homey kitchen. On a worn butcher's block, in the middle of everyone, is a pile of rotten meat.

"We're cleaning out the fridge today!" Kate announces cheerily. "By learning how to dissolve organic material in an acid bath! We'll be using a proprietary blend of commonly available chemicals we call 'Zap Sauce'!" She points out the four trays set out at intervals along the counter, each with a neat row of household cleansers and a graduated cylinder. "Who can tell me in what circumstances an acid bath is the best way to dispose of a target?"

I squeeze my eyes shut and swallow the rising bile in the back of my throat.

"When you can't move the body from a building without being seen?" Kurt offers.

"Exactly. Remember: if there's no body, there's no crime, and that equals more lead time to make your getaway. Some of your targets are going to be in urban environments with CCTV on the street, and you won't be able to just wrap them up and throw them in the back of a car. But as long as you have a plastic tub, some housekeeping supplies and a toilet, you can use this method. Because what did we come here to learn, guys?"

Kate raises her eyebrows and looks around the room.

"How to not get caught," we say in unison, and she smiles, her cheeks dimpling.

"Exactly. Now, safety first: put on your gloves and goggles," she says, and pairs us off, giving each pair a plastic tub filled with rotten meat. Dennis and I get three roast chicken carcasses. Kate explains how to combine the acids we'll be using, how to neutralize and dispose of them. Then she has us weigh our leftovers on the kitchen scale, measure our containers' volume and, using what she's taught us about the Zap Sauce, determine the amount needed to dissolve everything in two hours. I barely make it to the kitchen scale and back without heaving; if raw meat is gross after five years of being a vegetarian, rotted meat is positively harrowing.

Kate also hands out packets of worksheets with various word problems: given X amount of weight, Y amount of time, and Z being the volume of the container, how much Zap Sauce is needed to dissolve the target?

The smell of the Zap Sauce meeting the leftovers sends us all flying outside to the covered porch so we can breathe while finishing our packets, and gives me virtually no chance of surreptitiously sneaking back over to the pantry.

I look over my shoulder at Erik and Javier's table. Erik has gone over to talk with Troy, and Javier is staring at me. When our eyes connect he smiles, the flash of it sending the tiniest bolt of lightning through me. He left the note; now it's my turn to be brave.

"Hey," I say, walking over to him like I go up to guys all the time, no big deal. "Thanks for your drawing. It's incredible. I like, want it tattooed on me."

One of his eyebrows tilts upward in mild disbelief. "Do you have any tattoos?"

"No! I mean, I used to have big plans for getting one on my eighteenth birthday, but I'm not exactly sure if that's going to pan out."

"What were you going to get?" he motions for me to sit. I slide onto the bench across from him feeling like I'm at the edge of a high dive.

"I wanted a skull with roses in its eye sockets." I roll my eyes in embarrassment.

"That could be cool."

"Eh. It seems kind of cringe-y now. Or maybe it's just that everything death related has lost its appeal to me."

"Whereas before . . . ?"

"Don't laugh, but I used to be sort of a goth." Ooooh, why am I saying this? How did we get here? "Not like, *super* goth. As goth as you can be when you're broke." Better and better!

"So like, you went around in a trench coat and tiny sunglasses?" Javier's brow creases in something like concern, and I frantically shake my head.

"Noooo, just like, *a lot* of horror movie T-shirts. All black every day. Shared lots of Instagram quotes about wanting to hurry up and die."

"That's really hard to picture." He closes one eye, a slow smile spreading across his face. "But I bet you made it work."

"No, I did *not*," I laugh. Why am I sitting here laughing at myself?! What is wrong with me?

But Javier laughs too: "Yeah, right. I bet you were breaking all the goth guys' hearts." And I really do laugh at the idea of goth guys in

Ledmonton, and it's okay. Maybe I'm not that weird—he doesn't think so. He goes on: "Back before, death was just something in movies. It was more of like, an aesthetic than reality? Whereas now . . ."

"It's waiting at the bottom of the obstacle course?"

"Not while I'm around." He lifts his chin slightly at me. "So now that you've ditched the tiny sunglasses, how would the Signal of today represent herself?"

"Your dandelion."

His eyebrows go slightly up, his smile huge. "Seriously?"

"It's such a cool drawing. And dandelions are the best. They're sunny, they're strong—"

"And mislabeled?" he says, catching me off guard.

Can he tell I'm innocent?

I'm not sure how to react. If I smile back like I understand, am I telling him he's right? Or is this all just in my head?

"Well," Javier continues, smoothing over the hiccup of silence. "If you want I could give you a temporary version."

"Oh yeah? Do it."

He reaches for my wrist, then pushes up my sleeve and cradles my bare arm in his hand. With a ballpoint pen he slowly and deliberately draws a line up the inside of my wrist. The brush of the side of his hand as he works makes goosebumps rise along the back of my arm, and I can feel the warmth of his breath against the thin skin. Then he pulls away so I can admire it: a dandelion, on a strong stem, its face turned to the sky.

"That's perfect." My voice wobbles, his hand still holding my wrist.

Kate marches out onto the porch, holding up a beeping kitchen timer.

"Okay, campers! Time's up! Go check on your victims!"

Javier's fingers slide away from me, and when I stand I'm dizzy.

Dennis and I find our chickens are now a tapioca-colored slush.

Kate beams down at the beige goo. "This is by far the most successful application of Zap Sauce I've seen today! Well done, you two!"

Dennis and I high-five. It's disgusting, but I'm finally not failing at something.

* * *

I'd been counting on the group being sent off to the field or lake to give me an opportunity to sneak back to the pantry. However, Kate and Dave keep us close to the main cabin because of Dog Mask, whose presence hangs over the day like the promise of bad weather.

I'm feeling pretty hopeless until I learn Erik has kitchen duty tonight. He can easily get the clippings. I just have to get him alone and ask. Which, when you share a single cabin with seven people, is almost impossible.

I get so desperate as it gets closer to dinner I actually follow him into the bathroom; and of course Troy is already in there, and feeling chatty. I stare desperately at Erik in the long, speckled bathroom mirror, half willing Troy to leave us alone and half terrified he will.

"These water bugs are getting *bold*, man!" Troy brays at Erik, who is wrapping tape around the thumb he sprained on the obstacle course. "The other night I came in with my lantern when it was all dark, and one comes striding right up to me right when I'm peeing. And this thing is *huge*, I seriously thought it was like a turd, but then it walked. So I'm all, *BAM!*" he stamps, then sighs and shakes his head, "Dude . . . He just looks at me like 'You strike at the King, you better make sure he's dead!' and then *rushes my freaking foot!!*" Erik smiles, not looking up from his hand.

Can he tell I'm waiting to talk to him? Or does he think I just really need to wring every last bit of moisturizer into my hands?

"I booked it, I was *flying*," Troy laughs, oblivious. "Anyway, see you out there, man."

The second the door swings closed Erik and I turn to each other.

"I need your help," I blurt awkwardly. "I saw some newspaper clippings on Rose's trial." And for some reason I'm blushing, and I know it, the worst combination of two things you can be. "I hid them all under the bottom shelf of the pantry and if you get them then we could, like, read them later?"

There's a long pause during which we can hear the others exiting the cabin, Jada calling:

"Errrik, come on!!! Those onions won't peel themselves!!"

"You hate onions. You always pick them out . . ." Troy's voice fades out the door. And then there's a beat of silence that feels like the first dip of a roller-coaster before Erik says,

"Okay." And then, as he turns to walk away, "After lights out."

*   *   *

I have no idea what that means. *When* after lights out? Where are we going to read them? The bathroom has a back door that opens out onto the woods—should I meet him there? I lay in my bunk, duck boots laced up under my blankets, twitching every time I hear Troy and Kurt snore, waiting for the sound of Erik climbing down from his bunk. But I don't hear anything. Did he forget? Is he asleep?

And then a figure looms over me, darker and denser than the night filling the cabin.

"Erik?" I whisper, terrified it's not him.

"Shhh." I can just make out Erik's outline before he pivots and heads for the front door, so I crawl out of my bunk and follow him.

I have to practically jog to keep up with his long strides across the overgrown meadow behind our cabin, the grass gone purple in the starlight, and into the black shapes of the trees.

"You got them?" I whisper.

"Oh yes." He has his lantern but he doesn't turn it on, it just swings from his hand. "Right under the shelf, like you said."

"I kept wanting to get them during the Zap Sauce lesson, but I never got the chance."

"No? Too busy holding hands with Javier?"

"*Wow.*" My jaw drops. "I didn't realize you were monitoring my motions in class, creeper."

"*Creeper?!*" Erik stops short, his stricken expression rendered in indistinct blues by the starlight. "In *what world* am I a creeper?"

"Maybe in the world where you creeped, crept, whatever, into my cabin the first night I was here?" I point out. "Nobody even said you 'marked' me."

"*I* marked you? And what's this?"

He reaches out and pulls up my sleeve, exposing the dark line of Javier's dandelion.

"So Javier draws on your arm, even though he *knows* you're in a relationship." Erik's words get faster, along with his pace, as we wind uphill through the trees. "and *I'm* the creep?! Okay, Signal."

"Come on. Javier is a *nice guy*."

"Javier is a *sociopath*."

"Aren't we all!"

"*You're* not," he says, then flicks on a lantern, his green eyes iridescent discs like a cat's. The shallow light reveals a few rows of benches in front of a small raised platform and firepit, now filled with pine saplings. Erik sits on the first bench and pulls a roll of curled-up paper from inside his hoodie.

"Anyway. I am willing to look past your vicious name-calling," Erik says, "so we can discuss why a stack of year-old clippings on your case is hidden in the pantry. Someone's been hoarding them away, and they might be—pay attention here, because I'm about to use this word in its *appropriate context*—" His eyes flash. "They might be a creeper. Should we search Javier's bunk for scrapbooking supplies?"

"Seriously though." I bite the inside of my cheek to keep from smiling. "Who do you think collected these?"

"Kate and Dave, obviously. But don't worry about it too much, it's not like they hold life and death power over you or anything." He reaches for the "Remembering Rose" clipping, which is two whole sheets of recent newsprint, the paper still bluish and slippery. "Ready, Watson?"

"Okay, Sherlock," I say, and sit beside him on the cold bench. He spreads the paper across our laps and we both lean in and examine the smeary type through clouds of our breath:

LEDMONTON, OR — It's been a year since the small town of Ledmonton was rocked by the brutal murder of 16-year-old Rose Rowan, the Ledmonton High junior found decapitated in a woodland shed last October.

The popular teen's life was cut short by her obsessive classmate, Signal Deere, who clung to a grade school friendship despite the growing estrangement between the girls: Rose was outgoing, dedicated to her boyfriend and church community; Signal was a callous loner seemingly obsessed with the macabre. When Rose tried to distance herself, Deere snapped.

The lurid details of the "Girl From Hell" case dominated Oregon headlines last year, but less examined was the devastation Deere's crime wreaked on her once-idyllic community.

"He just up and left," Mrs. Lambe says, clutching a framed photo of her son, Michael Lambe, the Senior Class President and Rose's boyfriend when tragedy struck. "Right after the trial, he packed his car and drove off. Didn't graduate. Lost all his scholarships. He calls once in a while but won't tell us where he is." Mrs. Lambe's blue eyes, so much like her son's, fill with tears. "Mike, if you're reading this, we love you and we miss you."

Pastor Lambe and Rose's youth group hosted a service where parents, Tom and Janeane Rowan, and the trustees of the Windward estate announced they would be establishing a scholarship in Rose's name . . .

The low hoot of an owl makes me look up, straight into Erik's staring face, like he's reading me instead of the article.

"Did you get to the part about Mike yet?" I ask.

"I already finished."

"I'll save you a seat at the library," I joke, but feeling distorts my voice and I can't hold back. "Mike just 'up and left'? Why would he do that, unless . . ."

"Unless what?"

"Unless he felt guilty?"

Erik squints at me for a moment. "You really are, like . . . like a five-foot-tall piece of cotton candy or something."

"First of all, I'm five four and three quarters—"

"Signal, I'm sorry to tell you this, but whoever killed Rose feels no guilt." Erik is not smiling, "*Because he is a psychopath*. And they don't feel guilt, or fear, or love. They just *act* like they do. Nice Guys especially, they get a high from lying, it makes them feel superior. If Mike were our Nice Guy, there's *no way* he'd leave. Playing the grieving boyfriend would be *too much fun*. In fact, he'd probably do some big tearful speech at graduation about 'the one we lost,' then do the same speech again, howling with laughter, on the drive home."

I try not to picture it, focusing instead on the saplings and thin brush around us, thrown into sharp relief by the lantern light. Beyond them is just blackness.

". . . Are you a psychopath?" I ask him.

"You think I'd tell you if I were?" Erik smiles, the stark light of the halogen lamp dividing his face into light and dark, its symmetry undeniable. "At least you know I'm not a Nice Guy. Did you know only forty percent of serial killers are psychopaths? Not even a majority. And the percentage of Class As with psychopathy is even lower. Twenty-five percent." He tilts his head. "But then, what bearing does group average have on an individual? None whatsoever. I'm a Class A. So are you. But we couldn't be more different."

"We're not *that* different."

"We're a photo and the negative," he says quickly, then: "You don't remember seeing anything inside the shed at all. Not even like, looking over Rose's shoulder when you followed her inside—"

"Just blackness." I don't want to think about being inside the shed.

"I could try to hypnotize you?" Erik offers.

Absolutely not. "I tried that. With professionals."

"And nothing came back?"

"Nothing that made sense," I say, crossing my arms against my chest. "Pieces. I don't even know if they're real or forced memories or what."

"Okay. Tell me the pieces." His eyes are intent on mine.

"Are you trying to hypnotize me right now?!"

"No! I just have *dreamy eyes*."

I chuckle, but then Rose's face in black dots stops me. The page has slipped from our laps. I pick it up and smooth it as the wind rushes over us like a sheet pulled over our heads.

She was always so beautiful. Even at her worst, and I had seen her worst: I remembered Rose's face half-buried in her pillow, sickly pale under a net of dark hair, the morning after the very last time I slept over. She had come back a blurry, underwater version of herself at three AM, eyes glazed, so high she could barely form words.

"Rose, I have to go . . . ," I'd whispered.

". . . Okay." She ground the heels of her hands into her face. "Can you come back Friday? I can pick you up."

"I can't cover for you anymore. You need to tell someone about Mr. Moody, Rose. This secrecy is . . . it's just toxic, okay?"

"Um, I don't need relationship advice from a girl who's never been kissed, thanks."

I'd planned a speech the whole time she'd been gone that night, but I knew then it was pointless. No matter what I said, she would only hear a shrill loser who refused to grow up, demanding she become a kid again.

So I just walked out instead.

I was halfway down the street before I remembered my math book was still on her desk.

Hoping she'd gone back to sleep, I crept in the side door, through the kitchen, and tiptoed to the foot of the stairs, when Janeane's voice floated down from Rose's room:

". . . She's over here all the time now, she never says hello or goodbye, and your father and I are a little concerned—"

"You've known her longer than Tom," Rose snapped. "Who is *not* my 'father' and you know I *hate* when you call him that—"

"Well, Tom said you put a lock on the inside of your door."

"It's my door!"

"It's *his* house. It's *our* home. We don't need locks in our home. Whatever you and Signal are doing should not require locking out the rest of the family!"

"We're not doing *anything*. I'm just sick of you snooping through my room!"

"I don't snoop," Janeane said. "I would *never* snoop. I would only go into your room if I thought you had gotten hold of something that would put you in danger."

Rose laughed bitterly. "Let me guess. Tom's pills are 'missing' again?"

"Tom has chronic pain. He has a doctor's prescription—"

"Shame he can't make it last the whole month."

"Someone is taking those pills, Rose!"

I turned and padded back down the hall, back to the kitchen door, when a massive hand landed on my shoulder.

"Signal." Tom stood by the sink with a cup of coffee. He had a bull-dog jaw, a red nose with the coarse pores of an orange peel, and power-ful shoulders from college football, hunched from the years he'd spent behind a desk at the car dealership.

He held up a pack of American Spirits.

"I found these in the planter out back." He tossed them on the coun-ter between us. "You have any idea where they came from?"

Rose's mom was supposed to have quit years ago.

"They're mine," I lied.

"It's a filthy habit. And I won't have it around my Rose. I know your mom lets you run wild, but in this house . . ." In my peripheral vision, I saw Janeane's willowy shape hover at the kitchen door.

Sensing Tom was winding down, I nodded dumbly, crushed the cig-arettes into my pocket and stumbled outside.

"Signal!" Janeane ran after me down the driveway in her bathrobe, the tip of her nose pink. "Signal, I'm so sorry." She grimaced. "You didn't have to cover for me."

"I didn't take Tom's pills," I said, handing the cigarettes back to her.

"Well, thank you for telling me that." She had the grace to look ashamed. "You know, it's hard to believe, but I was sixteen once." It wasn't that hard. She was still beautiful. Just sadder. "I can remember how much I *hated* my mom. And now I find myself doing everything she did. And I get it." She looked back at the house, squinting in the morning light. "She was just trying to protect me."

She turned back to me, pleading.

"Signal, you would tell me if Rose was doing drugs, wouldn't you?"

I should've told her the truth. I should've confessed everything about Mr. Moody. But I didn't. And now Rose's smile is just a cloud of black dots.

That's why I said I was sorry in court. And that's why I owe them both the truth.

"I remember music." My voice warbles. "Not what song, or the lyrics . . . this is *so pointless*." I press my hands over my eyes so all I can see is darkness swimming with washes of staticky color.

"Tell me anyway," Erik says. "What else was there?"

"I remember a thermos."

"What kind?"

"The kind like you'd get in an old plastic lunchbox. It had the Transformers on it?"

"Really! Was there anything in it?"

"I don't know, this is stupid—" I'm about to sit up and take my hands from over my eyes, but his hands press gently over them, like he's leading me into a surprise party.

"Wait, wait, don't open your eyes yet. Just wait a minute. See if it comes." The heat of his fingers on the back of mine is searing in the cold night, but it anchors me in the safety of the moment. When his hands slide away, the thermos rises in my mind so clearly, like there's a spotlight on it. It tilts toward me, and the smell stings the back of my throat.

"It smelled alcoholic, but I don't remember any taste."

"Okay." His voice is so gentle. "What else?"

"Lightning." The word sticks in my throat. "A huge beam of light that blanked everything out. But there wasn't a storm that night, so that doesn't make sense."

"Don't try to get it to make sense. Just let it come up, and—" Suddenly he darts forward and snaps off the light, his voice dropping low:

"We have to go."

And directly below us, winding up the gravel path fast, are the searching beams of Kate and Dave's flashlights.

Chapter Ten

Color War

❧

"They're doing a bed check." Erik sweeps the clippings under the low stage and turns off the lamp. "Come on—" He takes my hand and we run downhill, racing to get to the cabin before Kate and Dave. When we hit the lawn, I head for the back door, but his iron arm sweeps me along the side of the cabin:

"*Window*," he whispers. "*The back door creaks.*" Erik effortlessly catches me up around the waist and lifts me to the window in one powerful gesture. I bruise my shin hard on the sill but manage to climb in and slide into my bunk just as feet land on the stairs. The hinge of the door sighs and a flashlight beam sweeps the mildewed wall. I struggle to keep from panting until the door closes.

"All accounted for," Dave says.

"I saw a glow on the hill." Kate sounds uncertain. "And we know he's still around. That campfire was only a few hours old."

"We just have to keep them close until we find him. And then . . . ?"

"I'll do it," she says, and I hear the flick of her lighter. "I owe him that much."

Their steps fade into the roll of the lake and the wind in the eaves and Dennis's soft, steady breath overhead. When I can no longer puzzle over Kate's words, the thermos tilts in my mind. Rose stands behind it, her face clearer and clearer as sleep pulls me into darkness.

"*Chug it, ho.*"

* * *

Morning comes before I'm ready to get up. But I pull myself out of bed with everyone else, and manage to not come in last on the obstacle course. I spend the second run-through watching from the tarp, and when Dave is out of earshot, lean discreetly toward Erik:

"Hey, uh, Erik?"

He turns to me. The missed sleep has made his eyes bloodshot so they glow green.

"Hey, I uh . . . I think I remembered something from the shed—"

Dave's shrill whistle cuts the air.

"Attention, campers! On your feet, on your feet, make a line! Camp Naramauke's first annual Color Wars starts RIGHT NOW!!"

We look around at each other uncertainly.

"Those of you who went to summer camp might have done a Color War before. There's teams and songs and talent competitions," Dave says, rattling a coffee can at the start of the line, right under Nobody's nose. It's full of brightly colored Sharpies. "Our version, as you might imagine, is a little different."

"We have three winners in our Color War. The first winner is whoever can 'slash' as many of their fellow campers' throats as possible. And it has to be a line that could kill: I want to see that carotid artery crossed, guys! The second winner is whoever manages *not* to get their throat slashed. And the third winner is whoever wins the Scavenger Hunt. Though it's very possible for all those wins to go to one camper."

"What do we win?" Dennis asks.

"One hour of screen time on Kate's laptop. No social media logins, but otherwise you're unsupervised. Watch a show. Check your sites. Whatever."

There's a collective gasp, then howling cheers, then the air goes tense as we hush ourselves and become as quiet and focused as runners before a starter pistol fires.

Dave starts down the line, holding out the can. "So pick a color, watch your neck, and we'll announce winners after dinner."

I choose blue and immediately am on my guard, stomach turning over, arm hairs on end. We all move warily on our way down to the lower field to eat, walking far apart and eyeing each other between nervous giggles.

Once on the field, we sit in a circle facing each other. I get so distracted keeping an eye on Erik I almost don't hear the soft footsteps in the grass behind me, and whip around to find a sheepish Dennis hovering, his orange Sharpie uncapped.

"Nothing personal, Signal," Dennis says, actually starting to smile at my betrayed expression. "You're just my only chance."

"Then you've got *no chance!*" I say, uncapping my Sharpie with a flourish and giving him an overly dramatic grimace. "I'll be right behind you *when you least expect it.*"

"Challenge accepted," he says, and slinks back to his lunch bag. I figure when we get up again I'll strike.

But before lunch is even over Jada makes the first move, springing herself on Troy. They go end over end across the quilts in the center of the circle as the rest of us hoot and cheer. Neither will let the other stand—they roll around clutching each other's wrists and staring into each other's eyes like the rest of us have disappeared. Jada, a good foot shorter than Troy, eventually manages to get her knee in the middle of his chest and pins him down like she did with me in the field, but Troy seems reluctant to wrestle her off. He's got her wrists in each hand now, his face gone bright red, and he laughs, "Whoa, you got some arm strength!"

Troy lets his hand flicker on her left wrist, gazing up at her curiously as though wondering if she'll notice. The second he gives, her arm slips across his throat and she bows over him, her short hair nearly brushing his face, and gently swipes the marker tip from ear to ear. Then she rolls off of him, giggling uncontrollably.

Troy's face matches the magenta stripe she's left across his neck. "Can't I try to get her back, Dave?" he calls, his eyes not leaving Jada's face.

"Nope, you're out," Dave says. "But you can still participate in the Scavenger Hunt. Kate will give you the list of things to find down at the Arts and Crafts table. So get moving, campers!"

We all stand slowly, nervously laughing as we gauge each other's proximity. I'm about to make my approach on Dennis when I notice Javier in my peripheral.

"What!?" Javier grins when I spring away.

"You KNOW what!" I can't hold in my frantic laughter as I wheel away from him. Dennis has disappeared over his shoulder, Jada on his heels. So I turn and run, almost sideswiping Kate in my hurry.

"That's the spirit!" Kate calls after me.

"You can run but you can't hide!" Javier calls, footfalls hard behind me. I race down the hill toward the picnic table under the sycamore, the water sparkling a deep blue in the midmorning sun, and grab one weathered corner like it's base, but this isn't tag.

Javier catches my arm and spins me into him like we're dancing, my back pressed against his chest, his strong arm across my collarbones, the scruff of his chin catching in my hair. I can't pull his arm away even with both hands, but I wriggle enough that he ends up spinning in a circle to keep hold of me, the blue and green whirling in a dizzy, gold-rimmed blur. My face hurts from laughing.

"Go on. Do your worst!" I cry at last, grateful he can't see how hard I'm blushing. The cold tip of the marker lands under my ear and makes a quick line across my throat just as Erik crests the hill. My eyes connect with Erik's, and I swear I hear his thoughts, his deep voice as clear in my head as though he were whispering in my ear:

What a Nice Guy that Javier is.

My laughter sputters out like a spent firework and I sink to the picnic bench, a shiver snaking up my back. But is the shiver from a fake throat slash?

Or from hearing Erik's voice in my head?

"Okay, okay, settle down, everyone in their seats for the time being," Kate laughs. "Plenty of time for slashing throats left before dinner. Now. Today we're going to be practicing our suture stitching." Kate puts a green plastic strawberry container in the middle of the table. It's full of travel sewing kits the size of a matchbook, like you get in hotels. She has us each take one, then hands out pieces of plastic the size and shape of credit cards, only they're coated on one side with brown or beige silicone and feature two bright red ridges, one curved and one straight.

"When you're out in the field, accidents happen. You might tangle with a target, break some glass clearing a scene, or catch your arm on barbed wire. And obviously you can't just waltz into an emergency room. You'll have to patch yourself up as best you can, so knowing how to stitch flesh wounds comes in handy. We'll get some practice in today. And for our Color War . . ." She waves a stack of papers. "We also have the Scavenger Hunt."

She puts a sheet in front of each of us, face down like a test, and then announces we can begin. I flip it over hopefully: if it includes forageable plants, I might still have a chance at the screen time.

Surprisingly the list is just eight items long. And each one begins with "Find the camper who . . ."

"Find the camper who wet the bed until they were thirteen?" Kurt reads the first one out loud. "No one's going to come clean about that. How are we supposed to figure that out?"

Jada, across the table, is frozen in place.

"That's the game." Kate smiles a tight smile. "Find a way to make them tell."

Troy is pale. For once he isn't joking. "That's a messed up game."

"Which of the campers' first kiss was with their—" I read out, then stop on the word "stepbrother."

My eyes connect with Nobody's, and we both look at Jada, whose head is hung down like she's staring at her sheet, shoulders hunching forward, curling in on herself like burning paper.

"Well, that was me," I tell the table. "You can all me put me down for that one."

Erik's eyebrow goes up, and I widen my eyes at him.

Troy clears his throat. "Cool, thanks, Signal. You can put me down for number seven."

Dennis looks up from his sheet, sincerely confused. "You can't be number seven. You don't have third-degree burns, Troy, that's clea—"

Dennis stops talking abruptly. "Oh, okay. Sorry. Um. I'm number three then."

Erik sighs, stands up, stretches his long arms, and walks over to the tree. He hauls himself up on his customary branch and leans back against the trunk.

"Thanks, Dennis. I'm the bedwetter," Javier offers confidently, as a knowing chuckle goes around the table.

"Nice try, guys." Kate puts her hands on her hips and glares at us. "Dave and I know the right answers. If you don't turn in a sheet with the correct camper matched to each item, then you don't get dinner tonight. Now get to work."

Just the thought makes my stomach hurt. Hunger here is not a joke. Our days are physically exhausting, our nights are cold, and a bag lunch won't cut it until breakfast. On top of which, the chance to search online for what Mike and Vaughn are up to might never come again.

Maybe I can just guess? The others are all still reading.

Guiltily, I scan the list:

1. Find the camper who wet the bed until they were 13.
2. Find the camper whose first kiss was with their stepbrother.
3. Find the camper who never had a visitor in prison.
4. Find the camper with the lowest Class A score.
5. Find the camper who doesn't remember murdering someone.
6. Find the camper who grew up in a trailer park.
7. Find the camper whose parent gave them 3rd degree burns.
8. Find the camper whose Wylie-Stanton result led to the bullying and suicide of their younger sibling.

Some are obvious, most aren't. Figuring out who goes with what for some of these would require borderline psychological torture. Ashamed of myself for even considering the list, I ball the sheet up.

The sound is deafening in the silence around the table. Heat flushes up my neck as everyone turns to look at me.

"Congratulations, Signal," Kate snaps. "You're the first person disqualified from the Color War. Enjoy missing dinner."

I throw the ball in the center of the table and cross my arms in response.

And then, in the ensuing tense silence, there's a crumple sound overhead and a second ball of paper falls from the tree.

Kate's expression darkens, but Troy laughs and Jada claps, and the sound of crumpling paper rises around the table, except from Nobody, who folds her sheet into a paper plane and sends it shooting toward Kate's back as she turns and heads up the hill, her walkie-talkie off her hip, radioing to Dave.

We don't care. We're all still laughing when there's a yip from Jada, her hands slapping over her throat. She spins around and we all see Dennis, Sharpie uncapped, give her an apologetic grimace.

"Dennis!! Oh no, you didn't!" she laughs, throwing her paper ball at him, and that launches the paper fight. We throw the balled-up lists at each other, pulling the sheets from each other's hands, tearing and twisting the paper and throwing it across the field until we've turned each other's darkest secrets into white confetti.

* * *

When the air horn goes off, there's only three people left without Sharpie marks, and Erik gets Nobody on the way to the field where Dave is waiting.

"So it's just me and Erik now?!" Javier says. He and Erik lock eyes. "Game on."

Erik bares his teeth in a smile, and there's a few encouraging hoots from the twins, but they break off as our huddle gets closer to Dave.

He's in the tall grass where we had the pop quiz that first day, so I don't quite see what's happening at first. From a distance it looks like he's holding a decomposing hand.

"Where's Signal? Where is she?" Dave says in a voice that makes me go cold. Then, seeing me, he strides over and grabs the collar of my shirt and slings me face first into a pile of mannequin limbs on the ground, so hard the knee of my jeans split on impact.

I try to get up, but he kicks behind my knee. I hit the ground, a wheeze rattling out of my chest as I collapse in the cold grass, Dave standing right over me.

"I told you, Signal," Dave says through clenched teeth. *"No more chances."*

Chapter Eleven
What's Buried

~

"Was I not clear?" Dave yells. "I told you to hide the body. So what's this, Signal?"

Something dense glances off my shoulder: a silicone hand flops in the grass in front of me. I wince away before the next body part catches the back of my head.

"What's this, huh? And this?" he screams, pelting me with parts of the plastic corpse.

In two strides his hand is on my collar, he hauls me up and stares me down. I'm so close I can see the tiny black spaces between his too-white teeth and smell the chemical sting of his harsh soap.

"You FAILED the same test TWICE. You FELL OFF the obstacle course, you FAILED Color War. You're a FAILURE, Signal. SAY YOU'RE SORRY FOR BEING A FAILURE!"

"Sorry, Dave," I wheeze. But I guess it's not sincere enough for him because he shoves me backward, hard. I wind up on my knees again, the others watching in stunned silence.

"You *are* sorry, a sorry excuse for a Class A! You're a *disgrace* to the work we do here. Let's see if you've figured it out yet: what did you come here to learn, Signal?"

He's angry I'm not afraid of him. But how could I be? What could he do to me that's worse than what I've been through? I woke up wearing the lifeblood of my best friend. I am the Girl From Hell.

"WHAT DID YOU COME HERE TO LEARN?!"

"Not to end up like you," I spit back.

"What did you say?"

I pick up the head, pressing its cheek to my chest, and look Dave in the eyes.

"You take broken kids and make them worse. That's not work. That's a waste. Of all of us."

"Oh, you're a waste all right, Signal. No need to convince me," Dave says, and his key fob rattles in his hand as he points it at me. Finally, he gets the fear he wants. I hold very still. "One of the bodies in front of me is going to disappear tonight. You understand?"

I manage a nod.

"Go," he says. "Everybody else, with me."

"She gets a buddy," Nobody creaks. "Dog Mask—"

"Jada!" Dave orders. "Make sure Signal does her own work this time."

The rest of them move off, leaving just Jada and me.

I gather up the burnt mannequin parts, aware of her moving around behind me. I turn to see her pulling off her large yellow sweatshirt and laying it on the ground. I figure she's going to sit and watch me scrounge, but then instead she drops to her knees and helps me pick up the pieces.

"If we put them on the sweatshirt," Jada says, "we can bundle it up after. Maybe we could do two bundles? That'd be easier to carry."

". . . Okay." I take my fleece off and lay it by hers.

"Good work back there," Jada says, not looking at me. "Telling Dave off. The face he made was really beautiful. Like his brain was constipated."

My own laugh surprises me. She smiles almost shyly.

"Any ideas where you want to hide it this time?"

"No clue," I sigh. "It won't burn, it won't sink . . ."

"So we bury it," Jada says. "I know just the spot."

We take a detour to get shovels from the shed behind the obstacle course. When she slings a sharp spade over her shoulder, I feel a twinge of misgiving.

"You don't have to help dig," I say uncertainly.

She tilts her head back. "What, are you like, scared of me or something?"

I grip my shovel uneasily, fighting to keep my voice calm. "Why do you think Dave had *you* stay? He's hoping you'll attack me again. He knows you hate me."

"I never hated you, wow." Jada rolls her eyes. "I hated how *boy crazy you were* when you first got here."

"*I* was boy crazy?!"

"Yes. You were boy crazy," Jada snaps. "Remember running down the field after Javier? Laughing with Erik all the time, all that 'I'm a virgin he he he' stuff? But then when I asked your girlfriend why *she* was cool with it, she said you had a hard time making friends with girls."

Ouch. "That's true," I admit. "I mean, I have a hard time making friends with anyone."

Jada nods, her eyes wary. "Yeah, well . . . me too."

We walk along the forest path through the forgotten playground.

"I had a best friend," I truly have no idea why I'm telling her this, "and then when we got to high school she sort of stopped talking to me in public." My face burns, but Jada doesn't laugh.

"Lucky you. I never even got a best friend," Jada tells me. "Every time I invited a friend over, my stepbrother would mess it up. I just stopped asking people." She smiles an angry smile. "I always thought, when I get to high school, I'll get an amazing boyfriend! He'll come home and kick my stepbrother's ass! So stupid . . ." She laughs, shakes her head. "Like I thought everyone got some perfect boyfriend in high school. Like in a TV show."

"Yeah!" I nod. "In middle school, I thought, like, there would be some group just waiting for me in high school."

"Yeah." Jada grins. "Barbie gets a Skipper! That's how it works."

I laugh. "Oh, I was the Skipper. A Skipper without a Barbie."

"Yeah, well, *I'm* a Barbie. One of the special edition ones with the big box and sparkly dress and little brush and everything." Jada lifts her chin, then laughs. ". . . No Ken though."

"Yeah? It's all, um, over? With you and Erik?" Why am I bringing this back up?

But Jada just shrugs, if a little too carelessly. "Eh, we were never official. He's hot but he knows it, you know? Like he'll never be some perfect boyfriend, he'll never be *all about* one girl like that. And after what I've been through?" Jada sighs. "I need to be straight up adored."

"I mean, that does sound nice."

"Doesn't Nobody adore you?" Jada asks.

"You know, we, um," I hurry to cover. "We mostly sent letters in prison so we're sort of adjusting to an in-person relationship. Now where are we looking to dig?" Smooth.

"We're looking for a patch of skinny white trees." Jada says.

"Like, birches?"

"Maybe? I don't know all the names of the trees. Right there. Those."

She points to a grove of slim white trunks ahead, their small yellow leaves turning the air around them gold, and I smile.

"Yeah, those are birches."

"Right. The ground there's super soft. And we need to dig the hole seriously deep because we *cannot* have your girl turning up again."

* * *

When Jada finally declares the hole deep enough, it's almost sunset. Winded, we open up our bundles and shake the limbs into the dark earth, then take a moment to rest before we have to shovel the massive pile of wet dirt back on top of the mannequin.

"What about Troy?" I ask her as we lie, collapsed, on the cold ground.

"What *about* Troy?"

"He likes you." I pause. "He might even *adore you*."

A smile flickers across her face. And then a distant whistle carries through the trees:

"JADA! LIGHTS OUT! LET'S GO!!!" Dave calls.

She looks confused. "I'm supposed to leave you here alone . . . ?"

"I guess Dave figures if it takes me much longer to hide this body then Dog Mask can have me." I try to sound cavalier, rising to my feet and giving her a hand up. The birches have dimmed from white to lavender, their long shadows blurring into the darkening air.

Dave's voice calls again, angrier.

"Well, you *do* have a shovel if Dog Mask turns up. And it *is* a full moon . . ." She looks doubtfully up at the sky, then back at me. "Just go fast, okay?"

"Okay." I smile, Dave's voice calling louder in the distance. "And thank you."

"I'm glad we got to hang out," Jada says, and then, her eyes sparkling: "I forgive you for being such a skank before, okay?"

"Wow, thanks. I forgive you for slashing my face."

"So dramatic! It was a SCRAPE, Skipper." She laughs, pushing my shoulder as she gets up, and disappears into the trees.

And then the only thing in the woods is me, and the wind, and somewhere, a man in a mask who apparently intends on killing me. But it's fine, I'm fine, everything's fine.

And then I hear a twig snap.

I hold completely still, and whatever is behind me does too. Slowly, I slide my hand down my shovel handle, gripping the wood like a baseball bat.

I swing around, raising the shovel to confront: nothing. I plant the shovel in the earth, my hands shaking.

"You're fine, *you're fine*," I say out loud.

"No you're not." A mocking voice answers, and I instantly flood with relief. "You're not even halfway done. What have you been doing out here since Jada came back? Making dirt angels?"

"Erik!" I turn and immediately wince from the glare of his flashlight. "You scared me for a second!"

"What else is new?" he says. "Kate asked me to track you down and make sure you hadn't run into Dog Mask. How's it going?"

"Well, hmm. I'll probably just be another, like . . ." I squint at the hole speculatively, "Fourteen hours?"

He takes my shovel and indicates a pack of water bottles he's dropped to the ground.

"Take a break, weakling."

He gets no protest from me. I settle on a tree stump and empty two bottles, barely pausing for breath, as Erik sets the flashlight in the crook of a tree to illuminate the ground and begins digging. The flashlight's beam cuts a stripe of color across his face: a flash of green eye, his flushed red cheek, the purple shadows cast by the constricted muscles of his clenched jaw.

"Everything okay?"

"What?" he starts, surprised, like someone pulled from a deep sleep. "Sorry if I'm not *chatty*, I just think I have a pretty good idea how to put Dave's eye out without him figuring out I did it—"

"Don't!" I laugh. "Dave is such a loser, he doesn't deserve anything as cool as an eye patch."

"It's not a coincidence your mannequin turned up after your stand-off with Kate at Arts and Crafts. They had to make an example out of you." Erik leans into shoveling. "But it's my fault they got the opportunity. We should've buried it where they couldn't find it and use it against you like that."

"That's not your fault. I'm just really bad at camp," I sigh. "Anyway. Who won the screen time?"

"None of us. No dinner either. You really put Dave in a *mood*."

"Wow . . . I'm sorry."

"Don't be. If we'd done that Scavenger Hunt, camp would've been a dismal place to live. And we probably would've done it, if you hadn't refused." When I look up at this, Erik's eyes flash away from me. "So. You remembered something?"

"Yes!" I cry, "Erik, I remembered inside the shed!"

* * *

The only light came from Rose's phone; its dim blue glow slipped across a mattress on the floor as she crossed to the corner and kicked loose a floorboard: "He always keeps some potion in here," she said, pulling out the Transformers thermos. She set her phone on a card table against the

far wall, its surface mottled with candle wax, and I watched her silhouette pour something into the Thermos lid.

"You up for a little pre-party?" she said, holding it out to me.

I almost choked it all up, it was so bitter. She didn't see—she was
busy pulling things out of her backpack: the ends of two candles, two
bowls, a hacksaw, and a package of Hostess cupcakes.

"Ugh. This is gross. How about we break into those Hostess cupcakes instead?"

"You can't eat the cakes, but I might have a granola bar or something . . ." She fished around in her bag, pulling out a white plastic dis-
posable camera left over from her parents' long-ago wedding reception.

Two cupcakes. Two people. I could do the math.

"Does Mr. Moody know he's meeting me tonight?"

"It's a surprise. And it'll be a good surprise if you're fun, happy Signal instead of nervous, weirdo Signal! That's what our little pre-party is
for. Chug it, ho!"

I finished the cap, my mouth going weirdly numb. Rose put her phone
in a bowl on the card table and pulled up a playlist, the music quickly filling the small shed. Then she stood two plastic figurines beside the bowl.
They weren't large, maybe the size of wedding cake toppers, yet the flickering candlelight sent their long shadows dancing around the room. One
was a stiff plastic Elvis with a blank pink face, the other a plastic Marilyn
Monroe, her feet splayed, her white skirt floating around her hips and her
head thrown back. Her face wasn't blank, but the paint was messed up;
her red mouth was one scarlet blob that dripped down her throat.

I knew they were just junk souvenirs, but as I watched I realized
they were pulling the light out of the candles, pulling the music from
the phone. I tried to tell Rose, my words like cotton balls in my numb
mouth, and she tilted her head back and laughed. And then all the light
was coming from her. She was the light, and she was the music, and she
wanted to dance.

* * *

"So, Mr. Moody didn't drug you," Erik says, leaning on his shovel and staring at me. "Rose did."

"She didn't know it was drugged." I shake my head quickly. "We drank from the same thermos."

"You're sure she drank as much as you did?"

I picture Rose's lips pulling away from the lid, their gloss undisturbed.

"Even if she wasn't aware the thermos was drugged," Erik goes on, "she *was* trying to get you drunk. Why? If she needed something from you, why not ask while you were sober? Especially considering you did everything she told you to—"

"That's *not* true."

"Yeah, it is." Erik shovels faster, as though to burn away some building energy. "You're bending over backwards every week so she can get high with a ghost. Why did you put up with all of it? Were you in love with her or something?"

"What?! No! Rose was like my sister. It was just . . ." I screw my eyes closed and say it. "Sometimes, in high school, a terrible friend is better than no friends, okay?" The sadness of the confession flattens me. "The article got that right at least. I was a loner. A sad virgin loner 'seemingly obsessed with the macabre.'"

"Signal." Erik frowns sternly. "Please stop hitting on me."

And I laugh. In the dark, beside a mock grave, he makes me laugh.

"So the hacksaw Rose brought . . . Was that the same one that was used on her?"

I nod. "It was a really common type, brand new. The police thought it was shoplifted."

"And it was under your hand when you woke up."

"Where Mr. Moody planted it."

He steps out of the beam cut by the flashlight, his face disappearing for a long moment.

"Have you been thinking about the newspaper stuff?" I ask.

"Yes. A lot," Erik answers, sending another shovelful of earth into the grave, "Especially about the Windward trust. Rose was a Windward as in, like, *Senator* Windward?"

"Sort of. Rose's mom was from a branch of that family. But when she got pregnant at sixteen they pretty much disowned her and cut her off. That's how she and Rose ended up next door to us in the trailer park."

"And her real dad?"

"He parted ways when Janeane found out she was pregnant. Rose always wanted to find him but . . ." All the things Rose will never do bump up at the back of my throat.

"So Janeane was cut off, but Rose had a trust, right? The newspaper said something about trustees and a scholarship."

"Yes. The Windwards set up a trust for her, but she couldn't touch it until she turned eighteen."

"Interesting," he says, then: "I wonder if it's set up to exclude spouses . . ."

"What, like what if Rose secretly married Mr. Moody? I mean, it'd be very out of character. But it would explain the secrecy."

"The secrecy was because Rose was banging Mr. Moody," Erik says flatly. "Considering what you've remembered about the shed, let's review her possible admirers: there's her churchy boyfriend, his violent best friend, and the local drug dealer. You see any obvious overlap?"

There's something about him putting it so cleanly that makes me see it in a flash. The tension. The love triangle.

"*Vaughn*," I say breathlessly. "Vaughn was Mr. Moody!"

Erik walks toward me, wiping his mouth on the back of his hand, and grabs a water bottle. "Nope. The guy most likely to stash an old thermos full of liquor in a shed is Jabberwocky Whatshisface. He's our guy."

"Jaw Itznicki?!" And then, feeling prim, "No way. He wasn't Rose's type."

"Bad boys are *every* girl's type." Erik grins.

"Where do you get your girl information, a T-shirt from 2002?"

"Come on, Signal. How hot was Jaw?" Erik's grin gets wider. "Rate him on a scale of one to me."

I roll my eyes, but guiltily remember seeing Jaw at work on Rose's lawn, looking much the way Erik does now: shirt plastered to his chest, clipping hedges or taking smoke breaks by the planter. I once pointed out the bruises on his neck and Rose cackled: "Um, you mean hickies?"

"Look, I get that the shed is more of a match for Jaw," I concede. "But *what if* Rose went to the shed to get drugs from Jaw's stash . . . for her and Vaughn? Vaughn said he was getting high with Mike that night, right? I *still* can't see Mike doing drugs, but Vaughn? Absolutely."

I get up and start pacing.

"So what if, after I passed out, Rose went to meet Vaughn at the party, and when they're high, Mike finds them. And it all comes out."

"And Mike kills her?"

"I don't know. I don't know what happened. But I could see there being a fight. I could see Rose denying everything and Vaughn losing his temper. And lashing out." My hands are shaking, my voice trembling as it all slides together. "Erik, that would explain Vaughn covering for Mike! *Because Vaughn would need an alibi too.* But Mike has a conscience. He couldn't live the lie. He had to leave town . . ."

Erik watches me silently, leaning on his shovel.

"Don't you see? One of them hurt her, and they both covered it up. Maybe initially Vaughn thought he could throw off police by leaving her in Jaw's shed. Make it look like an overdose. But when he gets there . . . there I am!" It's so obvious. How had I not seen it before? *"The only person who knew about Mr. Moody!"*

Erik tilts his head. "So why let you live?"

Cold shoots through me, though it doesn't come from the air or ground.

"So he could frame me instead." *Obviously.*

But Erik frowns. "Framing someone is *hard*, Signal. A spur-of-the-moment framing? Before I met you, I would've said impossible. Put yourself in the killer's position: you've just killed Rose."

My chest tightens.

"Your reflexes are on a hair trigger, the woods are full of your classmates, and then you stumble across *the only person alive who can tie you to the victim.*"

I hold very still.

"He'd kill you. I'm sorry, nothing personal." Erik puts a hand on his chest in a gesture of feigned apology. "But you'd be gone. But you're saying *instead*, Mr. Moody decides to use his precious getaway time . . . posing Rose in your lap? Planting false evidence? Who even does that?"

"Oh, I don't know," I snap. "A *homicidal maniac*, maybe?"

"A homicidal maniac might have the urge to frame you, but they couldn't pull it off. Only a psychopathic mastermind would be capable of that. So if Mr. Moody framed you—"

"*If?*" My voice breaks. "What do you mean, 'if'?! There's no if. He either framed me, or *I killed her.*" And there they are, the words I never thought I could speak out loud. "I killed her and then blocked it out. Is that what you're trying to say?"

Chapter Twelve
The Slumber Party

❧

"That's what the prosecution thought. And the jury too." Erik takes the flashlight from the tree. And then the world disappears as he turns its beam directly on my face.

"No evidence anyone else had been in the shed. You were found soaked in her blood, the weapon in your hand." Erik's voice for once is painfully slow. "No thermos was found. No drugs in your bloodstream. The only evidence we have Mr. Moody even existed is that Rose told you he did. And she lied to everyone."

The world is a haze of blinding white, my eyelashes refracting into dark rainbows at the edge of my vision as my eyes fight to close. But I stare at him through the light, hands balled into fists.

"But I don't buy it," he says, and the flashlight cuts away.

"Why not?" I ask the dark.

"Call it instinct," Erik says. "I see the angel and I want to set her free."

So he still doesn't believe I did it. I could sob with relief. But why does it matter what Erik thinks? When did he get so much power over me? Erik's pop idol dimples flash as he keeps talking, but I'm not listening anymore. I'm remembering one of the first things he said:

"You find a person's weakness, right . . . Then you get friendly and slowly make them believe that weakness is gone. Once they believe that, boom. You break right through it, right into their heads."

Erik said he wanted to talk over my case because he was bored. But maybe what he saw in me wasn't a new puzzle, but a new victim. He never believed I was innocent. He thinks I killed Rose and she's his way into my head. Why else would the deadliest guy in camp spend so much time with me?

"So, Watson, here's the questions we need to ask to solve this crime," Erik goes on. "Why did Rose keep Jaw such a huge secret? Why did she need to get you drunk? And who drugged the thermos?" He looks over his shoulder toward me. "Any thoughts?"

"No," I say, gripping the other shovel. "Look, I can take it from here. You can go back to camp."

"Uh, what?" He frowns. "Why?"

"Maybe because you just stuck a flashlight in my face and interrogated me?" I snap.

"Yeah? And? I wanted to see your face." Now he's acting baffled. "I told you. Everything comes through in your expressions."

"How stupid do you think I am? This whole time you've just been trying to get in my head!"

Erik's eyebrows shoot up. "Oh. Okay. I see." He stabs his fingers into his chest in a flash of anger. "I'm out here burying *your* mannequin, trying to *help* with *your* wrongful conviction, and you still think I'm just some creeper out to get you, right?" He lets out a sharp, exasperated laugh. "I'm sorry, Signal, but if you'll let me just make myself a little vulnerable here, you're starting to hurt my feelings."

"Come on, Erik." I roll my eyes. "We both know you don't have feelings."

His mouth contracts and some unnameable expression flares up and is gone before I'm sure it's there, the air going stiff as he turns away and tamps the earth down on the grave. He doesn't say anything, won't look at me as he finishes. Like he's actually *offended*. Like he was really being sincere, as if he's even capable of sincerity. Everything he does is a manipulation.

"You know those scars on Javier's knuckles?" Erik says at last, kicking leaves across the packed-down dirt. "He tore them open on his victim's skull. Javier banged his victim's head on an asphalt drive so many times they had to identify the dude with dental records *after they picked his teeth out of the pavement.* You should ask him to tell you about it the next time you're mooning over each other in a dandelion patch." I open my mouth, then close it. He snatches the flashlight from the tree, catches up the two shovels, and starts sauntering back through the birch grove toward the woods. I fall in beside him, the silence between us extended and uncomfortable.

Then he starts in again once we've returned the shovels to the obstacle course shed, blurting: "Your silence speaks volumes, by the way."

"There's a reason I didn't want to do the Scavenger Hunt today, Erik." I stare icily straight ahead as we cross the obstacle course field. "I'm trying not to judge everyone by their past. Only by how they act here and now."

"Except for me," Erik says viciously. "Everyone gets a fresh start except mean old Erik."

"You've been calling me a weakling and telling me I don't belong since I got here!"

"Yeah, and I'm right!" he says with cold fury. "Maybe that's what *really* bothers you about me. I don't pretend either of us is something we're not. I don't ask you to make me daisy chains in a meadow or tell you you're a flower. I'm just myself with you, *terrifying though I may be,* because I trust you can handle it. But you can't. You're *determined* to think the worst of me!"

"Erik, you killed ten people!"

"And you haven't even asked my side of the story!"

"Erik!!" I almost laugh at the audacity of the statement, yet his stung expression is completely serious.

"I asked you, at least," he says, and now the cabin and Kate's glowing cigarette are in sight, he strides head of me without a backward glance.

"You finish with the body?" Kate extends her arm, blocking me before I can follow him into the cabin.

"Of course."

"Then get right in bed. No talking, straight to sleep."

I guess she's still mad about me ruining their stupid Scavenger Hunt. My head is buzzing with everything I still want to say, but Erik's vanished up to his bunk, and I know everyone is lying there awake and starving and at least a little angry at me. So I shut up and go to bed.

* * *

Night bird sounds, the rustle of dry leaves overhead. I'm in the shed.

Dark lines of Rose's hair trail over my knee in one slow, steady pull, tickling the back of my hand. Because Rose's head is rising. It floats up from my lap and her body like a balloon. Her face is turned away, I stare at the bluish white of her scalp through her thick hair. And then once her head is level with mine it slowly, slowly starts to turn.

I can't move.

For a moment Rose's profile is cut out against the dark in perfect detail, and then those blank eyes lock with mine. Her lips part, her bloodstained teeth clatter, her thick tongue worms in the dryness of her mouth, but no voice comes out. She will never speak again.

In my lap, her body twitches. Her pale hands walk themselves like spiders up to her neck and clutch there, fingertips digging into the red meat. The body rolls into a kneel across from me.

I watch, paralyzed, as Rose's hands rake the air, catch her head and awkwardly pull it onto her neck. Rose, back together, kneels across from me, a line of red across her throat.

There's a figure behind her, and at the sight of it a burning scent fills the shed. The figure is too tall, too thin, saggy gray skin hanging from its bony frame. It doesn't have a face, just a flat flap of pale skin. It ducks behind Rose and then starts crawling around the room, hands moving back and forth, the burning smell so harsh I squeeze my streaming eyes closed.

Rose screams, a howl that cuts through me with almost physical force, it is so deeply animal, so full of fear.

White fills the air, obliterating Rose like an overexposed photograph. Then the white narrows down to two bleached rainbows arching through the window, and Rose is gone.

In front of me are the Marilyn and Elvis figurines, grown life-size. But Elvis has white-blond hair, and Marilyn's curls are dark brown. They're embracing, faces smashed together, their hands moving over each other's bodies.

A male voice, strange and slow: *"Come here and I'll give you a real kiss."*

Marilyn turns to me, her dark hair spiraling down over her shoulders, and the room goes white again, but slowly this time. As though fading into gathering mist.

Click!

The mist clears at once, and Elvis's blank face is right next to mine, his hand splayed across my cheek. He has no eyes, no mouth, his features are just blunt shapes. His formless mouth covers mine and I taste sweet smoke.

"This is messed up," he laughs into my ear.

"She's completely out. Just one picture." Marilyn's mouth is a red streak all the way down her throat.

"How much did she drink?" Elvis says, on all fours, backing away, then he rolls himself up to standing. "What if she wakes up? Sorry I'm so late." Elvis walks backward out the door and down the path, as Marilyn rushes over and kneels in front of me, her hand on my cheek. But she's not Marilyn anymore. She's Rose: whole, unbroken, alive, and I start to cry.

"Why isn't he here? He'll know what to do," Rose says, her fingertips brushing at my hair. "I'll have to tell you all about it when you wake up."

"ROSE!" I wail. *"ROSE!!!"* I reach for her, but she slips away, the shed dissolving as a strong hand reaches through the wall and grabs my shoulder.

"Signal, wake up!" Nobody cries, shaking me.

The lantern next to my bed blinks on. It was just a dream. It was just a dream.

Javier stands just behind Nobody, a red Sharpie slash across his throat.

"Troy?" Kurt calls, high and panicked. "Where are you?!"

"Right here," Troy answers. "Chill out man, you're okay."

"You kept calling for someone named Rose?" Nobody says in her gruff voice.

Confusion melts into the sick awareness that everyone is looking at me, all curled up, crying. "It was just a nightmare." I sit up, scraping my hair back from my clammy face. "Sorry guys, false alarm. Everything's fine."

"Um, *I'm* not fine!" Troy announces. "I thought Dog Mask was dragging one of the girls out of the bathroom or something."

"You okay?" Javier asks quietly, settling onto the bunk beside me.

"I'm fine, I . . . It just felt so real." Javier rests a hand on my shoulder and I sag with relief at the contact, my hand flying up to cover his, and that's when I feel them.

Javier's knuckles are crisscrossed with raised, wormy lines of scar tissue, like beads of badly welded steel.

That's when I see Erik, sitting on his top bunk, hair mussed but his eyes clear, staring at me through the haze of the lantern.

I hold Javier's hand tighter.

"Wait a second, is it . . . is it raining?" Dennis says sleepily, and a momentary hush follows as we listen. There's a sporadic drumming on the tin roof, and in the silence it grows steady.

The boys all groan, and Erik turns and spiders down from his bunk, then yanks down his sleeping bag. Dennis's pillow lands on the floor beside me, thrown from above.

"What're you guys doing?" Jada yawns.

"Last time it rained the water leaked down the inside of the walls. Everybody's bedding got wet. We'll be drier in the middle of the cabin."

"On the *floor?*" Jada gasps. Erik throws his bedding down just a few feet from my bunk. He stretches along it, hands under his head, and peers up at me, his expression impossible to read. There's a small rumble in the distance, and the drumming on the tin roof grows harder.

"The girls' cabin never leaked. Why didn't they just move us all in there?!" Jada grumbles, pulling her sheets away from the wall.

"Too close to the woods," Nobody says darkly. "Where Dog Mask is."

"Hey, Signal, c'mere . . . ," Javier says softly, and leads me over to the bathroom. He looks around furtively, making sure no one has followed us in, then leans in and says, "I managed to get these from the pantry before lights out. When Jada came back and said you'd been digging, I figured you'd need them."

He pulls back a towel from a stack on a metal chair to reveal a family-size bag of Ruffles and a *giant* bag of trail mix. *With M&Ms.*

I turn back to him, touched. "Is it cool if we share them with everybody?"

". . . They'll go pretty quick."

"I know, I know, it's just everyone's hungry and it's my fault."

"It's not your fault. Not at all." Javier's face softens. "But if you want, sure. Let's make it a party."

"Hey guys?" I announce as we walk back into the cabin. Everyone is sourly staking out space on the cramped floor and looking vaguely miserable. "Who wants some snacks?"

The drumming of the rain is all I hear for a moment as six stunned faces stare up at me.

"Are you serious?" Dennis says at last.

"PUT IT IN MY MOUTH!" Troy bellows, springing to his stocking feet.

The bags are torn from our hands. Jada runs and gets brown paper towel squares from the bathroom to serve as plates. A couple of lanterns are brought to the center of the floor, and everyone pulls their bedding into a ring to better oversee the even distribution of the trail mix elements. By the time I get my sleeping bag and join the circle, the only open spot is right between Nobody and Javier and across from Erik, who're establishing each person's preferences for dried pineapple over M&Ms, or banana chips over yogurt raisins; it all feels so strangely normal for a moment. This is real. The nightmare was just that, a nightmare. I push it out of my head.

"It's so weird, being up late eating snacks in our pajamas like this. It feels like a slumber party!" Jada chews on a banana chip.

"*That's* what a slumber party is?" Nobody asks. "Eating in bed?"

"What, you've never been to one?"

Nobody shakes her head.

"Then welcome, this is now your first." I look around the group. "Nobody's first slumber party, who's in?"

"I smell a MAAAKEOVER MONTAAGE!" Troy yells, with jazz fingers.

"Boys do slumber parties, right?" Jada screws up her tiny nose.

"We call them sleepovers."

"Uh, yeah, and they're the best. Video games all night and then everybody draws dicks on Kurt's face when he falls asleep first, and then we dunk his thumb in warm water and he pisses himself and it's just a great time."

Kurt jokingly narrows his eyes at me when I laugh at this. "Oh, so it's cool if we all draw dicks on your face, then?"

"Only if I fall asleep first. Which I won't." After that nightmare, I may never sleep again.

"My sisters would always play light as a feather, stiff as a board," Dennis offers.

"We could tell scary stories!" Jada's eyes go wide in the lamplight.

"I don't know if that's the best idea for Signal right now," Javier says to her quietly.

"And that's your business how?" Erik sits upright, his expression hidden from my view by the fall of his loose hair.

"Bro, she just woke up screaming. I don't think it's a great idea to scare the hell out of her."

"I grasp your logic, Jav, but as you're well aware, Signal has a mouth." He lets the word hang. "She can speak for herself."

"What's your problem?" Javier says just a little too loud. Erik starts to answer, but before he can Nobody cuts in.

"Are fistfights part of slumber parties too?"

"Nope, no, not at all," I interrupt quickly. "Javier's right, I can't handle ghost stories. But maybe we could tell, uh, non-scary stories? Like um, I don't know, maybe—"

Erik pulls his pillow over his head. "Boring. If you're all going to stay up telling each other fairy tales I'd honestly rather just sleep."

"Who said anything about fairy tales? I'm just saying we could tell stories where people don't, you know, die gruesomely-"

"Everyone dies," Erik says sharply. "Any story that doesn't deal with that is a fairy tale. Where do you think 'and then they all lived happily ever after' came from? The *best case scenario ending* is 'and then they each died alone after the humiliating torture of old age.'"

"That's awfully nihilistic, Erik."

"Whoo, slow down, Kurt and I didn't get to that part of SAT prep." Troy munches on honey-roasted peanuts. "Nia-listic?"

"Nihilism is the rejection of moral and religious teachings in the belief that life has no meaning," Dennis says, as though he's reading from a flashcard.

"It's a more official term for common sense." Erik's eyes flash but his tone is elaborately casual. "Now maybe Signal thinks the meaning of life is to share and care with us like Heidi of the Swiss Alps even when she's trapped in a damn murder machine—"

"I am no kind of Heidi of the Swiss Alps." I widen my eyes at him. "I wish you could have met me two years ago. 'Life is meaningless' was like, my personal motto back then!"

"And now?" Javier turns on his side and looks up at me. And I was about to try and pull my tough girl routine, but I can't with Javier watching. Because being a flower for sure means something to him, and it means something to me. So I go with the truth instead:

"Now . . . I feel the opposite way about it."

"What, that life has *too much* meaning?" Erik snaps.

"No," I say. "Or . . . well, kind of. I mean . . . it's not as simple as one meaning for everybody. Life isn't just some math problem with one solution, right? It's . . . a force. A force that gives and gives . . . We get a body, and a mind and time, and this huge urge to *do* something with all of it . . ."

"That's the hardest part of prison," Nobody says, staring down at a line of pretzels on her napkin. "Feeling like you can't do anything with your time. Like it's just going to waste."

"Yeah," Jada agrees.

"So maybe the meaning of life is what we give back when we answer that urge," I ramble on. "We create the meaning of our lives, by finding our individual purpose. By pursuing what we love."

I glance up at Erik, waiting for his sarcastic laugh, but it doesn't come.

"Whoa, man. Deep, that's deep!" Troy laughs, pulling on the rust-colored beanie he always wears to bed, then shrugs. "So the meaning of my life is to bang girls and eat candy. How about you, Kurt?"

"I don't know. I always thought it was like what Dad always says, the most important thing in life is family. Being loyal, having their back."

"I'm with Kurt," Javier's low voice rumbles close to my side. "Life is about protecting the ones you love."

"What does it mean if some of us think the meaning of *our* life is to end other people's lives, though?" Dennis asks. My smile drops.

"Yeah, how does that fit into your vision of life as a force that gives and gives?" Erik demands. "It's almost like you're conveniently forgetting the part where life brutally takes everything back, whether you serve your 'purpose' or not."

Javier laughs. "You and Dennis are part of Team Take, that's for sure."

"Oh, don't be so modest, Jav. Sure, you lost our Sharpie fight. But you're still just as much of a murderer as I am." Erik smiles at him coldly, and I notice he alone has an unmarked throat. "Everyone in this room is! We're all Class As. Sounds like we're *all* on Team Take to me."

Jada's face falls, and Nobody's shoulders seem to slouch. Troy and Kurt avoid each other's gaze and Dennis pulls his blanket closer.

"I know I'm a Class A. No one lets me forget it," I grimace. "I'm sure that's true for all of you too. The world keeps telling us we're evil. But what if we proved the world wrong? I am what I choose to do. I am the choices I make."

"You *chose* to come here to learn how to *kill people*," Erik says. "That's what this program is. We all made that choice."

I stare at his stern face. What must it be like to be Erik, to have that insistent voice inside your head all the time, picking you apart?

Something else is going on too—there's more anger in his words than I could inspire, about what I don't know. Because, as he pointed out, I have never asked his side. I don't know his life or his past. Maybe he hurts as much as I do.

Maybe everyone does, all the time.

With that in mind, I try and talk to him the way I wish someone would talk to me.

"Well then, this program is not working," I say gently. "Because if 'Class As' are supposed to be so terrible, no one here acts like a 'Class A.' You really helped me today, Erik. So did Jada. I wouldn't be here right now without you two. And we all protected each other from that Scavenger Hunt."

There's a murmur of agreement around the circle.

"So what if we keep doing that? Keep protecting each other? What if we turned this camp into a place we actually want to be?"

"In that spirit . . . ," Kurt asks seriously, "can I have the rest of your Ruffles?"

"Absolutely not."

"I have three pieces of pineapple."

"Okay. For three pineapples I would trade three Ruffles."

"Now that the speeches are over," Jada says in a dramatically bored voice, a low growl of thunder approaching overhead. "Can we do something *fun* please?"

Nobody lurches upright and stares straight out the dark window. *"Look."*

A bolt of lightning throws the figure outside into sharp relief: Tall, hunched shoulders, the features of his dog mask slick with rain, staring in through the window at us.

And before the next bolt of lightning flashes, he's gone.

Chapter Thirteen

Pop Quiz

❦

There's a moment of silence, like one collective intake of breath before diving into deep water. And then everyone but me leaps to their feet, *laughing*. Like the last period bell just rang on the last day of school— *that's* the kind of sudden joyful excitement that fills the air.

A masked assailant is here to kill us all, and these ruthless predators, these bloodthirsty Class As, these friends of mine couldn't be happier.

They huddle up as I stare down at our scattered pieces of trail mix, my stomach in free fall.

"He went left. He's gonna try to come in through the back."

"Why wait? Let's go out to meet him!"

"Nice try, Erik, you just want him all to yourself. Let him come in here and then we can all take turns."

"What weapons have we got?" Javier addresses the room.

"I got a shiv." Jada pulls a plastic toothbrush handle scraped to a sharp point from one of the pockets of her pink sweatpants. She's had a shiv on her this whole time?!

"I got some stones in a sock," Kurt offers.

Troy wordlessly walks over to his bottom bunk bed and pulls out a short-handled hatchet, grinning broadly at the others' impressed surprise.

"Squirreled this away the first day when they made us clear the saplings off the soccer field. Dave never missed it."

Nobody grabs the sleeve of my gray Mickey Mouse sweatshirt, yanking me to my feet. I've been frozen on the floor while they've been excitedly planning.

"I *had* a kitchen knife under my mattress." Javier glares at Erik. "But it went missing a couple days ago."

"Is that an accusation?" Erik snarls.

"*I* have it, Javier," Nobody says, still hovering at my side, and my jaw drops. "And I'm not giving it up. It was dull when I took it and it was hard work getting it sharp again."

"Okay." Javier takes my arm. "You take the knife, and I'll guard her?" Nobody looks to me for approval, then agrees to the trade-off.

Javier reaches down for the lanterns on the floor and snaps them off: *snap, snap, snap,* plunging the room into blackness.

CREEEEEEAAAAK.

The rusty hinges of the back door to the bathroom are pulled open from outside.

BANG!

The back door slams against its wood frame: he *wants* us to know he's coming.

Javier puts himself between me and the door to the bathroom, and walks us back between Erik's and Kurt's bunks, into the darkest shadow of the cabin, while everyone else gets into position. Hidden behind him I break down, choking on my own breath, fingers digging into his sweatshirt. I could bolt out the window, but what if Dog Mask saw? I'm trapped. We're all trapped.

Javier takes my hand in his, his thumb moving slowly over the back of my hand until that's all I can feel, the calm steady pressure, though he doesn't look back at me. He stares straight forward, ready to take whatever comes next. I grip his hand, scars and all, and squeeze back with all my strength. Javier doesn't even flinch.

Another bolt of lightning turns the room into a black-and-white photo: Nobody crouched by her bunk, gleaming knife in hand; Troy standing with his back to the front door, hatchet raised; Erik at his side, clutching one of the heavy halogen lanterns by its base. Jada has shot up the ladder of Erik's bunk beside the door to the bathroom, so she can strike first from above when Dog Mask comes in.

The rain seems to hammer down faster and faster as we all watch the bathroom door. Any moment now. Why is he just standing in the unlit bathroom? What is he waiting for?

The sigh of the front door breaks the silence and a scream rips from my throat. Dog Mask bursts in behind us, catching us all by surprise, his heavy steps shaking the thin floorboards. His shoulders are level with the top bunks, his eyes flat behind his smiling mask. He's so close I could reach out and touch the gleaming edge of his axe.

Erik throws the lantern at his head, hard, but Dog Mask blocks it with the axe, sending it crashing to the floor to light him from below in blinking, sputtering bursts as he swings the axe down at Troy.

With a grunt Troy throws up his hatchet, one end in each hand, and Dog Mask's axe head catches awkwardly on the thin wood handle. Troy's arms tremble frantically as he fights to keep the axe from bearing down and splitting through his chest.

Kurt darts forward and jabs Dog Mask's ribs, but Dog Mask doesn't flinch, he just sends Kurt flying into the wall with a half-hearted backhand. But the momentary distraction allows Troy to slip away, and then Javier shoots forward before I can stop him.

He stoops to picks up another lantern, and Dog Mask whips around, axe flying up, and a high, wild shriek escapes me for an endless instant until Dog Mask's throaty voice eclipses mine. Dog Mask spins away from Javier, one arm curling to his side, and we all stare as Nobody pulls her knife from under his arm and it drips a dark, black red onto the white sheets below.

Tall Nobody looks like a child across from Dog Mask, but she steps forward and they circle each other in the center of the cabin, stepping through the blankets and paper towels where a moment ago we were giggling and safe. Erik moves forward but Nobody puts out an arm without even looking at him.

"*Me first*," Nobody whispers.

Dog Mask's axe sighs through the air, held one-handed now, and Nobody dodges it. Dog Mask lunges, but she feints left and his axe head bites into the side of Erik's bunk.

Nobody, taking advantage, swipes at his other shoulder, but he pulls the blade from the wood with a rain of splinters and cuffs her hard with his forearm before the knife connects. Her foot catches on something and she tips to one side, falling.

"*NO!*" I shriek, straining forward, but Javier's hands clamp me in place.

In the nanosecond Dog Mask's axe swings high enough to expose his neck, Nobody impossibly recovers, surging up in a perfectly planned swoop that ends with her knife buried in Dog Mask's throat.

She buries the blade deeper, leaning in toward him until their faces almost touch.

His axe clatters to the ground. Guttural whimpers and thick, broken groans spill from him as his broad, bloody hand claps onto her black ski mask.

Nobody stands completely still, grasping the knife with both hands like a fishing line that might at any moment jerk her into the tide, her scarred arms twitching with effort. His knees sag and she sinks with him, onto first one knee and then the other, so they're kneeling across from each other in the middle of our blankets, dark blood soaking the sheets around them.

Whether she's making sure he dies or making sure he doesn't die alone, I don't know.

Dog Mask's fluttering hand clasps her hood. And then, with an almost delicate gesture, he pulls it away.

Nobody's face is not burnt. Unlike her scarred and melted arms, it's untouched and perfect. She is ludicrously beautiful. She stares back at Dog Mask with the kind of face perfume companies use to remind you how it feels to fall in love: heart-shaped, high cheekbones, with a clear-cut flower of a mouth and large, striking eyes that burn into his.

Nobody reaches over to Dog Mask and pulls off his mask.

The man underneath is maybe thirty-five. His head is large and heavy, his eyes sunk deep in his face, and a mass of scar tissue from his nose to his chin is made more grotesque by the blood bubbling out of his lips. The others all draw forward in a circle around them, except me. I'm frozen where I stand, in the deepest shadows, trying to reconcile the angel and demon kneeling in front of me.

"Tell . . . Kate . . ." Dog Mask's head lolls, sweat standing out on his cheeks.

"What?!" Nobody asks in her familiar coarse voice, her long, delicate eyebrows drawing together. "Tell Kate what?"

"We won't go quiet," he sputters, choking on his own blood. "Deal with . . . the devil. S'all it's ever been . . . tell Kate . . ." His eyes shut against the pain. "Won't go quiet."

And then his breathing stops, and all I can hear is the drumming of the rain.

Nobody gently lets go of the knife, and he slumps onto his side. She reaches forward, feels his neck, withdraws her hand, and nods.

The guys rush Nobody in an ecstasy of whoops and high-fives.

"Hey, great work there, Nobody. Wow." Kurt sounds more than a little smitten.

"You kind of hogged the kill, but I'm prepared to let it slide," Erik says.

Nobody looks through them to me. It's so weird to think this gore-spattered angel is the same person as my fake girlfriend Nobody, but as she gawkily walks over she becomes more familiar. And when she drags the back of her hand under her nose and then roughly puts an arm around my shoulder and says in that same raspy voice, "What's wrong?!" I get it. It's still her.

"What's *wrong?*" I wipe the tears from my cheeks and look around our circle for some understanding. But no one else is crying. Not even Javier.

I stare at the disfigured man below us, with his sunken, staring eyes. How did he look as a baby, when his mother first held him? How does a person become a monster like this?

And I know he would have killed us, that Nobody is a hero, that I owe her my life for what she did. But it's beyond awful. Seeing the light go out of his eyes will haunt me as long as I live. But I can't *say* that. Not to them.

"He was supposed to kill us all!" I manage instead.

"Well, he didn't."

"Yeah, he got his own butt killed! BA-BWAAAMP!" Troy does an elaborate air guitar lick right over the slumped body that makes Javier crack up.

"Stupid." He shakes his head as Troy continues rocking out.

"But why did he say that?" I plead. "How does he know Kate? What the hell is going on?!"

"Um, can we talk about the real issue here?" Jada puts her hands on her hips. "Nobody, why have you been wearing a mask all this time, girl? You're like . . . a supermodel."

"Seriously," Kurt says a little too warmly.

Nobody looks down at her ski mask as though debating whether to put it back on. It's saturated with thick, warm blood.

"I mean *damn*, girl," Troy says, trying to keep from cracking up at what he's about to say. "I never knew I wanted a knife to the throat *so bad.*"

Nobody tosses the bloody ski mask at him like a water balloon, he sidesteps it, and it lands with a big red splatter that trails all the way to the front door just as Dave and Kate rush in.

"What's all the ruckus in here?!"

Kate's eyes land on Dog Mask, and she freezes.

Dave steps in front of her, chuckling.

"Well, looks like you found the hiker! Thought he was going to have some fun stabbing some poor defenseless teenagers, huh? Instead you guys got a bit of a pop quiz!" He pulls back his rain hood and steps pluckily over to the body on the floor, nudging it with the toe of his boot. "Aaaaand you passed! Now you can work together to dispose of this body by morning. Kate, you and I should report an intruder to HQ."

"Right." Kate's voice is thick. She reaches blindly behind her for the door.

"*Wait.*" I stare past Dave at Kate. "He had a message. He said to tell Kate that 'they' wouldn't go quietly. How did he know your name?"

Dave lets an uneasy silence fill the cabin. Then he says, "He's been skulking around for a while. Guess he picked up that Kate was in charge!"

"*Why* was he skulking around? Why did he target *us*? Why hike out to *this* camp?" I press.

Dave shrugs, his smile disappearing. "Why do *any* of you kill? I don't know. I don't want to know. I just need you to be good at it. You have obstacle course in three hours, so I suggest you all clean up this mess."

Chapter Fourteen

On the Water

~

The blood seeps through our blankets and streams between the gaps in the plank floor, dripping into the crawlspace under the cabin. We stand around the body after Kate and Dave leave, staring.

"'Clean up this mess!'" Troy mocks, punching Dave's slight Midwestern accent. "I guess that's his new catchphrase now, since he can never use that stupid call and response again after Signal DESTROYED IT!"

Everyone laughs and I look around, confused. "What?"

"Earlier, when you told Dave you were learning not to end up like him. It was great."

"Great?! It was freaking *legendary*." Kurt holds up a hand until I high-five him.

"Jada did say he looked like his brain was constipated," I say, and Jada smiles as everyone bursts out laughing again.

"Okay. Let's start carving this big boy up!" Troy crouches down beside the body, and I have to grab onto a bunk to steady myself.

"No." Kurt shakes his head, passing a hand over his face. "We can't."

"Why not?"

"We don't have a tarp or anything sharp enough to cut bone."

"Yeah, he's too big to chop. I say we wrap him up." Erik nods at the corner of one of the sleeping bags. "Roll him, tape him, weigh him down, throw him in the water."

"After what happened to my mannequin?" I point out. "You really think that's wise?"

"You threw a *plastic mannequin* into ten feet of water, Signal. I'm talking about rowing this meaty beast half a mile out and dropping him in the middle of the lake and letting the Circle of Life handle the rest."

"Yeah." Nobody nods slowly. "That's our best bet. With the storm passing through it's too wet for anything else."

My stomach flips over at the thought of what "anything else" could mean.

"I can't handle this," I mutter.

"Surprise, surprise," Erik says under his breath, but waves me toward the bathroom. "Could you go find some mops and a bucket for the blood? I think there should be some in the main cabin kitchen."

I almost run out of the room while the rest close in. I hear a giggling Jada say something about how his hands are so floppy before I have to stop, throw on the faucet in the bathroom sink, and retch over the last toilet stall. The handfuls of trail mix I had for dinner come back up, and once I stop gagging I quickly brush my teeth, then run out into the rain, toward the main cabin.

I land on the front porch, teeth chattering, and as I open the door, muffled voices echo down the hall, from the nurse's office where Dennis and I were the other day.

"We can't tell HQ who it was," Kate insists.

"They'll figure it out. If we don't volunteer the information, we look complicit."

"If we tell HQ they'll send the campers out early. You want to risk that?"

"If we hide this, we *are* complicit."

"We both know if the Director sends the kids out now, we could lose them all."

A tense throb of silence, as though Dave knows she's right. Then a chair creaks as though he's dropped into it:

"That's the whole point of the attack, isn't it?" Dave says. "To force our hand."

There's a long moment, then steps cross the room. I race back down the hall and duck into the kitchen, my heart in my throat, trying to piece together what I've heard as I dig around for cleaning supplies.

The door creaks and I brace myself for Dave's voice, but instead hear the squeak of wet sneakers and then Javier is standing beside me.

"They need some trash bags."

I hand him a giant box and keep rattling through bottles looking for the Lysol. But Javier still stands there, and after a moment I sit back on my heels and look up at him, self-consciously pulling my hair back from my face.

"Was there anything else?"

"Nah, I just . . ." There's a small crease between his eyebrows. "Your girl is really pretty."

"Oh, Nobody, yeah." And I mean it when I say, "She's actually perfect."

"Yeah. Well, I think I owe you an apology because . . . before . . . I thought maybe you and her . . . like, it was a relationship of convenience or something?" He laughs nervously. "I made a lot of arrogant assumptions, and I'm sorry for that. So seeing her just now . . ."

He fumbles for words and I brace for where this is going, neck growing hot.

"It's just that, like, when Dog Mask came in . . . and you were holding my hand . . . I promised myself I'd ask you something." His eyes meet mine and he steps closer.

"Ask me what?" Why am I getting excited?! He's probably about to ask me if we'd consider a threesome. Get a hold of yourself.

"Wow, I feel so stupid right now." He sweeps his hands along the back of his neck with an embarrassed smile that is utterly charming. "You have a gorgeous girlfriend, I *know* the answer is going to be no, but I still have to ask—"

"Ask me *what?*" My cheeks go hot as my fingertips turn cold.

"Do you like me?" Javier gives me the sweetest, shiest half-smile I've ever seen.

"HELLOOO!"

We both spin around as Jada throws the kitchen door open with a bang, her wet hair clinging to her face.

"Javi! You find the trash bags? We're all waiting on you!"

"Right." Javier steps back from me, his face falling back into its familiar guarded expression.

"Uh, Lysol?" She takes the Lysol out of the bucket and throws it back into the cabinet. "Lysol's no good disinfecting blood. I know you missed the first week, but that was literally our first lesson. We need bleach. Focus, Skipper!" Jada claps for emphasis. "And both of you hurry up! Come on, Javier, let's go!"

I crouch in front of the cabinet again while she leads Javier out of the kitchen, barely seeing what's in front of me.

He wouldn't ask me that unless he liked me too, right? No way. So he must like me, right? Javier . . . *likes* me.

So what am I doing in the kitchen?

I dash through the cabin, throw open the door and leap down the porch to the gravel path, where I can just make out Javier and Jada disappearing through the dark.

"Javier! Wait!"

The motion light above me snaps on and captures him in a halo, and he's too handsome. I just stare at him for a moment as the conviction he *must* like me fights with the certainty I'm wrong. His hair glitters with raindrops in the motion light, little drops dot his broad shoulders, but he doesn't go, he stares up at me. I feel like I'm in a dream as I walk toward him, the last of the rain falling softly around us.

"What you just asked me?" I tell him. "Yeah. I do."

He's in front of me in two steps, but he hangs back as though he's afraid he's misheard.

"Does Nobody know?" he asks.

"I'll talk to her. But it'll be fine—"

"JAVIER! COME ON!" Jada screams from the porch of the boys' cabin.

"It'll be fine." I smile. "It's just . . ." There's no way to say this without sounding like a desperate idiot. "You do like *me*, right?"

And then his lips are pressed against mine, his stubble rough against my chin.

The fog of unreality that's been surrounding me since he asked if I liked him evaporates against the warmth of his pressing mouth. My spine melts, I sag against him as one of his arms winds around me, his other hand reaching up and slipping into my hair.

"JAVIER!" Jada calls. "EARTH TO JAVIER!"

"You better go," I whisper, pulling away once it's clear he can't hear her. "But we'll do this again soon?"

He shakes his head as though coming out of a trance. "Very soon," he says, jaw clenched, eyes pleading.

Pleading to kiss me again.

An unreal joy bubbles up inside me as I turn and practically fly to the kitchen. I put bleach in the bucket and set it under the running faucet, then dance around in a circle. *My first kiss.* I can't believe I just had my first kiss! And it was a perfect kiss. With *Javier.*

Because Javier likes me.

Is he my *boyfriend* now?

I don't know, the kiss alone is enough, is everything. I flit around the kitchen on my tiptoes as all my favorite love songs fight for space in my head. I'm weightless, if I jump I'll float up to the ceiling, bounce out the window, fly into the night.

I wish so badly I could tell Rose.

I haul the bucket and some mops over to the cabin, feeling like I'm glowing in the dark with Javier's secret revelation. Everyone's talking too intently to notice when I come in, except Javier, who looks up with shining eyes. I smile so hard I have to duck my head, as Troy's voice booms out:

"We're going to need everybody helping if we're going to carry him down to the dock."

"Okay, well, let's just get it onto the porch first so they can mop up," Erik says.

"Who wants a mop?" I flourish three handles and Jada grabs one.

"C'mon, Dennis." She foists one on him, and I grab the last, stepping out of the way so Javier, Erik, Troy, Kurt, and Nobody can haul the body to the porch.

"*Somebody* can't stop smiling," Jada remarks to Dennis as she wrings her mop out over the bucket, grimacing at the burning bleach smell. It's true, I'm smiling down at a pool of blood. But I can't help it. The best thing just happened to me and nothing else is real. This blood certainly isn't. I'm not really here cleaning it. I'm going through all the moments I've had with Javier in the last few days, trying to figure out when he started liking me.

Because *Javier likes me.*

"Must be the adrenaline," Dennis comments, pushing his glasses up his short nose. "We all probably gained a big rush of endorphins after our flight-or-fight responses were triggered."

"Totally," I nod.

Once we've finished swabbing up, we join the others on the porch around the body, and my warm glow fades pretty quick. They've built up several layers of trash bags, each sealed with duct tape, one over the other until Dog Mask, zipped into a sleeping bag with a footlocker of stones on his chest, is cocooned like a plastic mummy. If I pretend it's just a mannequin inside those trash bags, maybe I can get through this without vomiting again.

"On three," Erik says. "One . . . two . . . three!"

I'm between Nobody and Jada and across from Troy, positioned right at Dog Mask's knee when we all come to a standing position. It's way heavier than I'd imagined. I lock my elbows at my sides as we coordinate, in counted-off steps, to carry the dead weight down off the porch and into the wet grass.

"He's soooo heavy!" Jada groans.

"It's three hundred pounds of dead weight and a box of rocks. What do you expect?" Kurt says.

After all the digging, my arms twitch with exhaustion and my hands are freezing, but I still flinch away from the folds of the plastic where warm blood pools.

We thread our way through the trees, shivering as the last heavy raindrops fall from above, the wet grass soaking instantly through our shoes. At least we don't need flashlights. The night has gone from black to royal blue, and I can just make out the treetops against the sky.

When we get to the open field, we move faster as the ground slopes to meet the water, and then Dennis says "uh oh!" in his monotone, and the body tilts ominously. Despite all our hands shooting forward to stop it, mummified Dog Mask tips forward and topples onto the ground with a sickening squelch.

"Dennis, you STUPID BUTTMUNCH!" Troy bellows.

Dennis scowls, rubbing his hands together. "I couldn't hold it. My fingers are too cold. Kurt let him fall too, why don't you yell at him?"

"Oh please. The kid who comes in last on obstacle course every day is going to blame me for this?!" Kurt's face is pale, his shoulder high and tensed from when Dog Mask slammed him into the wall. "You and Jada—"

"Jada what, Kurt?" Jada glares at him. Her hands are as raw as mine from digging. "Did you not see me back in the cabin wrapping this whole monster? Meanwhile you were playing around with his stupid mask—"

"Hey, my hands are cold too!" I blurt, and everyone looks at me. "Why don't we hold onto each other's hands instead of the body?"

"Like the body just rests on our forearms, and we hold onto each other?" Kurt asks.

"Yeah?" I breathe on my hands and rub them together. There's a collective pause. We don't touch a lot in Teen Killers Club. Not a lot of hugs. But Dennis, clenching and unclenching his fists, nods.

"That could help."

Erik says matter-of-factly, "Sounds good to me. On three, we lift him up again. Ready?"

We squat down and with a monumental effort somehow lift the body to waist height again. Then, standing in place, we fumble our hands toward each other, grabbing onto each other instead of the corpse. Troy and I lock eyes as both our hands connect, his warm rough fingers digging into my forearms, and I cling back.

"Good?" Javier calls down the line, looking at me.

I nod as everyone else agrees, and then we go on, determinedly clutching onto each other, until we reach the small wood dock and the rack of sunburnt canoes.

The sky is going pale over the water, the stars fading as the black blood of night drains away. I can hear the far-off cries of birds beginning to wake.

Jada and I, being the smallest, pull one of the canoes off the rack and set it halfway in the water so the others can settle the body into it. There's a collective sigh of relief as the body eases into the narrow boat, and Erik and Javier pull down a much longer second canoe and fasten it to the first one. We all grab paddles, load into the long boat, and push off from shore into the thick gray mist that hangs over the lake.

Two strokes out and I can't see in front of or behind us. The fog turns the world into a flat gray blank, and as we glide forward trails of mist eddy away from our paddles, giving us glimpses of the black water below.

Erik's voice cuts through the fog. "This is far enough, yeah?"

"Yeah," Javier agrees.

Erik and Kurt, at the very back of the boat, tilt the canoe with the body onto its side until Dog Mask slips into the still black water. It swallows him without a splash, only the slightest gulping sound and a swirl of fine bubbles, and then it's as though he never existed. We sit shivering in silence, waiting to see if he'll come back up.

"I heard Dave and Kate talking," I begin. I tell the group what I overheard the other night, and what I'd heard just now while getting cleaning supplies.

". . . Whoever headquarters is," I end.

"Probably whatever deeply buried government program is funding this place—and I'm guessing it's *very* buried, considering the shoestring budget we seem to be on," Erik says, thoughtfully biting his nails.

"I've been thinking about this since you told us he tried to set off your kill switches," says Kurt, hunched in his blue hoody, squinting into the water. "Maybe Dog Mask guy started out as a counselor with Dave and Kate, right? But then he started really thinking it over, learning more about the program, and he couldn't handle it. So he came back to end the program before it even began."

"That would fit with wanting to force us out."

Troy frowns. "But he was also like 'we won't go quietly.' So who's the 'we'?"

"I'm telling you, he was a Protectionist," Jada mutters.

"I guess I just went to prison before Protectionism took off or something. How many of these guys are there?" I ask.

"It's hard to say. They're not just in one political party, everybody seems to agree with them on some level," Javier says.

"'Class As are evil. We know how to test if someone's a Class A. So let's just get rid of them all.'" Erik stares across the water.

"Stupid dumb-ass Protectionists," Jada grumbles. "I swear as soon as I get retired out of camp, Protectionists are the first people I'm going after."

"We get *retired?*" I blink at her.

"After fifteen years, remember?" Jada looks around the boat. "That's what Dave told me when I signed on. And we get paid for every target we do."

"I thought it was ten." Dennis frowns. "Did anyone keep a copy of their contract?"

"No." Kurt sounds exasperated. "It's not like we were in a position to negotiate. I didn't even read the whole thing, because Dave told us the bus was about to leave and it was sign on or stay in prison. But I remember him saying we'd get paid when we retired, because I remember thinking, like, *retired?* How old will we be, sixty-five?"

"They'll probably just keep sending us out until we don't come back," Erik says flatly.

"Why do you have to be like that?" Javier snaps.

"Be like what, be *honest?* I don't know, maybe because it's an insult to other people's intelligence to sit here and act like everything's fine? Protectionist terrorists might be trying to shut down camp so they can pick us off one by one, but by all means, let's pretend everything's just—"

"He wasn't a Protectionist." We all look to Nobody, sitting bolt upright in the middle bench of the canoe. She nervously keeps trying to pull down Troy's beanie to conceal as much of her perfect face as she can, but it only emphasizes her high cheekbones, softly backlit by the rose gold break of dawn.

"When we were fighting, I felt it," she shrinks back a little as we stare, blinking her huge sweet blue eyes and speaking in the voice of a grizzled barfly. "He was having fun."

"Going back to what Kurt said," I say after we all recover from the continual shock that is Nobody's appearance. "Let's say Dog Mask *was* a counselor, like Dave and Kate, but then something changed. He left or got fired, whatever, something turned him against the program. So why would Dave and Kate pretend they don't know who he is? And why would Kate feel like she should be the one to kill him?"

"Does it matter?" Javier's voice is almost pleading. "He's dead now."

"Don't you want to know who else out there is targeting us?"

"Everyone is. If we're *being honest*." Javier shoots a look at Erik. "The police, the Protectionists, everyone who's not a Class A—like you said, I know what the world thinks of me. How is that different than how it's always been? It's never been a fair fight, but I'm still standing. Whoever wants to take me down, they can come try it!

"*COME TRY IT!*" he yells across the still water, and then his voice drops again. "Plenty more room where we put the last one."

The fog has begun to thin, and through it the rippled surface of the lake is blushing pink, warmed by the sunrise.

"Yeah," Jada whispers, smiling at Javier. "Whoever they are, what difference does it make? We'll take them."

"I'm up for another round." Nobody smiles beatifically, and we all melt at the sight.

"Can I just tell you guys . . . ," Troy sighs. "I was saving all my M&Ms for last and then that asshole had to come and die on them and I'm mad about it."

I burst out laughing, realizing I had saved my chocolate for last too, and maybe we all had been secretly regretting our lost trail mix, because then they all join in, we're drifting in the boat in the middle of the lake, whooping with laughter.

"Can I give you a makeover?" Jada asks Nobody behind me.

"No."

"Can I braid your hair at least?"

Nobody considers this. "Okay."

Jada immediately stands, making everyone cry out as the boat rocks, then hops behind Nobody's bench and buries her hands in Nobody's hair. Nobody makes little grumble noises, like a wary cat in the arms of a toddler.

"Watch out!" Troy elbows me. "Jada is making a move on your girl."

"Signal and I broke up," Nobody announces, and everyone gasps at the drama. I nod, going along with it but more than a little confused, and then Nobody adds: "We're still friends though."

"Always," I say quickly. I have to admit, there's a weird surge of rejection involved in getting fake-dumped by my beautiful fake girlfriend. *What did I do?* I look over at Javier, though, and his knowing smile makes my heart race.

I can say, for the rest of my life: I have been kissed. And it was perfect.

"Troy, you hungry yet?" Erik calls.

"Yeah, man. Let's head back!"

"All hands on deck!"

The canoe moves much faster now. Maybe because our arms got a chance to rest. Maybe because there's no body dragging behind us. Maybe because we can see the vivid green horizon growing closer, the dewy grass shimmering in the earliest light of a new day.

We climb up onto the shore, and Javier's arm brushes mine as he falls in beside me.

"So you talked to her?" he asks brightly.

"Actually no. I should check in with her real quick," I say, cheeks hot.

"Okay. I'll save you a seat at breakfast?" he says, reaching down to squeeze my hand.

So we're like, a couple now? Am I still dreaming? No, this exhaustion is real. My sore arms are real. If bad things can be real, good things must be too.

"Yeah, okay," I want to kiss him on the cheek but it seems like too much, and I see Nobody approaching, so I squeeze his hand back and pull myself away.

"Hey, you." I wave to her, and she gives me a stiff nod. "So uh . . ." I slow our pace so we hang back from the others, who are surging toward the main cabin. "Are we okay? When you said we'd broken up I thought, maybe . . . like, you're not mad at me or something are you?"

"No," she says. "You just seem like you're on the verge of a real relationship. So, thought I'd cut you loose publicly."

"Wow . . . that obvious, huh?"

"Yup." And she gives me an unearthly smile, then drops it, her angelic brow furrowing. "Don't get me wrong. I still think he's dangerous. But it's your life, so . . ."

"Dangerous?" I slow to a stop. "You think Javier is dangerous?"

"Javier? What?" Nobody frowns. "We're talking about Erik. You like Erik. It's obvious."

"It is?" Erik's voice, half-choked with laughter, interjects right behind me. I turn and find myself staring into his smiling face as he claps the water off his hands. He just put away both canoes, he's been walking right behind us.

Nobody rolls her eyes and walks on without us, since I'm apparently frozen in place and Erik is hovering over me delightedly, waiting for my response.

"I don't," I stammer. "Like you. At all."

One eyebrow goes up, his dimples deepening.

"*At all*," I repeat.

"Yeah, well, you would if I *wanted you* to. Like me. Love me even."

After a moment, I'm able to swallow. "Not a chance."

"Desperately." He draws the word out. "It'd take, hmmm . . ." He closes one eye, calculating. "Three weeks? A month tops."

"Right."

"And after all those accusations of me getting into your head about Rose, a Signal with a crush on me sounds like a way more fun person to hang out with—"

"Um, I have never believed you could actually get in anyone's head, to be clear—"

"Then this is the perfect way to prove it. Three weeks." Erik's grin is cocky when I dare a mortified look at him. "Starting from today. I'll make you fall in love with me if it's the last thing I do."

"Um, literally impossible." I laugh too loud, trying to make it clear I don't take any of this seriously.

He stops me short, hand on my shoulder, barely suppressing his own laughter, then swallows his smile and says in a serious tone: "Do you even know how beautiful your eyes are?"

"I know you're joking," I sigh. "But just FYI, I'm about to start a new relationship with Javier so I just *can't* with the compliments. Even sarcastic ones."

Surprisingly, this is met with silence from Erik. When I glance over, he's furiously biting at his nails, and then—

REEEEEE-BOOOM!

Jagged planks shoot sideways out of the trees ahead of us, followed by a ball of smoke and the thud of what sounds like stones raining down on the main cabin's tin roof.

A second blast tears through the air and my ears go silent. A high shrieking note repeats again and again inside my head as Erik's hot hand closes on my arm. His mouth shapes the words but I can't hear anything, I only see him shout:

WOODS! NOW!

And then we sprint for the trees as fast as our legs can go.

Chapter Fifteen
Field Trip

❧

The walls of our cabin collapse in on themselves like the sides of a stomped cardboard box. Dark smoke rises as Erik and I watch through the trees. Nobody sprints over to us and I fold her in my arms, then Dennis appears, followed by a wide-eyed Kurt, Troy trailing him and half-carrying Jada, then at last Javier comes running over to me as Erik slips away. I'm starting to wonder if my hearing will ever come back, when it does, all at once: Nobody's groan next to my neck, the hiss and crackle of the flames, and Kate calling our names in the distance.

"HERE! OVER HERE!" Jada screams, and Kate hurries through the trees, cat's-eye glasses askew, soot streaks across her face.

"What's *happening?*" We mob her.

"Everything's under control." Kate clears her throat. "We just had some issues with the facilities—"

"Seriously?!" I snap. "*Issues with the facilities?!* That was a bomb!"

"It was a boiler malfunction," Kate says firmly.

"Boiler? To heat up all the water in the showers, right?" Erik is furious.

"It's Protectionists. We're being attacked!" Jada wails.

"Quiet! All of you! Please!" Kate grits her teeth and then levels with us: "Listen. Our visitor last night left an incendiary behind, alright?"

I imagine Dog Mask crawling under our cabin to place the bomb, while just overhead we sat obliviously talking about the meaning of life, and feel sick.

"So we need to stay away from all the cabins until they've been swept for explosives. Dennis, you and I are going to go through the wreckage with fire extinguishers, find the device, and examine it. Javier and Erik, you are going to stay here until Dave has finished sweeping the main cabin, and help him get supplies together. Everyone else will go up to the obstacle course field and find whatever tents or tarps are in the shed and set up a place where we can camp tonight. Alright? Everyone clear on what they're doing?"

We all nod. "Then let's get moving!" she says, and blows her whistle to send us on our way.

* * *

The morning is unusually warm, and by the time the four of us have raked and cleared a patch of lawn and staked a few big tarps over it for tonight, we're unspeakably gross. Kurt's and Troy's shirts are both soaked through with sweat, Nobody's nails are black with dried blood and Jada's Spongebob Squarepants nightshirt is stiff with it. Itchy mud squelches between my toes inside my canvas sneakers.

Dave appears with Erik and Javier toward midday; they've gotten a chance to shower and are hauling up bags of food and sleeping bags. When he sees me, Javier drops the bag and starts walking toward me, but Dave blows his whistle:

"Girls, hit the showers! Kurt and Troy, you'll go when they come back!"

For once I'm grateful for Dave's control freak tendencies; I want to shower before getting too close to Javier, and also am sort of unsure how close to get or how to act now we're a couple. Do we, like, tell everyone? It's such a petty thing to announce, considering camp is under siege. I fret about it on the walk down to the cabin, while Jada grills Nobody on why she wears a ski mask.

"People can be weird when they think you're pretty," Nobody shrugs.

"What, like they're too nice?" I laugh.

"*Yes,*" she says, and her tone makes me stop laughing.

Dave and Kate's shower is just as cold as ours, it turns out. And finding clothes from the lost and found is impossible: everything that fits and isn't hideous was already scavenged; what's left either doesn't fit or is, well, hideous. Jada makes it a game: who can put together the worst outfit?

We're all laughing uproariously at each other's clothes as we return to the obstacle course, hair still damp, with me the declared winner: I have too-tight red track pants that say "CHEER" on the butt and a massive navy Big Dogs sweatshirt. (It features a Saint Bernard on a surfboard and the caption "If you can't surf with the Big Dogs, stay off the Net.")

When Erik sees me from across the field, he throws his head back and laughs.

"It's called fashion!" I cry at him.

"Wow." Javier leaps up from the quilt where he's helping Dave with dinner and hurries toward me, and everyone is watching. "How do you look gorgeous in everything?" Javier says, and he twirls me around like he actually wants to get a better look, scanning me up and down.

Kurt wolf-whistles and Troy yells "Smooth!" and my face heats. Is this how we're letting the group know we're together?

Apparently yes, because then Javier brings me into him and kisses me hard, his stubble scraping my face as wild catcalls echo across the field, until Dave's whistle cuts through and Javier pulls away. I stagger a few steps when he lets me go, overwhelmed, but not with the giddiness from before. I feel blindsided and a little embarrassed as Jada gives me a playful shove: "You and Javi?! Whaaaat?!?! That's so cuuute!!!"

Nobody widens her eyes at me before Kate calls her over, and the twins high-five Javier when he returns to Dave. I look across the field to Erik. But he's deep in conversation with Dennis and doesn't look back at me.

Dave calls everyone to dinner and we gather on the picnic blanket, and it seems like Nobody is giving me space; she sits at the other end of the quilt instead of next to me. Jada and Troy sit across from me and Javier, talking to us both at the same time, like we're a unit. I can barely follow the conversation, I'm so conscious of Javier next to me. He keeps his long arm draped loosely behind me, his head occasionally dipping closer to say little sweet things: "You cold? You want my fleece?" And "Did you want me to get you another granola bar, gorgeous?" Or I'll catch him just looking at me. Like he doesn't want to take his eyes off me.

Erik sits with Nobody and Dennis, his back to us.

When the sky starts to blush with the sunset, Javier drapes his huge fleece over my shoulders, and I'm surrounded by his warmth. It's surreal, being treated like someone's girlfriend. I don't know why it makes me so uneasy. Maybe I'm just not used to belonging.

After the sun sets, Kate suggests we make up for lost sleep by going to bed early, and Javier takes two sleeping bags over to a corner of the tarp away from everyone else. And this is easier: to be him and me, instead of us and everyone else.

"My tattoo needs a touch-up," I tell him as the first stars start to tremble overhead. He takes my forearm, his finger tracing inside my wrist. It feels like sparkling wherever his finger touches.

"Or I could do a new one somewhere else?" His eyes glint in the dark.

"I *cannot* lose that dandelion."

"You're missing the lesson of the temporary tattoo," he says, teasingly, his finger moving from the tattoo to trace from my elbow to my wrist. "The moment you start stressing about how to keep something, you lose it forever. Because you're not *enjoying* it. You're just *owning* it. Temporary tattoos are about living for the moment."

"Whoa!" I laugh, tucking my arm back into my sleeping bag with a heady shiver. "I had no idea you were such a philosopher."

"I'm full of surprises." He smiles. "You'll see."

He falls asleep midsentence not long after, the field growing quiet, everyone's exhausted. But I can't sleep, I keep staring at the stars overhead. In Ledmonton, I thought the night sky was flat. But now I see trenches and waves and chasms that must be millions of miles deep.

I realize he's beside me before he speaks.

"Signal," Erik whispers. "Come with me."

I don't answer, afraid to wake Javier, I just rise and follow him.

I follow him to the last obstacle on the course, the fake apartment building. I follow him all the way up the fire escapes to the small platform of fake roof at the top. The wind is higher and colder three stories up, the treetops billowing below us like an ocean before a storm. I have never felt closer to the stars.

"Erik, if this is about—"

"Dennis told me something interesting," Erik cuts me off. The moonlight turns him black and white, like a silver screen idol. "Kate is taking down the fence tonight, in case we have to make a run for it. Just until dawn."

"So what, you're going to run away?" I don't know why that comes out. But Erik shakes his head.

"It doesn't work like that. The way Dennis explained it, if we're on the wrong side of the fence but still in range when it comes back on, our kill switch still goes off. And the range is over twenty miles." He bites his thumbnail. "I can't cover twenty miles before dawn. But I could get there and back."

And he points to a small grouping of lights past the first ridge of trees, maybe a dozen city blocks away.

He pulls a flashlight out of his hoodie. "What if we could get that screen time after all?"

A night hike with Erik? I should be exhausted, but instead an almost manic energy steals through me.

"Okay. Let's go."

Erik puts a leg over the edge of the fake apartment building, turns, and drops out of sight. I lean over in time to see him jumping from the top of the doorsill to the ground and roll my eyes. I take the fire stairs, like a normal human being.

When I get to the ground he's pacing impatiently, staring out at the forest like it's a pool he wants to dive into.

"Could you have possibly taken longer to get down here, Grandma?" he says as we make our way down through the forgotten playground. Shielded from the field by the trees, he turns on the flashlight. A bleached-out circle floats across the ground ahead of us, the ghost of a sunbeam.

"Now, now," I say. "Calling me names is *not* going to make me fall in love with you."

"*What?*" Erik sounds genuinely puzzled. "In love with me? What are you talking about?"

Utter. Mortification. "Remember? Before the bomb went off?"

"Oh, right, when I made that joke." Erik's face clears. "Sorry if I got your hopes up there, Signal, but I wouldn't *dream* of intruding between you and Javier. What you've got going is so healthy, so real: he gets to play at being high school sweethearts and you get to pretend you can change a cold-blooded murderer—"

"We're not *pretending* anything. We're both broken people. I know you see me as some sweet little weakling, but I've got my share of regrets to carry, believe me."

"Yeah, I can only imagine how many flavors of lip gloss you used to shoplift," Erik snaps. "Have you told him you're innocent yet?"

I take a deep breath. "It hasn't come up."

Erik looks smug. "Well, the good news is I don't actually care. I'm sure it's all very exciting, but as an onlooker you two bore me to tears. I'd much rather ask more questions about Rose, if I'm *allowed*."

"Actually . . . Would it be alright if we talked about you for a little while?" I say as nicely as I can. "You know things about me I've never told anyone else, and I don't even know your last name."

"You wouldn't believe me if I told you." He mutters in a low voice.

"You don't have to answer anything you don't want to," I continue. "But we only ever talk about me. I'd like to know more about you."

He doesn't say no.

"Like, who were you in high school? Did you play sports? Were you in all AP classes? Backpack or messenger bag?" I smile in the dark, trying to imagine Erik with either. I truly can't.

"I never went to high school," Erik says. "I was pulled out in sixth grade and home schooled."

"Oh." That would explain the precocious way he talks. "Was your mom, like, a stay-at-home mom or something?"

"She was a forensic psychologist."

". . . And your dad?"

"A computer programmer."

"Why did they home school you?"

I can hear Erik smiling his heartthrob smile.

"They didn't want me to hurt a classmate and end up in prison."

"Oh."

"Am I creeping you out again?" he asks, still smiling.

"A little, yeah," I confess. "That's quite a statement, Erik. You want to give it some context?"

"Context, context . . ." I'm sure he's about to blow me off with some pithy remark. Instead, his words rush out with strange intensity: "When I was thirteen, I attacked an emotionally abusive narcissist who deserved it. He was over twenty at the time, so it's not like it wasn't an even match. And face stitches look cool! I *still* don't see what the big deal was. But I was informed that I lack in *empathy*. So my mom pulled me out of school and tried to fix me."

"Fix you how?"

"Oh, she tried everything. Medications. Music. Aromatherapy. 'Incentivizing kindness,' that was a big one." His disembodied words in the dark feel so intimate, like a voice on the phone late at night. "*Lots* of reading. I am definitely the type who spent his weekends at the library."

I really wish I could see his face.

"... Did it work?"

"Well, no, obviously," Erik laughs, and my blood runs cold. "Or maybe it did *sort of*, but that's a story much longer than this walk. Next question, please."

"What do you mean, 'sort of'?"

"Next question."

"I'm really supposed to let that one go?"

"Another time. Next question."

"Ooooh-kaaay. What's your favorite color?"

"Gray."

"Favorite food?"

"Pop rocks."

"What do you mean by *sort of*?"

Erik's hand grazes mine briefly as he swerves in the dark, so I know to follow him. The sensation reverberates up my arm like a struck bell.

He stops, and gestures to lights up ahead. We circle the small cabin, staying just inside the tree line.

"No signs of a dog. One station wagon. Motion lights by garage." He frowns and suddenly is halfway up a chain link fence. I follow him, and we land in a small grassy yard. From there it's strictly hand signals between us as we pause, check for motion lights, then dart up the steps, pressing ourselves to the side of the house, holding our breaths and straining to hear if anyone inside has seen us.

And then a tinny scream pierces the night, and a sting of synth swells.

"Someone's up, watching TV," I hiss at Erik as he steps to the nearest window and looks in. "We need to go!!!" But he turns to me with a dismissive half-smile and shakes his head.

"It's just a little kid watching a scary movie. I'm guessing he snuck out of bed, so probably his parents are asleep. Come on."

"Probably?!?"

Erik kneels by a tiny basement window, which looks about the size of a shoebox. He slides open the glass and fiddles with the screen so it pops and falls backward into the room below, noiselessly.

"Carpeted. Nice," Erik exhales.

"Yeah, right, you'll never fit through that win—"

Erik, who is over six feet tall and has almost disproportionately broad shoulders, is through before I've finished the sentence.

Erik smiles up at me from the basement window.

"You want to find Mr. Moody or not?" he says, and disappears from sight.

There's only one answer. So with the deepest sense of dread I lower myself through the small window and into the unknown.

Chapter Sixteen
Creepy Crawl

∾

The moment I breathe the still, warm air of the house I know we shouldn't be here. The drone of the heater, the alien weight of the unseen people overhead, the lingering smell of their dinner, it's too familiar and foreign at the same time, my skin crawls with alarm.

"*Erik this is crazy!*" I whisper as he gives me an assist down. "What if someone wakes up? What if they call the police? *What if they have a gun?!*"

"What if they just stay asleep?" Erik is completely untroubled. "I know what this is about: you don't want anyone to catch you in that outfit. Can't blame you there. But we can only stay about twenty minutes, so let's just focus on getting what we need and getting out without exposing those pants to any innocent bystanders." His flashlight sweeps one side of the room, then he coolly pulls a kids' chunky plastic playhouse from the corner and positions it directly under the window, a makeshift ladder if we need to climb out quickly.

The bright flashlight beam moves deeper into the room, throwing the furniture into sharp relief, and lands on a couch with a laptop on its arm. I gasp, but the circle of light keeps moving until he finds a tablet in a kid's chunky pink case.

"Here we go," he says, snatching it up.

"Don't you want to use the real one?"

"You can try it, but it'll probably have a password, whereas the kid's stuff . . ." He taps the tablet, and an unprotected home screen glows in answer. He hands it to me. "Have at it."

"I should still be Facebook friends with Mike from like, back in elementary school. I still want to know where he went, Nice Guy or not," I say, navigating to my scarcely used account. Tapping over to Mike's profile, there's a video posted in the last couple of weeks with at least *five thousand* likes.

"That's like, the population of our entire town," I mutter.

Erik leans in as I press play:

Mike's face, glistening with a day's worth of blond stubble, stares back at us somberly. His hair is swept to the side and it's clear he's in an urban apartment from the sounds bouncing up from the street.

"Hey guys." Mike sounds nervous. "I know since me and Vaughn left Ledmonton there's been a lot of talk. Then with that newspaper piece coming out, we've heard from a lot of friends and family and we decided it's time to be open. So here it is. Vaughn and I have moved to New York City. And we're boyfriends. We've been boyfriends for a long time."

"Wait—*what?!*" I cry, and Erik shushes me.

"For years I had to hide this aspect of myself. I knew there wasn't anything wrong with being gay . . . ," Mike continues, his eyes edging with tears. "But there was something very wrong with *me* being gay. That was impressed on me by my family, my parents, my church. The pressure only went away when Rose and I started 'dating.'" He makes air quotes when he says it. "Rose helped shield me during the hardest time in my life. And it wasn't until we lost her that I decided to stop lying and living in fear. And to start being who I am."

Now I'm going to cry. "I had no idea. That must have been so hard for him—"

Mike goes on: "Signal Deere, a Class A, is now in jail for Rose's murder. And I believe with everything in my heart that she will burn in hell for what she did."

Erik nods along in mock agreement. "Finally, someone talking some *sense.*"

"It's not his fault. He thinks I'm guilty." I blot at my eyes. "And if I thought he did that to Rose, I'd probably say the same thing about him."

"Is *that* what empathy is?" Erik says, one eyebrow up. "Thanks but no thanks."

"At least," I go on, "this explains Rose's weird rivalry with Vaughn. Vaughn must've been so jealous, with Mike all over Rose at school . . . And why Mike lied about getting high: it was easier than telling his parents the truth, that he and Vaughn wanted to be alone together . . ."

"There's a site I want you to see." Erik snatches the tablet and navigates to a message board called Armchair.org, then taps "Girl From Hell" into the search bar.

"One of my mom's tactics was to channel my more morbid impulses toward 'being a helper,'" Erik says, his voice low. "She encouraged me to try and solve true crime cases. This board is pretty reputable, lots of freelance crime journalists and retired cops . . . Anything catch your eye?"

I scan the short list of thread subjects:

>**GIRL FROM HELL: THE ROSE ROWAN MURDER:**

>>MIKE & VAUGHN: Mike Comes Out in Facebook Video!!

>>Tom & Janeane RECENT PHOTOS// Award Ceremony for Rose Rowan Memorial Scholarship

>>$$$The Windward Connection$$$: Rose's Murder Not First Brush with Teen Tragedy in Famous Family's Past

>>MUH ALIENS: UFO Spotted Over Park Woods the Night Of!

>>NECKLACE THEORY: Complete Breakdown of Why Signal Murdered Rose Over a Necklace.

"What's all this about a necklace?" I tap on the last thread.

>>NECKLACE THEORY: Why Signal Murdered Rose Over a Necklace

According to local sleuth/armchair contributor CC_ CUBA, Tom Rowan told members of his Bible Study group that Janeane had found a <u>pentagram pendant</u> in Rose's room days before that fateful night. Tom confronted Rose with it the day of her murder. She had explained the necklace belonged to Signal Deere, and Tom prohibited Rose from inviting her to the house again. Tom put the necklace in a bedside table drawer.

Flash forward to that night. Signal somehow gets Rose to meet her in the shed, and Rose tells her their friendship is over. As Sherpop&lock89 pointed out in a previous thread several elements of a traditional pagan altar were found at the crime scene: burnt down candles, a bowl of salt scattered on the floor, part of a cupcake wrapper (food, especially sweet cakes, is a common pagan offering), and of course the 10-inch mini utility saw found under Signal's hand (likely shoplifted from Ledmonton Hardware Supply) would have stood in for a pagan atheme, or ritualistic dagger.

Lets_Get_Em has theorized that when Rose ended their friendship, she triggered some kind of emotional meltdown in Signal, who was possibly high as well (as RETIREDPHD points out, the drug tests administered to Signal when she was first processed did not include specific assays needed to identify a variety of opiates).

Signal strangled Rose, then incorporated her friend's body into an occult ritual.

The necklace was not listed in discovery, suggesting Rose returned it to Signal, who alone knows its location. Tom finding Signal's necklace lines up perfectly with explaining the "table of junk" (the altar) the mutilation of Rose's body (a magic ritual) and a compelling motive for why things came to a head that night.

!!UPDATE!! Check out Signal's meltdown in AP Biology, the day of the murder, in Katie Williams' Instagram!!

I click on the hyperlink to Katie Williams' Instagram. She has a clip of me, beet red in AP Biology: I'd forgotten a worksheet packet at home and had a small panic attack. I totally forgot about that, but apparently it's one of many reasons everyone back home thinks I should burn in hell for eternity.

"We should go," Erik urges.

But I can't stop scrolling the comments on Katie's post. Everyone talking about how they could always tell I was a Class A, how I "always creeped them out."

The only comment that has anything even slightly positive to say is . . . Jaw Itznicki's?!

JawsItz: aw she's not so bad is it for sure she did it?

I click over to Jaw's Instagram feed. The square that pops up is all blue sky and hot pink bougainvillea. And his location is now Oxnard, in Southern California.

"Erik, look!!" He's half risen out of his seat, but he gets back down beside me.

"We should go."

"I know but look, Erik, Jaw's in California now—"

I scroll through picture after picture until I see one of him leaned up against a front door with the numbers 1227 in frame. All I need now is the street.

"Come on." Erik takes my hand and almost drags me to my feet, but I can't put down the tablet.

"Wait, just one more thing—"

At last, a picture with a location attached, a taco shop which Jaw describes as being "Just down the block" on Silver Strand Ave—

SNAP!

The room bursts into color around me, and in the doorway two little blue eyes connect with mine. My heart jerks in my chest at the little boy's face, peeping around the doorway.

But he's way more scared than me.

His freckled face goes white as a sheet and he disappears with a gasp, his steps scrambling up the carpeted stairs.

"Time to go!" Erik rushes me toward the playhouse, and gets neatly through the window. I step up onto the playhouse roof, and it buckles under my weight. I let out a cry just as Erik's hand shoots through the window and grabs mine, so I'm hanging from the basement window.

"Mom! Dad! There's people downstairs!" the little voice cries as my sneakers rake the wall. Erik grabs my other arm and pulls me until my torso is through the low window. From there I crawl on my elbows onto the cold dirt at the side of the house, frantically wriggling my hips through the small window, all too aware my butt currently says "CHEER."

I squeeze through just as a sleepy dad's voice floats out the window above us:

"Garvey, have you been up watching scary movies again?"

We run through the backyard, then up the steep incline into the shelter of the trees. I want to slow down, but Erik keeps sprinting, his flashlight's circle getting smaller and smaller in front of me.

"Erik!"

He doubles back and links his iron arm through mine, and suddenly I'm pressed tight to his muscled side like we're in a three-legged race, scrambling and sliding as we thread through the densely packed trees.

I've never run this hard, this long, in my life. But it's a release: all I can think of is how to clear the next obstacle before we meet it head-long, my body burning with the animal joy of escape.

At last the trees open up and I recognize the playground, we're past the fence, we're safe. Erik breaks away from me, his grin taking over his entire face as he jumps up and grazes a high branch with his fingertips.

I bend over double, gulping down air, sides burning and cramping.

"You have *zero* stamina," Erik says. "That was three quarters of a mile, not even, and I carried you for most of it."

"I never had . . . a pentagram . . . necklace," I pant. "But Jaw . . . you were . . . right, Jaw . . . was Mr. Moody . . . after all." I hang my head for a moment. "Only thing that fits."

"But you said he had no motive," Erik reminds me, the sky above us almost lavender. "So what's his motive?"

"Like what your website said. Some kind of ritualistic murder."

"If there was going to be a sacrifice that night, why wouldn't it be you? And not just because you're the virgin—"

"*Obviously*, it should have been me," I say, exasperated. "The only person who would've missed me is my mom! And even my mom would've been better off with me dead—"

"You never say that again. Ever." Erik's voice is so hard it frightens me, his hands gripping my shoulders. "Listen to me, Signal. We're going to clear your name and get you out of camp, I *promise you*—"

But his words are drowned out by rhythmic thunder overhead. We look up to see a helicopter pass above us. We watch it descend, the trajectory leading just past the trees to the field in front of the main cabin.

"This isn't good," Erik says, tense. "Can you handle more running?"

"Try to keep up," I gasp, and slip my arm through his.

* * *

But by the time we get to the obstacle course field I'm flailing with exhaustion; my foot catches under the edge of the staked-down tarp and I go sprawling into the middle of the sleeping bags with a wild cry.

Nobody leaps up, poised to attack, Troy and Jada's sleeping bags jerk apart, and Dennis is scrambling for his glasses as I roll onto my side, panting.

Javier sits up, his puzzled gaze going from me to Erik, and before I can say anything, everyone else gets in the way.

"Where were you guys?"

"Did you hear the helicopter?"

"Kate and Dave weren't here so this whole time Troy and Jada've been making ou—"

"Shut UP, Kurt!" Troy pounces on his brother, who laughs hysterically.

The talk cuts off as we all hear it: a car engine. Driving up to the field.

"Everybody get back in bed!" Javier bellows. "Lay down, lay down!"

I race over to the bedroll next to him, but Javier doesn't look at me. I start to speak but he turns away on his side. I freeze, curled up next to him, bathed in cold sweat from running arm in arm with Erik, the headlights arcing over us as the car chugs to a stop.

What's going on? Did Kate and Dave see me and Erik cross the fence? Did that family call the police, and they've tracked us down? Is Javier upset? Is he going to break up with me?

The tarp is flooded with light as the driver switches on the high beams; a car door slams and we try to see who's rushing toward us, but we're blinded by the glare.

"GET UP! ALL OF YOU, GET UP!" a strange male voice yells.

"I'm sorry, who are you? You work with Dave and Kate?" Javier calls, shielding his face with one hand.

"I said GET UP!" the stranger yells, and kicks the nearest sleeping bag. Jada yelps in pain.

"What the hell, man?!" Troy moves to shield her.

The stranger holds up a fob and clicks it at Troy.

"*NO!*" Kurt screams.

But Troy is already on his knees, frozen in the beam of the headlights. His skin turns a neon red, like the worst sort of sunburn, burning him from the inside out. Within seconds it's deepened to purple, bruises blooming out across his skin as corrosive acid dissolves his veins. His eyes, fixed on the man, go crimson and then he collapses forward onto the cold blue tarp.

He didn't even get a last breath.

Chapter Seventeen

The Director

❧

"*Troy!*" Kurt screams.

Jada curls over Troy's body. "*No no no no . . .*"

The stranger levels the fob at Kurt, who freezes in place.

"I am the Director of this camp." The stranger's cold tone cuts through Jada's sobs. "We have some developments to discuss at the main cabin. You will proceed there in a single file line, without talking."

Numb, I climb out of my bedroll and fall into line with everyone else. I can't look at the poor figure huddled below the headlights, the thing that used to be Troy.

As we walk the familiar trail to the main cabin, I'm vaguely aware of Kurt crying and Jada sobbing far behind me, but too afraid to turn and comfort them. None of us do. None of us want to be next.

When I surface from the shock, we're all in a line across from the Director in the main cabin as he addresses us. He's tall, spare, white-haired, and looks so . . . reasonable. So relaxed.

"Training is over," the Director says calmly. "You will leave on your first mission in twenty-three hours."

What?

"I don't have the time," the Director goes on, "to deal with the Class A sense of entitlement." He shoots a look at Kate and Dave, who stand in the far corner of the room. "There's a clean-up back on the obstacle course."

Kate and Dave exit at his command, to "clean up" Troy. Troy, who held my wrists so tight under Dog Mask's body and hadn't gotten a chance to eat his M&Ms and let Jada Sharpie his throat just because he wanted to see her win. I will never hear his laugh again. And all I can do is stare at the wood grain of the floor between my wet, grass-stained sneakers.

The Director casually holds up a stack of folders, like a high school English teacher going through examples of a book report they assign every year.

"As this is your first mission, you'll be sent out in pairs to help each other with execution and concealment of four high-priority targets, targets you have been matched with based on the strengths you've displayed."

This is how they plan to keep us from striking out on our own once we're past the fence? *The buddy system?*

I'm going to be free. I'm going to be free in twenty-three hours. The relief is so intense I have to choke back a sob.

"So. First pair: Jada and Erik."

Erik is expressionless. Jada walks behind him like a zombie. The Director hands them each a folder.

"Javier and Lark." *Lark?*

Javier and Nobody walk up to the Director to take their folders. If Nobody is angry he used her real name, she doesn't show it.

"Troy and Kurt."

Kurt walks up alone.

"Dennis and Signal."

I can't bring myself to look into the Director's face, I just take the folder and follow Dennis into the dining area, the room so much emptier without the usual rowdy laughter.

"Read over your briefings in silence, please."

I look up to see Javier staring at me from across the room. I offer a minuscule smile, but he looks away as Nobody, beside him, raises her hand.

The Director stares at her for a beat, but she doesn't drop her arm.

"Yes?"

"I've been assigned a primary target, but it seems like there's also a lot of . . . potential casualties."

"Yes," the Director says. "Casualties may be required to escape from the Ojai compound."

Ojai? That sounds so familiar. Some kind of celebrity got married there . . . Because it was close to Los Angeles, in Southern California. Where Oxnard is.

Where Jaw is.

"It seems like the potential casualties would be teenage girls," Nobody continues, her raspy voice firm. "So I can't do that."

"You're refusing your mission?"

"I'm not going to be any good to you on this one," Nobody insists, and the air goes electric. What is she thinking? *He'll kill her.*

"You don't have a choice in the matter." The Director's voice is a warning. Nobody is about to respond when I swing my arm into the air. I force myself to meet the Director's eyes, flat dark holes in a thin pink face, shielded by thick glasses.

"I'll trade with her." I can barely get the words out.

"Trade?" The Director's upper lip curls, revealing teeth the color of old piano keys.

At last Javier looks at me, and almost imperceptibly shakes his head: *Don't.*

"Your targets have been assigned to your skill level." The Director walks slowly toward my table. Dennis, next to me, shrinks into himself. "You're Lark's inferior. If you trade, you dramatically reduce your odds of getting back to camp alive."

I hold his gaze. "Okay. I'll still do it."

There's a long moment, and the Director flicks his wrist so the fob lands in his palm. He moves the pad of his thumb over the button.

"Very well," the Director shrugs at last, letting the fob slip from his hand and rattle around his bony wrist. My teeth unclench. "Leave your folder at your table and exchange seats. But there will be no more trades. And this one is final."

I push back my chair, the scraping sound harsh in the silence. Nobody reaches out and squeezes my hand quickly as we pass by each other, and then I'm next to Javier.

I look over at him, long enough that he should be able to tell, but he won't look back at me. He stares down at his folder deliberately instead, so I open mine and see the face of the man we're supposed to murder.

Angel CHILDS: 30, 5'8", brown hair, brown eyes.

First noted in Santa Cruz two years ago, in a small camper van with glow-in-the-dark stickers adhered to its side.

Angel spent approx. last two years traveling the California coast, playing his guitar in coffee shops and tourist spots. He met a freshmen co-ed who subsequently dropped out to join Angel on his tour of the PCH and help recruit others. Within four months six college drop-outs were living in Childs' van.

They traded up to a decommissioned school bus, which they drove to musical festivals throughout SoCal until they arrived at a collective in Ojai, called Owl's Nest.

Once an active commune in the 1960s, Owl's Nest was home to three older artists who had lived there continuously for over fifty years. They reportedly invited the newcomers to stay.

By spring, all three artists had disappeared. Childs claimed they left after signing the property over to his first recruit, called "Compass" by his group, who refer to themselves as "The Constellation."

Since the disappearance of the original owners, the population of Owl's Nest has risen to approx. fifty adults between the ages of eighteen and twenty-four.

Neighbors have reported hearing gunshots, as well as sightings of Childs driving down horse trails on an ATV while wearing a holster. Members of a prominent California biker gang known as the Death Heads have been seen going in and out of Owl's Nest at night.

Childs himself never leaves.

Ergo, this target must be dispatched from within the compound, which will take considerable strategy to infiltrate. They are highly selective in deciding which guests may enter, and within their own hierarchy access to Childs is highly limited.

Furthermore, if The Constellation detects Angel Childs' assassination before agents leave the compound, the agents will almost certainly be terminated.

A picture paper-clipped to his profile, taken from social media, shows him sun-soaked and square-jawed, long dark hair cascading over his shoulders, strumming a guitar and smiling a large, toothy smile.

*   *   *

Once we've finished reading, the Director tells us to make our way over to the Arts and Crafts table to meet with Dave, and we all flee.

With a small, shared glance of understanding, Javier and I sprint ahead, running off the path and into the trees, out of the sight of the others.

Once we're hidden in the cool shadow of the woods, the sparkling blue of the lake breaking through in pinpoints between the pine needles, Javier turns on me.

"Why would you trade with Nobody?" he cries. "What were you thinking?! This is a suicide mission!"

"Javier, I didn't have a choice."

"You chose to trade!"

"Because the mission is in Ojai," I confess. "I need to investigate a guy in Southern California. This way I'll have the whole trip down as a head start before they realize I've taken off."

"Whoa, investigate? Investigate him for what?" He blinks at me. "What are you talking about?"

"Javier, last night I found out the guy who killed Rose lives in California."

He stares at me for a long moment. "The guy who killed your *victim*, Rose?"

My stomach starts to sink.

"Wait . . . so, what, you're innocent?" There's a panicked note in his voice, something between a laugh and a sob. "Like, you've never killed *anyone?*"

"I'm sorry, is that a bad thing?" My voice comes out high, brittle. "Didn't you . . . couldn't you tell? All that stuff about being mislabeled, 'flower for sure,' I thought . . ." I reach for his hand.

He flinches away. "So that's where you and Erik were? Off 'investigating' all night? You told *him* you were innocent, but you didn't tell me?"

"I *didn't* tell him, he guessed! He guessed the first day he met me."

"I really don't know what to say." Javier shakes his head. "I thought we were on the same page. I thought you were someone who'd messed up and was trying to do better. But you're *nothing* like me." His jaw is set, his nostrils flaring, his eyes won't meet mine. "Signal, *you* might be an innocent, but I'm not. I killed a guy with my bare hands."

My eyes go to his scars. He sees me look, and he draws himself up straighter.

"You know something else?" Javier says, lifting his chin so he looms almost a head taller than me. "I don't regret it. When I let myself look back on that day I feel . . . satisfaction. Yes. *Satisfaction.* If I could go back to that moment? I'd do it again. Only thing different, I'd make it last longer. Try and enjoy it."

I feel sick.

"So now what, you want to make out?" He takes a sudden step toward me and I step back involuntarily. "Didn't think so," Javier says quietly, and walks stiffly past me down the field.

* * *

Dave blows the whistle in front of the Arts and Crafts table as I stumble down the hill and join the stunned group of campers facing him.

"Well, campers, we're going to be really busy for the next twenty or so hours—"

"Who the hell *is* that guy?" Kurt interrupts in a strangled voice.

"He's the Director," Dave says tensely. "After we reported the intruder last night, HQ put him in charge of camp. Believe it or not, he's here for your protection."

"He *killed my brother!*"

"We could all rush him at once," Erik says in such a serious tone that Dave lunges forward and grabs him by the collar.

"If you want HQ to simultaneously activate all your implants at once, then go ahead, by all means. Play your asinine games with the man who planned and built this place." There's a desperate edge in Dave's voice as he pushes Erik away. Erik bristles, rage and restraint fighting in his face, and I put my hand on his shoulder without thinking. He turns on me at the contact, breath catching, but something in my expression makes him calm enough to hold back.

Dave looks at each of us in turn, then snatches up his walkie-talkie and yells for Kate to come handle us, disappearing up the hill. We all stand there, left without answers, and a small, muffled sob escapes Kurt as he sits down in the grass, hands over his head, his back to us, and I can't handle it anymore.

I kneel down beside Kurt and put my arms around him and he sags into me, the muscles in his neck and back rigid, his voice broken and jagged as he cries:

"I don't know where he is. I don't know where he is."

I don't know what to say, so I murmur nonsensically, "It's okay. It's okay . . ." and rub his back. Light footsteps, and Jada kneels down beside us. And then Nobody's fingertips graze my hair as she winds her arms around Kurt and Jada, and then Dennis's fine curls graze my hand as he closes around the other side of Kurt, and I can sense Javier in the huddle across from me, and the unmistakable heat of Erik's arm reaching across my shoulder so he can rest his long, broad hand on Kurt's back. Kurt's neck and shoulders release then, and he lets out a long, broken sigh.

"You know, in ancient times . . . ," Erik says, and Kurt lets out a dry, hot laugh, and then weeps again, but these are good tears. Necessary ones. Like he's getting something out of him. We sit there in the long grass, huddled together against the wind coming off the lake, just holding on to each other as hard as we can.

I've dozed off by the time Kate arrives. There's a sick pallor over her usually cheerful features, and the sky is the color of milk. She clears her throat and asks us to come to the table, so we help each other up and sit in a tight knot as she passes out eight stapled packets of Google Map printouts.

"I know this has been a difficult morning," Kate says at last. "But in spite of all the arguments I could possibly make against it, you guys will be leaving tomorrow at dawn. So we need to get serious about getting you ready. The routes to your targets are in front of you." I look down at the national view of our map, a pink squiggle that runs from Washington to California. "Study them carefully. It will be crucial that you stay on this route once you're out of camp. You'll all be given burner phones. Camp HQ will be programmed in as 'Mom and Dad.' If you need to make a detour for any reason, pull over and call us, and wait for us to give you the all clear. Because if you go a mile off your route in any direction, your kill switch *will* be triggered, and obviously we do not want that to happen—"

"Wait, what?!" I blurt. "What are you talking about?"

"Your kill switch, Signal," Kate says in a tone like this should be obvious. "Until now, it could only go off if you crossed the fence or we clicked a fob. But when you go off on your missions, we activate the GPS, and your kill switch conforms to your route. You travel to your target, complete your assignment, and come back the same way. Or it will go off. Understand?"

Chapter Eighteen
Becoming Someone Else

I clench the packet of maps in front of me, my field of vision narrowing. I force myself to take deep calming breaths like my lawyer told me to the day my verdict was announced.

This actually feels worse.

Because back when they condemned me to life in prison, I half expected it. And I had been able to openly break down in tears. And I had the comfort of knowing I was in the right and they were in the wrong.

But this . . . I am going to have to choose between dying and killing someone. That's what this boils down to. I can't escape and I will not be allowed to return until my target is dead.

How could I have been so stupid? How could I have held on so tight to the illusion I could escape this place, this place so clearly designed to use us, to break us down, and stab us into other people as broken as we are?

Kate looks at her watch, the wind ruffling her short hair. "I have to go back to the main cabin. I'll see you campers back there in an hour?" The others nod and she heads up the hill, the grass bowing in ripples under a sudden rush of cool wind.

"Since we have this time alone," Dennis says to the table calmly, "I want to tell you what we found searching the cabins yesterday."

We all turn to him.

"Not a ton of the bomb survived." Dennis pushes his glasses up his short nose. "But what we did find indicated a beautiful, homemade device. On a timer. Dog Mask planted it under the cabin on a delay, in case he didn't get all of us."

"So you think he made the bomb?" I ask Dennis.

"Frankly, no," Dennis says. "Because it appears he got the AM/PM setting wrong."

"He probably got it from someone in the Protectionist network. They blow places up," Jada says softly. "They targeted a cell block full of Class As in Massachusetts. Fourteen prisoners killed."

"What was the headline?" Erik asks. "'Good Riddance'?"

"There's something else," Dennis continues. "Dave wouldn't let me in the nurse's office while he was sweeping the main cabin. Because he didn't want me around the laptop. So he put me in Kate's room. And I used the time to search her stuff."

With a swift furtive glance toward the hill, Dennis pulls out a crumpled sheet from the band of his Bugle Boy shorts and lays it on the table. "I found this. A spreadsheet with the exit dates and money given previous campers."

"Previous campers?" Javier's shocked tone speaks for all of us. "There's no previous campers. This is a new program."

Dennis shakes his head. "Not according to this."

We crowd around, scanning the fine print. It's a long list of ID numbers, then a range of years and amounts paid. Several entries end in "KIA." Killed in action.

"They had them going out on mission for seventeen years," Javier whispers.

"This doesn't make sense." Erik sounds genuinely troubled. "They didn't know how to identify Class As until two years ago. What, they just rounded up random homicidal teens? How did they keep them here? You're saying they had *kill switches* in 1999?"

"And what happened here?" I ask, my finger tracing the shortest entry, the only one that doesn't end in "KIT" or "KIA." Instead, it shows an enrollment of two years, and ends in "PARDON."

"That got my attention too." Dennis nods to me. "But if we can't manage one of those, at least we know what's ahead of us. We *will* get retired . . . if we live through taking out targets for seventeen years. As approximately seventy percent of the last class did."

"My sentence was forty years," Nobody shrugs. "So. Beats prison."

"Does it though?" Javier asks. He looks as queasy as I feel. Seventeen years of killing strangers. How could I have ever signed on for this? Why did I agree to this deal—

"Deal with the devil." I lock eyes across the table with Erik.

"Dog Mask was a camper," he says immediately. "Seventeen years ago he would've been sixteen or seventeen."

"Just the right age for the Teen Killers Club."

Javier's eyes go from sad to alert. "That's how he knew where and what camp is! But why kill us?"

"Kate told Dave she thought the attack was meant to force us to go after our targets early," I remind them. "Before we were ready. And that's exactly what's happening. When we killed Dog Mask we didn't foil their plan. We just got the ball rolling."

"I don't like this man." Javier runs his hand over his hair, bouncing one leg on the ball of his foot compulsively. "I don't like this one bit."

"'Come try it,' right?" Jada says, her eyes staring a mile over the lake, which has lost its sparkle under a lid of heavy clouds. The wind is a steady, audible stream now, and a heavy drop of rain lands at the top of my scalp.

"I'm going back to the main cabin," Javier says, shoulders slack as he gets to his feet.

Erik stretches his head back as though to catch the next raindrop in his mouth, and there's the low groan of thunder in the distance and a dart of light far over the lake. Another storm is coming, the air feels pulled taut by it. We get up and start trooping through the damp field, and I fall behind the others to talk with Dennis.

"Hey," I start. "You caught what Dave said before, right? About HQ setting off our kill switches? That they can do that without fobs, like remotely, that's what he meant, right?"

Dennis quickly looks from side to side. "Yeah, that caught my attention too."

"If they can set them off remotely then couldn't you turn them off remotely? Like the pacemaker?"

Dennis looks at me for a long moment. I can see him weighing and measuring what I'm asking: Will you help me escape?

"*Theoretically* yes," Dennis says at last. "But keep in mind it took me hours to figure out how to turn the pacemaker off. There were plenty of times I accidentally restarted it, or slowed it down, or sped it up. Knowing that, whose switch do I start on? Because if I mess up . . ."

"They die," I finish.

More lightning silently glows on the other side of the lake and thunder sounds a moment after, the rain starting to fall in earnest. Dennis and I break into a run toward the covered porch beside the main cabin. When we get there, we're half-soaked and the rain is drumming hard on the corrugated plastic roof.

"Find your partner!" Kate announces, handing out worksheets. "Read over your character profiles!" Javier sits at the corner picnic table, face hard. He doesn't look up as I approach; he just slides my packet of handouts to the other side of the table, away from him. I sit shivering on the metal picnic bench, head down so he can't see my face, and scan the sheet: on this mission we will be acting as a couple, a boyfriend and girlfriend who go to school at USC, Jenny Smith and Hector Garcia. We're on our way up to San Francisco to see my family.

"That's ironic," I say thickly. "Acting like a couple now we're broken up."

"So we're broken up now?" he asks quietly.

I thought that was obvious? And not my call. I look up, his eyes are wide—

"Girls!" Kate claps her hands, standing in the doorway between the covered porch and main cabin. "Once you've finished reading your profiles, we're heading to your old cabin to do makeovers. Boys, Dave will meet you in the bathroom of the main cabin. And we'll all meet back up for dinner."

"Makeovers, hey." Nobody nudges Jada. "You always said you wanted to give me one."

"What?" Jada startles, as though pulled out of deep thought, and Nobody and I each take an arm and help steer her toward our old cabin.

* * *

Thirty minutes later I find myself staring into the photoshopped smile of a woman on a Clairol box, watching bronze-colored water circle my feet on its way down the drain. Blue hair is apparently "too memorable" for the mission, so Jada helped me cover my head in cheap dye.

When we'd arrived at the cabin, three JanSport backpacks were lined up for us with clothing chosen for our new identities, as well as the burner flip phones. MomandDad is the first number, Hector G is the second. There's at least ten more names, which Kate explains go to automatic voicemail proxies. I'd spent the half hour it took the color to develop sorting through clothes with Nobody, making sure we both had pants that fit, since swapping missions meant swapping clothes. Jenny Smith's wardrobe is heavy on embroidered peasant blouses and cutoff shorts, which are pretty forgiving for length.

When I get out of the shower Jada is at the mirror poking a safety pin through her ear. Her face is heavily made up and she's in a crop top, miniskirt, illusion tights, and three-inch platform creepers, all black. She's dressed the way I always wanted to in high school, except on her it looks right.

"Signal?" Kate's surprised gaze meets mine in the mirror. "I almost didn't recognize you without the blue! Here's your makeup kit." She puts a quart bag with "Jenny" written on it in Sharpie on the edge of the sink. I haven't seen makeup in so long, and there's a lot, the nicer brands of drugstore stuff. Rooting through it feels weirdly similar to combing through my candy haul on long-ago Halloweens.

Jada grabs my wrist and clings. "Can I do your makeup?"

"Please!" I say quickly.

"I love this kind of stuff," Jada sniffs quietly. "Put your hair back?"

The last time she was this close to me she had a sharpened arrow against my eye. Now she's dotting concealer on the scar she gave me, and all I can think is I hope she's okay. She becomes completely absorbed in making me pretty, staining my lips carefully, tracing precise lines inside my eyelids with infinite care.

By the time my hair has dried out, I'm in a slightly-too-big peasant top, low-riding jeans, and I look maybe the best I've looked in my entire life. Jada is seriously talented; after months of nothing more than cold water on my face it's amazing the difference some carefully applied brown eyeliner and blush can make. My hair has turned out pretty good, too. Instead of the usual blue over bleach and six inches of dark roots, it's a surprisingly convincing bronze all over.

Nobody looks stunning and miserable in her cotton sundress. She slouches around swearing she's going to buy some sweatpants the second she's out of camp.

"And a ski mask?" I prompt.

"No need," Nobody says simply. "You guys know me now. And it's not like Dennis and I are going to run into anybody."

The target she and Dennis are taking out is some paranoid recluse deep in Arizona, who never leaves his house even to get his mail, so Dennis will be doing everything online. All Nobody has to do is drive back and forth to the Best Buy to get him extra solid-state drives or whatever.

"That could have been you, Signal," Jada says. "Why did you trade?"

Because I thought I was going to escape, so it didn't matter. Because I came to camp to learn to hunt down Rose's killer, and now that I know who he is and where he lives, he's ironically safer from me than ever. Because I'm a coward. Because I'd rather kill than die.

"You know me: boy crazy," I tell her. "Still chasing after Javier."

"Listen to me." Her small hands catch my wrists and she locks eyes with mine. "You seriously need to stop playing games and just tell him how you feel. The guy you like is right there—" she gestures wildly toward the main cabin "—where you can see him and touch him and talk to him. You *both* need to stop playing games and just be real about it while you still can. Okay?! *Okay?! Promise me?!*"

I nod, stunned, and she releases me, then abruptly walks out of the bathroom, brushing by Kate with a look worse than a slap.

After a moment Nobody and I follow Jada to the main cabin. We wait for the boys to finish getting ready, warming up mugs of cocoa in the kitchen. I'm on my second mug when I hear Erik's throaty laugh and look up. My jaw actually drops.

In black jeans, a scuffed leather jacket, and worn Pixies T-shirt, Erik looks like a rock star. The change is so striking it's not till he ducks his head and fleetingly bites his fingernails that I remember he isn't a celebrity—just Erik, a real guy I actually know.

A gray-faced Kurt is dressed like a total jock in Seahawks Starter jacket, track pants, and Adidas shower shoes; Dennis wears an utterly generic navy blue sweatshirt and jeans but compared to the usual lost-and-found neon ensembles I've gotten used to him wearing it's nerd chic on a par with Steve Jobs.

And Javier stuns me in a tailored blue button-up shirt that shows off his broad shoulders. He's got a USC cap and—I almost laugh—a pair of *tasseled loafers*. A *preppy*. He looks like a total preppy.

And he's *staring* at me.

"Find your seats!" the Director's voice rings out as the door opens. We return to our seats from this morning and fall quiet as the Director scans us, his expression neutral.

"Tomorrow morning your first mission begins. We're sending you out while your training is incomplete, which increases the risk of your missions." He shrugs. "But given the state of the facilities, we can't guarantee your physical safety here either. If we have to lose Class As, we might as well lose them in action."

Computer genius Dennis; exquisite Nobody who saved all our lives; brilliant Erik, with his humor and intelligence and courage; gallant, artistic Javier; beautiful, burning Jada; sunny, steady Kurt—they're just "Class As" to him. As interchangeable and replaceable as gears in a machine. He'd use and discard them without a second thought, drown all their bright gifts in blood. Because he doesn't see any of the good in us. We're just monsters to him. And if we aren't monsters yet, by the time we get back we will be.

The Director clears his throat. "You have until lights out to finish studying your routes. Instant oatmeal is in the kitchen for your dinner. Make the most of the time."

I watch Dennis intently. When he gets up from his chair and heads for the kitchen, some greater impulse carries me after him.

Dennis is warming up cocoa when I barge in after him, the microwave's yellow window the only light in the dim room.

"Dennis?" I whisper, "Look, about the kill switches?"

He nods.

"I want you to practice with mine."

The microwave goes off with a ding, but he doesn't move.

"If I mess up, you'll die," he says slowly, like I'm not getting it.

"Yeah, but if you *don't* mess up, then you can turn off your own switch and everybody else's. And then anyone else as sick of camp as I am can leave."

"Signal—"

"It's worth it to me," I tell him. "Please, Dennis."

He takes out his mug, blows on the steaming cocoa, and sips it carefully.

"It wasn't an act, was it?" he says at last. "You're just, like, a nice person, aren't you?"

"Sure." I roll my eyes. "Will you try? Please?"

"Once I'm out of here I can. They're giving me a basically unlimited credit line at Best Buy to take out my target remotely, and not even Kate can follow my programming once I'm back online. As long as *you* know what you're risking."

"I do." And I mean it. "Thank you, Dennis."

I turn around before my eyes tear, surprised at the euphoria of relief that floods me. The choice is made. Whatever happens, I don't have to kill anyone. After Dennis gets a chance to hack my kill switch, I'll go off my route toward Jaw. If Dennis disables it, I can go find him and clear my name. If not, my switch will go off and I will die.

Either way, they'll have no power over me. My soul will be my own.

Erik said once there's no such thing as good and evil, just strong and weak. But I believe there is evil, and I believe it begins when we do things we know are wrong out of fear.

I feel sort of outside of my body as I return to the table where Javier waits, already seeing him like he's a memory. But then I notice his leg is going again, and he keeps shielding his eyes from the overhead lights as if they're too bright. Or he's holding back tears.

"What's wrong?" I finally ask.

"What's wrong? Are you seeing this?" He stabs the aerial shots of the compound with his finger. "Even if we *can* talk our way into this place, which is going to be next to impossible, there's literally no way out."

I try to focus on the image, but my mind is clouded by exhaustion and adrenaline.

"We'll figure it out," I say, not believing it at all.

"Right," Javier says, voice clipped, and we both sink back into our separate silences.

After a dinner of instant oatmeal, we push the tables to the walls and roll out bedrolls on the floor of the dining room. Kate hands out sedatives so we can "get some rest" before our big day, which is a kindness. I swallow the pill gratefully, and lie down fully dressed in my Jenny Smith outfit, hoping dawn comes before any dreams can.

But I don't wake at dawn. I wake in total dark, disoriented, and stumble to the bathroom. It's only on the way back I notice Javier's bedroll is empty.

The door to the covered porch creaks back and forth with the night breeze. I pad as silently as I can to the strip of light leaking in from the patio and peer through the tight space above the door's hinge.

Javier sits at a picnic table, across from the Director, talking low and fast.

"Even if Signal somehow talks her way into the compound—*which I guarantee she can't*—there's no chance she'll take Angel out. I'm *telling you*." Javier's voice drips with contempt. "She's useless. Worse than useless."

"So what exactly," the Director says, "are you proposing I do with her?"

Chapter Nineteen
Road Trip

❧

Javier leans toward the Director.

"I can get in the house easier than she can. I should be the inside man, and she can handle exit strategy."

The Director gives him a patronizing smile. "And how would it be easier for you to get inside? Angel is known to recruit young women. But men he doesn't know aren't allowed on the property."

"It said in the profile he hangs out with the Death Heads," Javier counters. "I know the leader of the Death Heads, Ray Gomez. His little brother is a friend of mine from way back. Put Ray's number in my phone and I'll take care of the rest."

The Director idly spins the fob on his wrist. "Won't he think it's strange you're suddenly out of jail?"

"Ray's got a lot on his mind. If I tell him I got out on appeal, he won't dig. And he won't notice when I go off the radar again."

The Director considers this. "Normally I forbid involving outsiders, but it's a valuable connection, especially if Signal is as inept as you claim. Of course, it would have to be *just* your friend Ray. Not him and his three best friends. *Just* him."

"Understood."

"Very well. I'll allow you to contact your friend, and he can bring Signal into the house."

"No, man, it's got to be me and Ray!" Javier has pushed back too hard, and a cold silence condenses between them. The fob stops spinning, the Director holds it, considering him.

"I'm starting to think that you're trying to *protect her*, Javier."

"I don't care about the bitch," Javier sighs heavily. "I just don't want to get caught out on my first mission!"

"Then why not follow the plan I've just described?"

"Because Ray is not going to ride in with someone he doesn't know. Ray will do it *with* me, but he won't do it *for* me. You understand the difference? I don't have a kill switch in his neck. I have to strike an actual deal with him, not just give him commands—"

The Director's voice cuts in: "Whoever goes into that compound is almost certainly not coming out again."

"I'm not afraid of some hippies," Javier says. "You want this guy dead or not? Because I promise you, Signal can't get it done. Sending me in is your only chance."

The long silence that follows is agonizing.

"All right," the Director says at last, his tone cool. "Both you and Signal will go in with your friend. And we'll see who comes out."

Javier pauses, then scribbles out Ray's number, which the Director assures him will be "assiduously checked."

"Okay," Javier says, putting out a hand. "Thanks."

The Director looks down at Javier's hand with disgust, like it's already covered in blood. Then he gets up and walks out from the covered porch, straight into the trees.

When I'm sure he's gone, I step around the door and into sight.

"Javier, what are you doing?"

"Signal!" he startles. "I thought you were asleep—"

The wind is so cuttingly cold, it's like walking through icy water to cross the patio.

"I get that I'm a burden to you, okay?" I wrap my arms around my chest. "But I never thought you'd go sneaking around to tell the Director you need to ditch me—"

"*What?*" Javier is aghast. "I'm trying to *protect you*, Signal. That's all I've ever done!"

"Since when?"

"Since I volunteered to do the obstacle course so I could climb behind you?" His eyes flare. "Since I traded mannequins with you? *Since the first time I saw you?*" His voice breaks in frustration. Then he bites his lip and says, with effort: "Forget it. Forget I said that. I swore to myself I was going to break it off with you."

"Whatever, Javier. Whatever you want."

"What I *want* is for you to be safe. And this mission . . . There's no way to make it safe, okay? I would have done anything to keep him from sending you in, but I'm powerless, okay? I'm completely . . ." His voice breaks, and he looks away quickly, one knee jiggling wildly above the picnic bench. He bows his shoulders, his hands covering his face.

I sit down beside him at the picnic table, chills cascading down my back, my arms, my teeth chattering.

"He's dead set on you going in," Javier blurts, face still in his hands. "Maybe because you traded? I don't know. But that place is a death trap. If we use you as bait? You won't get out." He shakes his head back and forth, and I realize he's keeping his sentences short because he's fighting back tears. "I don't know how to keep you safe."

I fumble awkwardly for his hand.

"I don't want you to like me anymore. I don't deserve it." Javier's tone is stern, but his fingers clutch at mine.

I heard him say the words myself: "I don't care about the bitch." But he was saying that to keep me out of a deadly mission. Or is he just saying all that to me now because I overheard? Was he just saying what I wanted to hear when he called me a flower? How could he think that, if he believed I was guilty? Is there a real Javier, or does he just say whatever he needs to?

"I'm *not* a good guy, Signal," Javier says, but his hand is still holding mine.

"Aren't you?" I ask, staring into his eyes.

His hand drifts to my neck, and it's the only warmth in the world. Our lips meet, and the kiss deepens; and it's not a performance or a claim on me. I let my fingers graze the plane of his cheek, his rough stubble, then force myself to pull back.

"What is going on with us?" I ask Javier. "Are we together? Or broken up?"

"I should just push you away and keep pushing until you hate me . . ." Javier trails off. "But it's harder than I thought, pretending not to care about you." And he traces the dandelion on the inside of my forearm. When he looks at me, when he touches me, it's like I transform into this beautiful girl. I know that feeling isn't true. But if a lie feels this good, does it even matter?

Is that what romance is? Pretending?

Oh, Erik, get out of my head.

"Can't we just try and enjoy this trip?" Javier goes on. "Considering how it could end? Can't we just try and make it a clean slate, like you said that first night? Enjoy ourselves while we still can?"

He has no idea.

"Okay," I say, wiping at my eyes. "Clean slate, starting tomorrow."

"Tomorrow." He smiles at last. "You and me. We start again."

He leans over and kisses me, fast and hard and with searing heat, and then we return to the silence of the main cabin, to our bedrolls at opposite ends of the room, to steal a little oblivion.

* * *

At four AM they wake us, to pitch black windows and the chill of night. Out front Dave and the Director are inspecting four cars lined up along the gravel.

We crowd around the kitchen counter, a cold excitement banishing the last of the sedative from our systems, and power down instant oatmeal as Kate hands out counterfeit licenses and credit cards with our new fake names embossed on them.

"You have fifteen hundred each for expenses. After you hit your target, a bonus will be deposited, so you can have a little fun on the way back home." She wiggles her eyebrows.

I'm taking my turn in the main cabin bathroom, trying to replicate what Jada did with my makeup yesterday, when Dennis knocks and I let him in. He scans the hall before closing the door behind him and then leans on the sink counter.

"You still sure about what we talked about?" he asks quietly.

"Yes, I am."

"Okay. Well, me and Nobody are going to be driving pretty hard the next couple days. But I should be able to find a couple hours on the seventeenth. If I hit some kind of firewall where I absolutely cannot jailbreak your kill switch, I'll try and text you or Javier—"

"You *can't* tell Javier."

Dennis frowns. "You're not going to warn him that he might lose his partner halfway through his mission?"

"I'm betting on you, Dennis. I think you can do it. And if you can't . . ." Then I don't want to spend the next three days with Javier trying to talk me out of it, or worse, physically restraining me. "Then the fewer people who know you tried, the safer you'll be."

"Okay," he says. "I'll be trying on the seventeenth. If something goes wrong, I'll text you a single asterisk. If it *does* work, and you cross the perimeter without activating the kill switch, I'll be able to tell from the code. Don't contact me, that'll draw their attention. Just keep going, and I'll go down the line and break us all out as fast as I can. But you have to understand, I won't know for sure if it's worked until you've crossed the perimeter. You are the test case."

"And I'm not happy about that, at all." He blinks, as though confused. "I'm a Class A who's always wanted to hurt someone. But I hate that you're doing this, Signal."

I'm aware this is as mushy as Dennis could ever possibly be, and I throw my arms around him in an impulsive hug I immediately regret. He remains still, arms at his sides, patiently waiting for me to get hold of myself.

"Thank you, Dennis," I tell him, tearing up again. Everything's very close to the surface today. "No matter what happens, never forget you're way more than a Class A. You're one of the most amazing people I've ever met."

". . . I also need to use the bathroom now," he says, and I suppress a laugh and return to the crackling energy of the central room, where the rolled-up bedrolls and backpacks are piled in the middle of the empty floor.

As Javier dips down and grabs our packs, I realize something is wrong with his face and blurt out, "Where's your tattoo?"

"Cover-up. Kate said the tear didn't go with my outfit." His tone is almost shy. As I reach over and pick up my pillow, he leans in and whispers softly,

"Do you have any idea how gorgeous you look right now?"

Before I can recover, Dave is thrusting a pair of keys between us, anchored to a USC keychain. "You're in the 2002 Volvo station wagon," he says gruffly. "With the 'Coexist' bumper sticker."

We walk out into the thin light of dawn, to the line of cars, and find ours. Behind us, the Director is talking solemnly to Erik and Jada, leaned up against a matte-black lowrider. Erik doesn't look at me, even though I stare at him, hard. He just nods, intent on whatever the Director is saying.

Behind them, Kate is instructing Nobody on how to stack several computer towers into the back of a gray Arrowstar van as Dennis punches buttons excitedly on the GPS.

Kurt, in a blue Jeep SUV with a surfboard mounted on the top, is at the very back of the line, engine idling. From the sound of it, he's programming radio stations.

Javier and I load in our backpacks and bedrolls, throwing pillows in the back seat in case one of us wants to nap. "I can take first driving shift if you want to sleep?" Javier offers, and I nod, though there's *no way* I'm sleeping. Every moment I have, I want.

I wander over to Nobody's van once she's got the computers loaded.

"Hey!" I reach out my arms and she hugs me, tight.

"I owe you one for trading, you know."

"What are girlfriends for?" I squeak into her shoulder. "Just be safe out there, okay?"

"Oh, you haven't seen the last of me." She grins.

Kurt jogs over to give us quick goodbye hugs, and I'm shocked to feel tears slide down my cheeks when Jada's tiny arms wrap around me.

"It'll be okay, Skipper. We'll all be back at camp soon," Jada comforts me. "Think of it as a little romantic getaway for you and Javier." Her voice goes grim, "Except the getaway part is *no joke*."

Before I can respond, the Director calls for our attention. We fall into a line in front of him as he flicks at his smartphone in silence.

"Okay . . . ," he says finally. "HQ confirms kill switch perimeters rerouted." He looks up from the display at last. "You're cleared to take off. Be sure to follow your routes, take care with clean-up, and good luck." He nods stiffly, then looks to Dave, who steps forward, clapping his hands like a coach giving a final speech on game night.

"You've trained. You've prepared. This is a way earlier launch than we expected, but you are exceptional young people, and we believe in you. We expect to see each and every one of you back at camp soon. So now all I have left to say is this . . ." Dave lets a smile spread across his face. "Just have fun with it."

Hoots and clapping at this. My arms stay at my sides.

Kate clasps her hands together, her knuckles going pale from the pressure. "We are so, so proud of you guys. And we can't wait to see you all safely back, very soon! Remember, guys: what did we come here to learn?"

An electric current of understanding passes down the line of campers, all of us thinking it: *how not to end up like you.* I have to bite the inside of my cheek. Kate looks confused by our silence so we all hurriedly jump in with "How to not get caught!" out of unison, knowing smiles flickering on our faces. Dave, staring straight ahead, seems paler under his tan.

The Director claps his hands, ordering us to our cars. I step toward the lowrider behind us to say goodbye to Erik, but Dave yells "Load *in*,

Signal!" and Erik's door slams. Unwillingly I turn and get into the passenger side of the Volvo instead.

But I don't want to leave without saying goodbye to Erik. I said goodbye to everybody but him. I twist in my seat, staring into their car. Erik, in the passenger seat, stares out the window with a pillow wedged under his head, his hair blocking most of his face from view. I wave, a lot, but nothing.

This is the last time I'll ever see him. After today I'll either be on the run from camp or, well, dead. *Say goodbye to me.* I *know* he can tell I'm staring at him, but it's like he's refusing to acknowledge me. I twist in my seat waving frantically, trying to get his attention, and finally stop when Jada, at the wheel, gives me a puzzled thumbs-up.

Javier hits the accelerator, our car bumps down the white gravel road, and I turn forward, hot tears starting to stream as we pass under the Camp Naramauke sign. Then, once we've jounced down the switchbacks and gotten off the access road, the lowrider growls behind us and Jada swerves past, incredibly fast.

"She's going to get pulled over!" I cry. "Isn't there some way to get them to stop or something? Warn her to take it easy?!"

"It's okay, she's just burning off some steam."

The lowrider shoots off into the distance before I can even see Erik's face one last time, and I burst into sobs.

Nobody pulls alongside us twenty minutes later, Dennis throwing us a wave, then they turn off at a southbound exit, and I wipe my eyes with my sleeve. It's impossible to think I'll never see them again, these maniacs, these killers, my only friends.

* * *

We go through a drive-through for breakfast, and after we eat hash brown patties and egg sandwiches in what can only be called ecstasy, Javier cranks back the passenger seat and pulls out a pillow, and it's my turn to drive.

Javier doesn't sleep, though, he chats with me, light and playful. He wants to know about my other boyfriends, refusing to believe he's my first.

"No way. I know you broke all the guys' hearts. Look at you."

If I could turn off the voice in my head that calls out every ridiculous thing he says, it would be pretty charming. But instead I just try to not to laugh and change the subject.

We don't stop again until lunch, pulling off at a low-slung building on our route with a blinking EAT sign out front and no further enticement. Their veggie burger is dry and the décor is dour, but the freedom of walking through the world, of ordering from a menu, of wandering to the bathroom or poring over the jukebox without asking anyone's permission . . . it's *everything*.

"It almost feels real, doesn't it?" I laugh to Javier as we walk back to the car hand in hand. "Like we're really a couple on a road trip together."

"We really *are* a couple on a road trip together."

"Oh. Right." I laugh.

"Don't worry. I won't let you forget it again, gorgeous." He gently twists the hand he's holding up to his lips and brushes my knuckles with a kiss. I, Signal Deere, am on a road trip with my handsome, adoring boyfriend.

Also, I might be dead in two and a half days.

Life is a fuse, and I am the red spark shooting toward its end, each moment burning away as soon as I exist within it, bright, sparkling, then gone.

* * *

Around ten o'clock Javier pulls up to the Sleepy Nite Motel. The smell of cigarette smoke almost knocks me backward when we get inside. Every sound echoes in the small room as Javier crosses to the far queen-sized bed and sets down his backpack on its plasticky quilt. I set my backpack down on the other bed, and then we turn and stare at each other.

"So . . ." He steps toward me. And then his phone goes off.

He's so intent on me he doesn't recognize what it is at first. I have to say, "Um, is that your phone?" and he pulls it out of his pocket.

"Hello?" A tinny voice from the other end. "Right. We are, we checked in. . . . oh yeah? Great! Okay, I will. I will right now. I appreciate it." He clicks the phone off and looks up at me. "That was the Director. Ray's number was just added to my directory." He's beaming. "I have to call Ray, set everything up." He strides over to me and wraps me in a hug. "Hopefully it doesn't take too long but . . . Ray can be a talker."

"Yeah, great, okay." I nod, head bobbing automatically as he scrolls through and finds the number. I go into the bathroom to brush my teeth. I can hear him speaking a rapid-fire mix of Spanish and English through the wall, so I take a shower as well. The hot water is absolute bliss.

Dripping in my towel and rifling through my backpack for bedclothes before I go back out, I'm stumped on what to wear. It's not like Javier has never seen me in my pajamas before, but still. It's different. We weren't boyfriend and girlfriend before. And I don't have to wear every piece of clothing I can fit into, because unlike the cabin, this room has heat.

Heck, I can wear underwear to bed if I want.

I stare down into my bag, heart hammering at the thought, then find the baggy red sweatpants and long-sleeved USC T-shirt tucked at the bottom and put them on as fast as I can before whatever mischievous mental voice that suggested the underwear gets louder. Dressed, I pad out of the bathroom to find our room empty. I go to the window and find Javier making loops under the sickly buzzing yellow of the parking lot lights, like a fish swimming in an aquarium.

So I climb into bed and click through the TV channels: the dire evening news, house hunting shows, *Wheel of Fortune*. I had *Wheel of Fortune* going the last time I saw Rose. She'd stopped talking to me when I stopped covering for her, but then one night she suddenly texted she was on her way over. Five minutes later a knock rattled the thin trailer door and Rose stepped into our scrubby living room, beaming at our old TV, at our stained couch covered in neat piles of folded laundry.

"Aww, Signal! It's all exactly the same as when we were kids! I'm going to cry!"

"Yeah, me too. I think this whole trailer would fit in your room. What's up?" I asked, wary. "Off to see Mr. Moody? You want me to cover if your mom calls?"

"No . . . I just had to get out of the house for a while." She shook her head, then: "Tom took the lock off my door again, so I go to talk to him about it, and he starts going off on my shirt? About how he can 'see everything' and I just . . . I grabbed my keys and left."

". . . Did your mom hear him say that?"

She nodded.

"What did *she* say?"

"Nothing. Not a damn thing." She laughed, but the corners of her mouth jerked down, and she ducked her head. I sat down on the couch next to her, my hand on her shoulder, unsure what to say. After a moment she threw her head back, shaking it off. "Anyway. Whatever. I turn eighteen in a month. And the second my trust comes in, the *second*, I'm going to buy a car, and drive straight to Portland." She tilted her head. "You'd come with me, right?"

I held out my pinky, and she smiled, and we promised.

I woke up with her in the shed a week later.

* * *

We check out when it's still dark. I huddle in the passenger seat, watching the sun rise. I don't know how many of these I have left. But I guess no one does. Javier takes my hand, his thumb moving gently over the back of it.

"It's going to be okay," he promises, his gift to me. I smile like I believe him, my gift to him. Erik was right. We are hell-bent on playing pretend.

We drive straight until lunch, stopping at a small diner, and while I'm in the bathroom washing my hands I glance up at the mirror and realize I'm beautiful.

Not beautiful in the magazine model sense, like Nobody. Beautiful as in incredibly well designed and capable. My hands can tie a braid without thinking, they can touch type, and once, briefly, played the flute. My eyes are 20/20 vision, my mouth can say or sing anything. My meaty little space suit, protecting me from all things in this world that are not me, has done a damn fine job the last seventeen years. I marvel at my own body for maybe the first time in my life, and yet I can't shake the feeling it's not mine anymore. It exists for the moment in limbo, like money placed on a table for a bet.

We decide to do drive-through for dinner and push through northern Nevada to the motel, getting there earlier than expected. The motel room is a carbon copy of the last one, except mercifully no cigarette smell. We set down our bags and stare at each other.

"Any calls or anything we have to do tonight?" I ask shyly.

"Oh, I think you know *exactly* what we have to do." Javier's eyes are intense as he strides toward me and takes me in his arms.

Chapter Twenty
Over the Line

～

Then, almost immediately, Javier frowns and steps back.

"You should try and kick my knee before I get to you. That's your best block."

". . . My best block?" Awkward. I thought we were going to make out.

"We need to practice for tomorrow," he says sternly. "If you're going in, then you're going in as prepared as we can get you between now and then. Let's see what kind of weapons they packed for you, then we'll go over some defensive moves."

"I don't think I got any."

He turns my backpack on its side and digs through to the zip-up panel in the very bottom, fishing out a small black canvas bag. Inside is a brand-new bowie knife with a four-inch blade.

"Nice," Javier muses. "But we'll practice with this."

He holds out my pink hairbrush.

"We don't have to do this—"

"Yes, we do," he insists. "I can't fight if I'm worrying about you."

I swallow my protests and take the hairbrush.

Twenty minutes later, after a great deal of jabbing, feinting, and blocking his approach by (gently) kicking his knee, I seem to be getting *worse*. Even with Javier coming at me slowly from well across the room in plain sight, my instincts are to flinch and run, not jab and swipe.

"There's no point!" I snap after managing to knock myself on the forehead with my own hairbrush. "I'd be better off dropping my knife and running for it."

Javier considers this. "You are pretty fast," he concedes. "But how far are you going to get in a fenced compound? I just need you to be able to hold off an attacker until I can help—"

There's no point, I want to scream. This is possibly my last night on earth. I don't want to spend it practicing knife-fighting!

"Again. Come on." Javier returns to his starting point, across the room, in front of the truly hideous drapes. "I'm going to keep coming at you until you fend me off, okay?"

I get in the stance he's shown me: chin slightly tucked, pink hairbrush firmly in hand, weight balanced, ready to go into a crouch. Punch for the throat. Jab at the eyes. Okay!

He crosses the room at half speed. I kick at his knee, jab toward his eye. He feints, his arms going around my waist. I put an arm around his neck, and then his mouth is on mine and we're on the scratchy duvet cover, pressed against each other.

Now *this* is how I want to spend my last night on earth.

I dig my fingers through his short hair and feel his muscled neck, his carved, stubbly jaw. His lips move to my throat, melting my brain. And then his hand slides up under my shirt, along my bare back, and his fingers wind around my neck, and all the heat in me drains away.

Why is he holding the back of my neck like that?

I twist my neck to get him to loosen his grip, but he doesn't seem to get the message, and the ridges on the back of his fingers swim before my mind's eye with terrible clarity, and I remember his words: *"I killed a guy with my bare hands."*

I push away from him, gasping, one arm straight out, elbow locked, like we're practicing self-defense again.

"What is it?" His voice is pained.

"I need to know about your one."

Javier rolls on his back, and the electricity fizzles out of the air. He crosses his long arm over his eyes. There's a long beat, filled only by the rattling swamp cooler in the corner.

"So all that stuff you said, about not wanting to know about rap sheets? About getting to know everybody as themselves? I guess that was B.S.?"

"Sometimes you say what you have to. Like when you called me a useless bitch."

"Jeez, Signal!" He sounds so stung. "Everything I said then was to keep you out of the compound! What happened to our clean slate?"

"Maybe clean slates are B.S. too," I say bluntly. "Maybe you can't clean a slate if you don't know what was on it in the first place. I don't even know what we're agreeing to not talk about!"

"Because I don't want you to know," he says softly. "I've done some seriously bad things, Signal."

"So *tell me about it*," I plead, though my pulse is racing at just these words. "What else do we have to do tonight? I think we can agree I have well and truly killed the mood."

He stares up at the ceiling, the face of a boy carrying the weariness of a man.

"I just wanted a new beginning," he says softly. "If only for a couple of days."

I'm acutely aware how these moments are slipping away. It's my fault, and I wish desperately I could go back to before I asked him about his victim, to the heat and magic of a few moments ago. But I can't.

I can only lie there, letting my unspoken refusal to accept so little from him hang in the air and condense into a silent anger.

"Okay. Well. It's late," I say dully. "I'm going to get ready for bed."

When I get out of the bathroom, Javier is in his pajamas, sitting primly on the side of my bed. I sit down next to him and give him a "*Well?*" look.

"Let me see your arm?" he asks quietly.

I let him take my hand, and he picks up the complimentary pen from beside the motel phone, turns my arm over and retraces the dandelion in black ink, then looks at me, something like an apology in his eyes.

"Can I hold you?" he asks.

I get under the duvet and he lies on top of it, curled up around me, his knees behind my knees, my back against his chest. Spooning, that's what this is called. What a stupid word for such an intimate gesture.

Finally he lifts his arm and pulls down his sleeve, tapping the figure of the boy on the inside of his forearm, which he holds out in front of me.

"You know that kid tattooed on my arm? That's my baby brother, Mateo. Loved machines, building stuff, taking it apart. He was smart the way Dennis is smart, but so emotional. I remember he cried when he was three and someone told him Spiderman didn't exist."

His quick, agonized chuckle makes me instinctually grip his arm.

"I had a friend named Ricky," he says at last, and the name comes out heavy, charged. "One of my best friends, till we got to high school. Then he got caught up with the Death Heads. So we kind of stopped hanging out—not like, I wasn't *angry* about it, it was kind of . . . his brother Ray had always been high up in the Death Heads, so he was always going to be part of that crowd. But it meant we were on two different tracks."

I nod in the darkness.

"But it's summer, so Ricky drops by one day and says, oh let's go to the corner store like old times, and Mateo wants to tag along. Except Ricky's wearing this black bandanna around his forehead. He's flagging for Death Heads—you know what flagging means?"

"Like . . . advertising he's one of them?"

"Right. Well, I didn't know, back then. I was such an idiot. It was just a black bandanna to me." He pauses, then forces himself on. "So we're walking along the street with Ricky, Mateo's asking me if I'll get him sour punch straws. And I was teasing like I wouldn't, but I always did . . ." His voice breaks off for a moment and I grip his hand. "But then this car slows, this red Mustang. I remember thinking, *these guys must know Ricky*, and that's when it happens, this huge bang. It was so loud. It's not like on TV, it's so much louder . . ."

No no no.

"They missed Ricky," he says simply. "Mateo was twelve."

I turn on my side to face him. "I'm sorry." How wholly inadequate. His hands slide up and cover his face for a moment and he just shakes. At last he comes up, with a sound like someone coming out of water for air.

"My dad? He's real tall, like I am? Built, just like, the strongest guy. But at the funeral? I had to . . . I had to lead him by the hand down the stairs. Like he was an old man." Javier's voice breaks, and I wait for him to go on.

"Two, three weeks go by, and nothing," Javier says, his voice low. "No arrests, no suspects, no witnesses. Everybody knew who did it, but nobody would give evidence. The shooters, you understand, they're with the Centro Street Gang, so nobody wants to get involved. Not even Ricky."

He's holding my hands now, so tight it hurts. I squeeze back.

"The day before the homecoming game, I get dragged to this house party, and *there's the same red Mustang*, parked right out front! I'm like, how many times did I describe this car to the police? And it's just parked right out front, in plain sight!" The frustration is still raw, his voice high and strained with disbelief.

"I walk in and there he is. There's the shooter. I recognize him *immediately*. It's the same guy who's been in my nightmares for weeks, when I see him it's like someone's punched me. This guy . . . he's drunk, fat, chatting up some girl, not a care in the world. Mateo is buried next to my grandmother, and this guy is just . . . walking around? It wasn't right. It wasn't right! My friends tried to stop me, but I go up to him and I say, you're the one. You're the one who killed Mateo Olivar."

He swallows.

"And this kid's like, 'Who?'"

Javier lets out a thin, joyless laugh.

"It's a blur after that. Something . . . just snapped. I was in football, I was a center my junior year, I was the strongest I'd ever been. After that first punch, I don't really remember anything. Not until the cops pulled me off him."

So this is why he doesn't regret it. He doesn't remember it. He lives my worst fear: he killed without even realizing it.

Javier lets out a long sigh. "The Death Heads claimed they ordered it, to make themselves look tough. Like: you shoot at us, you get your skull pushed in!"

I shudder at the image.

"So that's how I was charged, like it was a gang killing. Didn't matter that I was varsity football, honor roll, had stopped hanging out with Ricky the last three years . . . oh no, I was a *gang banger*. It wasn't till I got in prison—because they put me in adult prison, oh yes—it wasn't till I got in that I joined. To stay safe, I let the Death Heads put the tear by my eye. But I kept Mateo where I could always see him. So I can remember to try and be who he thought I was."

I lift his hand to my lips and kiss each one of his scarred knuckles.

"They scare you?" he says after a long moment. "The scars?"

"Not when I know where they come from," I tell him honestly. "Do you feel any better?"

"No, not really," he says bluntly. "Talking about this kind of thing . . . it doesn't . . . this pain is always going to be there. Whether I talk about it or not. Some things will never be right. No matter what you say about them."

I lay there, holding his hand, rubbing the back of it with my thumb.

"Tell me about Mateo?" I ask gently.

I carefully extract them: better and better memories, until I hear the smile come back to his voice. Once the smile is back the exhaustion creeps in, and our words start to trail off.

We wake up curled into each other like a figure eight, fingers entwined, him over the duvet and me under. He's already awake, staring at me.

"Morning," he says, voice gravelly from sleep.

I kiss him gently on the lips. (Carefully, because what if I have morning breath?)

"Thank you for telling me last night," I tell him honestly. "I'm sorry it hurt so much."

"Don't feel bad, gorgeous." He smiles, and it's a relief to see that smile again. "You know, I haven't slept that deeply in a long time. Maybe telling you is part of that." He tucks a strand of my hair behind my ear. "Or maybe it's just sleeping beside you." He leans to kiss me, just as the shrill bedside alarm goes off. We groan and force ourselves up and out to the car.

* * *

Stomach aching, hands clammy, mouth dry, I stare out at Ojai Valley as we crest the final hill before town and check my phone for the thousandth time.

Nothing from Dennis. No asterisks.

We pull into the Oak View Motel. Our room, for once, is inviting and smells delightful. I check my phone. It's half past one. No asterisks.

Javier's phone chimes. "Ray's on his way now. I might take a shower real quick before I meet him, unless you want in the bathroom?—"

"Javier?"

"Yeah?"

I walk over to him and throw my arms around his shoulders and he pulls me in even closer, his hands holding tight to strands of my hair, like I'm a balloon that might fly away. "It'll be okay, Signal. We're going to get you out of there safe tonight. I promise."

I lean back and scan his face: his large, gentle dark eyes; his sensitive, serious mouth.

"I'm not worried about tonight." It's the next ten minutes that really scare me. "I'm going to drive down the street to the store, okay?"

"Okay . . ." He can tell something is wrong. But so many things are wrong, that's perfectly normal, I guess. I float over to the door, looking over my shoulder one last time. He's about to disappear into the bathroom when something squeezes it out of me:

"Javier?!"

"Yeah?" He ducks his head past the door.

"Being your girlfriend is the best thing that's ever happened to me," I tell him. And without giving him time to respond, I shut the door and hurry to the car.

I left my phone in my backpack, along with my credit card. I just have the keys and my knife sheathed in the small of my back. Our route perimeter is limited to a mile around the motel, and a mile around the road to the Owl's Nest compound.

So if I drive over a mile down the road away from Ojai, I'll know if Dennis succeeded or not. Which presumably he has, since there's no asterisk. Of course, he could've not sent an asterisk because his mission went wrong. Or his phone isn't charged. Or he just plain forgot.

Or they figured out he was trying to hack into the kill switches and set his off first.

Stop being such a weakling. Do you want to free all your friends and get justice for Rose, or go into a cult compound tonight and watch Javier murder someone so you don't have to?

I pull out of the parking lot, gaining speed as I merge onto the rural, oak-lined street. I stay in the outside lane, so if I have to, I can veer off the road with my last conscious twitch and not endanger other drivers.

Stop it. Be brave.

When the balloon breaks, the helium escapes, and joins the air.

I cross the half-mile point and wonder what my mother is doing. Is she at her job, gray-faced and smiling, trying not to picture me in the cell where she thinks I am, forever?

I think of kissing Javier last night, the sweetness of it.

I picture Nobody in the desert with Dennis, dozing in the driver's seat of their parked van, head tilted to catch the sun on her perfect face. I picture Dennis in the back, watching a beeping point of light that represents my kill switch flying off course. Three quarters of a mile.

Kurt is off somewhere in sports gear, his heart still broken. And Jada and Erik in Portland. Just thinking his name hurts. *Why didn't I say goodbye to Erik?* Why didn't I do whatever it took? And this regret is what pierces through, a high note of pain above the low roar of despair, and knocks the tears out of me at last.

A sign looms up ahead, "Welcome to Meiners Oaks," and the last good feelings dissolve. All I have is the sound of my breath and the steering wheel in my hands. Did you do it, Dennis? Did it work? I step on the accelerator and my chest floods with fear.

Rose, if this is it, please come get me.

The sign shoots by, my heart throbs, and I am 1.1 miles off my route. I shout at the top of my lungs and punch the car's ceiling, and then shout again as I fly down the back road, crying and laughing like a maniac, pounding my steering wheel and yelling at the top of my lungs as I pull off onto the shoulder of the road.

"YEAH! *HELL YEAH!!*"

I get out of the car, shaking wildly as adrenaline cascades through my nervous system. I jump up and down, bang my fists on the hood and actually turn a cartwheel, enjoying the sharp pain as the gravel at the side of the road digs into my palms. Pain is a gift, just as much as my racing breath and the warmth of the sunlight; I am here for all of it. I catch the stunned expression on a driver of a passing pickup truck—he probably thinks I'm crazy. What's really crazy is that we aren't all dancing with joy every minute we're alive.

*   *   *

Oxnard is full of low bungalows and tall palm trees leaning in the breeze that rolls off the ocean. I find Jaw's duplex on a street of candy-colored houses, bleached pastel by relentless sun.

I knock three times on the door. Hard.

A seagull cries overhead as I wait, watching the palms sway like they're underwater. No answer. Two little girls cruise past on bikes, ringing their bells before turning the block's corner.

Go time.

I walk to the side of the duplex, slipping between two scraggly cypress trees and following a rough wood fence. Up on the second story of the duplex, past a white iron balcony rail, is a sliding door. Time to see if it's unlocked.

I grab the top of the wood fence, tuck the toe of my sneaker into a knothole and bounce upward, pulling myself to standing five feet off the ground, then throw myself toward the lip of the overhanging balcony. Thanks to the obstacle course, my practiced fingers hook and dig. I gain the railing, pull myself up and swing my leg over the rail like a cowboy mounting his horse.

The balcony door opens noiselessly under my hand and I step into the air-conditioning. There's a gentle clatter of vertical blinds as I step through, closing the door behind me, my senses on high alert as I listen for voices.

This must be Jaw's mom's room: there's a vanity covered with cosmetics and lingering perfume mixes with notes of new paint. As I move out into the hall I bump the bedroom door.

SKREEEEEEEE . . .

The hinges let loose a high-pitched, comically prolonged shriek that rings through the house. I freeze in place and listen.

Complete silence. Well then. The house is definitely empty.

With a sigh of relief, I spot a padlock on a door down the hallway. That's got to be Jaw's room. Thanks to a few hairpins from his mom's hairdresser, I get it open fairly quickly.

The smell hits me first, intimate and grimy like the bottom of a laundry pile. Though the hallway is bright and airy, Jaw's room is completely dark. Snapping on the lights reveals industrial-strength blackout curtains nailed around the windows. The walls are covered floor to ceiling with posters of black metal bands, turning the room into a dour patchwork of black, red, and purple.

I move quickly past Jaw's unmade bed to the rickety desk in the corner. It's dominated by an enormous gaming console next to a charging e-vape. I've tried three different passwords when the e-vape blinks on. I look down and freeze when I see the swirling image on its LED screen: a blinking purple pentagram.

The vertical blinds clatter across the hall, and my skin crawls. I must have left the sliding door open. It's probably just the wind. But I could have sworn I closed it?

SKREEEE . . .

Someone else is in the house.

Chapter Twenty-One

The Missing Piece

～

I press myself behind the door and take my knife from its sheath. I'm still listening for steps when a tall dark figure slips through the door, and I leap out with a cry, blade flashing.

"There she is!" He grins. "Nice knife!"

"Erik?!" And before I can stop myself, I'm hugging him as tight as I can. When I step back, he holds onto my arms and takes me in from head to toe as if to make sure I'm still in one piece. He looks pale, and there are dark circles under his eyes, like he hasn't slept in a while.

"You don't know how glad I am see you," I splutter. "How are you here right now?"

He blinks at me, then quickly turns his head away, scanning the room over my shoulder.

"We finished our target early. I was going to try and meet up with you and Jav after checking this place out." He turns back, eyes sharp and clear. "How are *you* here? How many miles are we from Ojai?"

"It's surprisingly close," I lie, not wanting to tell him about my kill switch yet, until I know if Dennis has freed us all. "You . . . finished . . . early?"

Erik shrugs, running a hand through his mop of stringy, dark gold hair. He looks like he hasn't had a shower in a while.

"Yeah. Our girl ran this dive bar in Portland that hosts all these bands. We went to a show and stayed until everybody else left. The weird thing is . . . she didn't like . . . fight us? We cornered her in this little backstage area, when she was unplugging all the tech. And then she pulled a gun on us. I thought that would be it. But then she just . . ." Erik puts two fingers in his mouth and lets his head fall back.

"*What?*"

"Yeah." He bites quickly at his nails, then shoves his hand in his pocket. "The shot was so loud we were sure someone heard, so we cleared out. Drove as far as our switches would let us, called 'MomandDad' and told them we needed to get further away. So they disarmed our switches for a few days."

A chill goes up my spine.

"I'm sorry," I tell Erik. "That must have been really disturbing."

"How are things going here?" he says quickly.

"I was only here for about five minutes before I heard the vertical blinds."

"Vertical blinds!" He shakes his head. "My Achilles' heel. And then that squeaky door!"

"We should start carrying WD-40 when we break and enter," I say seriously, and Erik lets out a little laugh, then scans the walls with a palpable shudder. He nods to the computer.

"Password protected?"

"Yeah. I have one more guess before it locks me out."

"Have you tried 'Sailor Moon'?" The side of his mouth twitches. "It doesn't matter, because he didn't do it." Erik taps the corner of one of the posters. "No one who puts Scotch tape on fresh paint has the foresight to stage a murder scene."

"Yes, he did," I insist. "Jaw got Rose into occultism. He has pentagrams on everything—" I hold up the e-vape triumphantly, then, in a flash of inspiration I try "pentagram" as the password. The error message comes up and I bang the keyboard. "It's locked me out!"

"Forget the computer. Are you looking at this room?" Erik sounds frustrated. "There's no . . ." he clutches at the air around him. "No *drive*. Nice Guys are driven to kill. It's a drive strong enough to split them into two different people. What drive do you see in Jaw? Besides maybe one day managing a head shop?" He kicks at some marijuana leaf pajama pants. "Also, I looked up that altar thing from Armchair.org on the way down. It was a Wiccan altar, and Wicca is basically Recycling the Religion. It doesn't require *human sacrifice*." Disapprovingly, he watches me rifle through Jaw's bedside table. "What exactly are you looking for?"

"Anything that links him to Rose." I pull open the bedside table drawer: glass pipes, a razor blade with black tar on the edge, a silver skull ring. Erik picks it up and frowns.

"Aside from dressing like the President of Halloween, Jaw seems like a pretty chill guy. He's fine with Rose dating Mike, he worships the Lord and the Lady, and keeps himself pretty sedated. What motive does he have to kill his hot secret girlfriend?"

"Who knows?" I take the ring and throw it back into the drawer. "Couples are weird that way. No one can really tell what goes on in a relationship except the two people in it."

"As a single person, I'd say *everyone* can tell what's going on in a relationship *except* the two people in it," he says meaningfully. "Different perspectives."

"Yeah. Well." I refuse to take the bait. "I remembered Jaw being inside the shed." I rummage through a low dresser, "And why Rose wanted me to meet him."

Erik's eyes are suddenly bright again. He looks so much like himself, I have to turn around and rifle through a bookcase to hide my relief.

"Well?" he presses.

"She wanted a picture of me and Jaw doing something. For the My Life thing."

"When did you remember this?!"

"At camp. When I had that nightmare." I run my hand along the tops of the stacked graphic novels, netting a few sticks of incense and a quarter.

"The nightmare that made you *wake up screaming?*" Erik's tone demands I turn and face him. "A picture of you and Jaw doing *what* exactly?"

"Kissing." I blush. But that's not the right word. "Well, I mean, I don't know how much kissing I was doing, I was mostly passed out."

"So Jaw assaulted you. Oh, okay." Erik tears his hand through his hair with a quick, suppressive gesture, then turns and kicks in an expensive-looking speaker near the door.

"Erik!"

"Whoops." He shrugs as the cone clatters off. "You were saying?"

"Rose asked him to," I say, and he starts excitedly biting his nails.

"It fits. *It fits.*" Erik's voice comes out half-strangled with excitement. "Signal, it's so obvious. Jaw was Mr. Moody. But Mr. Moody never killed Rose."

"Not that again." I heave the rat's nest of dirty clothes from beside the bed and lower myself to the carpet. I push myself as far as I can under the low wood bed frame, Erik's voice chasing after me.

"So what, you think Jaw met her at the shed, took her somewhere else, then brought her body back? The same Mr. Moody who won't even call Rose is crisscrossing the woods with a corpse in the middle of a kegger?"

"Maybe he didn't know about the party."

"Your high school's drug dealer didn't know about a big party in the woods? You're being purposefully obtuse, Signal."

Below the bed is a clear plastic bin, disappointingly full of shoes. I wrestle open a long cardboard box crammed beside a set of turntables, scraping my knuckles viciously in the process. Inside is an old skate deck, empty aquarium, and rock tumbler. I tear open a trash bag to find a worn sleeping bag that stinks of weed.

"She was killed in the shed," Erik insists. "They're drunk and high and doing an occult ritual. They're not going anywhere. But there's no evidence of a third party. So what does that tell you, Signal?"

The back of my head cracks against the wood frame, hard, as I back out from under the bed. I swallow a string of expletives before staggering over to Jaw's thin closet doors and throwing them open, Erik's voice right behind me.

"If you know Mr. Moody was in the shed too, then what does that tell you, Signal?"

Craning my neck, I scan the boxes on the shelves above Jaw's rack of dark clothes, the back of my head throbbing. There's a black cardboard box with a pentagram sticker on it.

"The only way to see the truth here is to strip away what you want to be true and face the facts, unpleasant though they may be," Erik continues. "But you won't. You can't. You keep turning away from the same key fact because it scares the hell out of you."

I reach for the black box, straining my arms as far as I can, teeth clenched against the pain in my head. My fingertips just brush the sides with me standing on tiptoe. Erik reaches over me, his chest brushing against my back, and lifts it easily from the shelf, setting it down on the floor. I fall to my knees and pull off the lid: it's just a bunch of old vinyl records.

"Signal. *Look at me.*" Erik sits on the corner of the bed, right across from me. A prickle creeps up the back of my neck.

"You're seriously trying that again?" I glare at him. "Trying to get into my head by 'proving' I killed Rose?"

He's about to retort something but swallows instead, hangs his head, then looks up at me with a wounded expression, eyes glistening like fresh scrapes. "Okay. Let's just play into your paranoid fantasies about me for a minute. Let's say *I am* trying to get into your head by proving you killed Rose. If you *know* you didn't kill her there's no way for that to work. I can't prove what isn't true." His face has never been more intent or more beautiful. "Don't you want the truth?"

Or am I afraid of it?

If everyone was somehow right, and I *did* kill Rose in some disassociated state, that guilt would destroy me. But walking around every day, half-believing it's true, that will destroy me too. If there is some buried memory of that night, don't I want him to find it?

"Yes," I tell him. "I do."

When he leans toward me, the corner of his mouth twisting, I flinch back a little. But it's the last twitch of prey in the shadow of its predator. Then I meet his eyes and all the noise in the world narrows down to Erik's deep voice.

"Signal, it's time to face some facts. Rose never left the shed. She died in front of you."

I start to object, but Erik goes on firmly:

"You remembered her drugging you. You remembered Jaw in the shed. You remembered her taking a picture of the two of you. If we had longer, you would remember her dying, too."

Rose's scream rings through my head, as it did in my nightmare. And part of me already knows that was a memory.

"But the next morning there was no evidence of anyone but the two of you in the shed. No picture of Jaw. No thermos. No drugs. So what does that tell you, Signal?"

Rose's scream, her kneeling before me. The red stripe across her neck and the burning smell. These were not dreams but memories.

"What does that tell you, Signal?"

I bow my head as it comes out:

"I'm a Class A, aren't I? Team Take." My voice breaks. "I would never consciously hurt Rose. But not all of me was conscious . . . Part of me was awake. And angry at her. And sick of being used. So when she had Jaw kiss me . . . that's what 'fits,' isn't it? After he left, that part of me took control. That's what you're saying, right?"

"No!" Erik reaches out and takes my hand: "Signal, I've known you didn't kill Rose from the moment I met you."

"How?" I say, tears streaming.

"Call it instinct. Or attention to detail. But I know it the same way I know you never had brothers or a serious boyfriend." Erik's jibe breaks me out of my daze. "Because you clearly have no idea how to search a guy's room."

And then he stands and flings the mattress off the bed, covers and all. In the corner, right under where he'd just been sitting, stuck between the slats and the frame, is a box wrapped in beige vinyl packing tape.

"Always start by looking under the mattress," he says, snapping it up, and then sits down cross-legged in the middle of the room across from me.

"The fact you keep avoiding, the fact there's no evidence of anyone but you and Rose at the murder scene, is actually what clears you, Signal.

If you were to consider it objectively." Erik scrapes at the packaging tape with his stubby, nonexistent fingernails. "This shed is the hookup spot of a vaping warlock. There should be *too much* evidence—of him and every girl who's ever been in there. Hair, nails, fibers, fingerprints, unspeakable forms of DNA—the backwash in that thermos alone, I shudder to think—"

The tape crunches into a wad and I hear the clink of a metal handle. Erik turns around the box to face me. It's a Transformers lunchbox.

"Erik."

He carefully opens the lid, and smiles. Then he pulls out a plastic Elvis and a plastic Marilyn. I reach out and take them with shaking hands.

"This proves it, don't you see?!" I whisper. "Jaw cleaned up the murder scene!"

"Whoa whoa whoa. We still haven't seen any evidence this kid knows how to clean. And whoever cleared that shed truly knew what they were doing. They fooled the cops, the defense, and a jury. If the crime scene had been an evidence drill? Absolute A+."

And then he takes out the Transformers thermos, and I can barely breathe.

Erik carefully unscrews the lid and turns it upside down. A small silver key and a steel-colored necklace slip onto the carpet. He picks up the necklace and holds it between us, a pentagram charm hanging from its ball chain.

"There it is," he says, as if he'd been wondering when it would turn up. "Jaw's necklace."

He takes my hand, then slowly lets the chain pool in the center of my palm, cold and surprisingly heavy. I look down at our hands holding it. My whole world was blown apart by a charm the size of a nickel.

"Let me just talk you through some thoughts. And if I don't convince you, hey, you still have the lunchbox. You can go see about making a case against Jaw."

"I'm listening."

"Since we started talking about your case, there's a contradiction that's always stood out to me." He leans forward, pulling his hair back from his face. "The crime scene is meticulously staged to frame you." He raises one trembling finger, nail bitten down to the quick. *"But you weren't supposed to be there.* Rose told you in the shed Mr. Moody didn't know you were coming. You were a surprise. How could Mr. Moody so perfectly set up someone who was never supposed to be there in the first place?"

Erik's eyes flash as he talks, his words crisp and sharp and a little too fast.

"So I thought, okay then, so what if Rose *hadn't* brought Signal? She and Jaw would have met in the shed. They would have shared a thermos that was spiked with something that could escape a forensic drug test. And, I'm willing to bet, Jaw would have woken up with Rose's head in his lap. So the killer had been to the shed and knew about the thermos. The killer had a reason to kill Rose and make Jaw suffer and *planned to do both*.

"I told you there were three questions we had to answer to solve this crime. Why was Rose so secretive about Mr. Moody? Why did she need to get you drunk? And who drugged the thermos? I have the answers, but I'm going to make a lot of leaps, so bear with me, it's just how my mind works."

"You see the angel in the marble and you need to set it free?"

"Exactly." His eyes, ringed with dark circles, burn in his pale face. "So first off, Rose brings you to the shed. She gives you a thermos, you do your best impression of a party girl and immediately pass out. Rose barely drank at all, because she had a goal for the night. Up until a few minutes ago, I didn't know what that was, but the picture fits. *It fits perfectly.*"

He smiles then, a smile of ecstatic satisfaction. "She needed you buzzed so she could get a picture of you and Jaw kissing. More on why later. The point is, when Jaw shows up, there's nothing left in the thermos for him and you're halfway to a coma. She gets the picture. Did you remember anything else after that in your dream?"

"I think they, um . . . made out after that."

Erik's eyes are focused on the wall behind me, as though he can see it playing out there in front of him like a silent movie. "The killer followed Jaw to the shed, where he was expected to split the thermos with Rose, and then *both of them* were supposed to pass out. But that's not what happened. When the killer comes in to stage the murder of Rose by Jaw, they're *wide awake*. And they've *seen the killer's face*. Time to recalculate! So our 'Nice Guy' demands that Jaw leave—"

"Wait, *what?*" I shake my head. "Why would Jaw agree to just leave?"

"Exactly what I asked myself. Jaw, moody warlock that he is, would only obey the killer if they had a high level of authority over Rose. The kind of authority where you can totally invade someone's privacy, tell them what to wear, forbid them from dating, and still take the moral high ground."

I shake my head, my gorge rising, refusing to follow where he's going. "Wait. Hold on. If Jaw saw the killer, why didn't he say something during the investigation?"

"Why put himself on the scene? He's the town drug dealer. Instead, he saw a chance to strike a deal with the killer: write me a check, and I'll get out of town. California is *not* a cheap state to live, and this is a nice place. What does Jaw's mom work as again?"

"Waitress."

He lets out a low laugh. "Yeah. Blackmail bought this house." He holds out the small key that slid out of the thermos. "This looks like the key to a safety deposit box. What do you bet that's where he's keeping his leverage? Evidence worth this kind of payoff might be enough to reopen your case."

If he's right, he's holding my freedom.

"The damning thing about the necklace was not that it was a pentagram, but *who it belonged to*. It was proof Jaw and Rose were together. That's why Rose needed a picture of Jaw kissing you—bad enough to get you drunk, bad enough to ask her secret boyfriend to kiss you right in front of her. She didn't need that photo for a project. She needed it to prove to the killer that *you* were with Jaw, and not her.

"Because the killer allowed Rose to date the pastor's closeted son, but sleeping with Jaw was a capital crime. The killer was locked into a sick dance of sexual suppression with Rose that had nothing to do with you. You got caught up in this mess, not because you're evil or crazy, but because Rose knew she could count on you, because you're the most stupidly selfless and kind person I've ever met." He rattles this last part off quickly, but so sincerely, his face a mixture of such sadness and anger, it catches me off guard.

"W-what?"

And then we both hear the front door lock turning, the door opening downstairs.

Erik shoves the key and the necklace into my hands, throws everything back into the lunch box and smoothly slides it under the bed.

"Go go go go go," he hisses in my ear.

There's the rustle of grocery bags downstairs and heavy footsteps as I shut the drawers of Jaw's desk, my hands trembling.

"C'mon," Erik whispers, and as I hurry ahead he hisses "Door!" but I've already done it:

SKREEEEEEEEEEEE

"Mom?" I hear Jaw call from the front. "You home?"

Erik pulls me into the bedroom, whipping open the sliding door, the blinds rattling like the plastic bones of a Halloween skeleton.

"Mom? Hello?"

"Don't go to the ground yet. Wait for him to get upstairs," Erik whispers as we throw our legs over the thin railing, and I nod. We cling side by side, clutching the bottom of the balcony floor, hanging off the side of the house, twelve feet above the narrow side yard.

"Did you mess with my lock?!" Jaw's voice echoes down the hall. Oh hell, I forgot to close the padlock. *"What the hell happened to my speaker?!"* he bellows.

"Now," Erik says calmly. We turn and drop down to the top of the wood fence, spider down to the pavement and run through the still, sun-bleached neighborhood to the car, fast as we can go.

Erik directs me up the block where he stashed his backpack, and then we're off with a screech in the green Volvo, all the windows down, the honey-colored afternoon sunlight so thick and warm it's like an animal presence.

"How did you even get down here without a car?" I ask Erik.

"Hopped a train in Portland. Did some hitchhiking. There's quite a network of voluntarily homeless youths in California. As your guy Angel Childs well knows." He looks at me, a strange hunger flickering over his face. "When is that going down?"

"Tonight."

"Fun stuff." Erik shakes his head in the stiff wind rolling in the window. He kicks back his seat and yawns, his heavily muscled arms twisting in either direction, so close his hand nearly grazes my cheek. "So," he says drowsily, "are you going back to help Javier, or just heading out into the sunset, now your kill switch is off?"

He's lucky I don't drive off the road.

"How did you know my kill switch was turned off?!"

"Dennis told me."

"I can't believe it!" I gasp, outraged. "When would he have even—"

"Before we left, he told me to visit the old Skullsex.com. It redirected to some weird proxy message board. We've been keeping up. So he did it? Turned off your switch?"

I nod, gripping the wheel.

"So now what?"

"Well, the plan was for Dennis to turn off everyone else's kill switch too, which I'm hoping he has. Once I know that, I'll tell Javier we don't have to do the mission, and then—"

"Then you'll *both* ride off into the sunset." He stares at me. "After risking your neck for him with your little kill switch plan. I can't believe he didn't make any effort to stop you."

"He didn't know. I told Dennis not to tell him."

"And why's that?" Erik's voice perks up.

"I was afraid he'd stop me."

"So, he's controlling? He doesn't respect your autonomy?"

"No! No, that's not it at all! He just cares about me too much."

Erik laughs, and I know he's rolling his eyes. "Oh right. Tender-hearted Javier. The man who feels too much. Did he ever get around to describing how he caved that one guy's head in?"

"Yes, as a matter of fact, he did," I snap. "He told me all about it."

"And?"

"It sounded like a one-off psychotic break brought on by overwhelming circumstances."

"Whoa ho ho, are you excusing the murder of a *fellow human being?*" Erik tsk-tsks. "Someone's been a bad influence on you, Signal."

"Javier's *not* a bad influence," I say. "As a matter of fact, he's bent over backwards to keep me from having to kill someone. He's doing everything he can to protect my innocence."

I regret my wording instantly. Erik lets out a whistle.

"Wow. Wait, hold on, so you're like, *proud* he sees you as utterly useless?"

For a few moments I follow the twisting roads toward Ojai before collecting myself enough to answer him.

"I'm not useless just because I don't want to *kill people.* There's different ways to be useful."

"Not in this situation," Erik says savagely. "And if Sir Javier wants to be your perfect white knight so bad, why didn't he just tell the Director he'd do it alone?"

"He *did,*" I shoot back. "He risked getting his kill switch set off! He has a kind of strength you don't value, Erik. The kind of strength that doesn't come from hurting people. It comes from *helping them.*"

Erik seethes in the seat beside me, his head turning completely to the window, and the minutes trickle by in tense silence.

How did this happen? How did we start fighting again, when we'd been so close back in Jaw's room? How can Erik be so helpful and brilliant one minute, and then so insulting and horrible the next? Why can't I control myself when he needles me like this? Why do I feel the need to justify myself to him?

I pull in beside the motel and cut the engine, but I don't make any motion to get out of the car. Instead I turn to him, taking a deep breath.

"Erik. I'm sorry. I don't want to fight with you, okay?"

He's still turned away, staring out the window. I soldier on with my planned statement, knowing full well any minute he'll burst out in his cutting laugh.

"What you did back there was brilliant. *You're* brilliant." I swallow hard. "And I . . . I'm glad I know you, okay? I'm *grateful* to have you as my friend. So if we're all going to be free now, I hope . . . I hope you *stay* my friend."

"We won't be seeing each other again." His voice is matter-of-fact.

". . . No?"

"Your mystery is solved." He doesn't turn from the window. "What else do we even have to talk about?"

It takes me a moment to find an answer. "I'd talk to you about anything, Erik." I take his hand, trying to get him to engage with me. His fingers are loose in mine. "I hope you know that."

"Cool, thanks." He leans his head back on the chair seat, exposing the muscular line of his throat. "But when all our kill switches go offline at once, I suspect our Director is going to get busy finding us. Keeping in touch would just help him do it faster."

My eyes are going all hot and itchy, which means I'm about to cry.

"So yeah, this is the last time we'll see each other."

I turn my head away as tears blur my vision.

"Heartbreaking, I know," he goes on sarcastically. "Seeing as we barely know each other anyway." Embarrassed, I pull my hand away. But his fingers tighten, and he pulls it back, pulls it so my hand hovers just a hair from his heart. The gesture is so small, but it makes the air go still around us.

"At least we got to say goodbye this time." He turns to me, all sarcasm gone.

"I miss you," I confess, tears spilling over. "I miss you every day."

Erik is momentarily at a loss for words, then he says, stunned: "Are you CRYING?! Signal, *I'm kidding*. I'm just kidding!"

And now I'm sloppy sobbing.

"Signal! Signal! Don't cry! It was just a joke! I'm kidding! You think you could lose me that easy? We still have to make sure your name gets cleared, okay? I was just giving you a hard time, I didn't think you'd CRY!" And then, delightedly: "*Why* are you crying, Signal?"

And he starts to laugh, an infuriating, surprised laugh, like he's just won some impossible bet he thought he'd already lost. I'm not sure what I'm doing as I curl into him, twisting his collar and cursing passionately, but his green eyes are fixed on my mouth, and when they rise to mine I cannot look away.

Then Erik reaches up and tilts my face toward his, so carefully, so gently, as though I'm precious, as though he's wanted to touch me for a very long time. And it's the unexpected gentleness that does it, that makes me reach up and bury my fingers in his hair as he closes the space between us and covers my mouth with his.

At the moment of contact a physical rush seizes my entire body, an awareness so intense it's almost panic. Most of my life I've been a head and a pair of hands, only remembering the other parts of myself when they hurt. But kissing Erik, I am the heart of an infinite universe of sensation: I'm the curved shoulder his hand has found, I am the soft skin inside my wrist as it drags against his back, I am the cheek his eyelash brushes, I am the thrashing heart and the repeating thought: *I can't believe this is happening, this cannot happen.* And I have never, not even once, felt so completely alive.

Erik pulls away, his smile dizzily bobbing in my vision like I'm somehow drunk, lost in the landscape of his face this close, and says with certainty:

"We aren't friends, Signal. Friends don't make each other feel like that."

I blink for a moment, speechless, and then I see Javier behind him, standing outside the car, phone to his ear, staring in at us.

Chapter Twenty-Two

Into the Night

～

I fling the car door open.

"Javier!"

He puts his hand up, his eyes not meeting mine.

"Okay, she just woke up—" He covers the phone with his hand. "It's the Director. I told him you've been napping for the last couple hours." He holds out the phone to me, his face inscrutable.

Erik, getting out of the car, shakes his head at me. "Don't talk to him!"

But I take the phone, pulse rising, stomach sour. I can't turn Javier into a liar, not until I know if Dennis has deactivated his kill switch. Besides, why not talk to the Director? What can he do to me now? Nothing. Right?

"Hello?" I say into the phone.

"Signal. Your kill switch briefly went off the grid. We've determined Dennis tampered with it. As a result, he has been eliminated."

My knees buckle and I sink to the curb, my hand over my mouth.

"I am calling to let you know that your kill switch is once again traceable. We can follow your movements currently, and full function will be restored within a few hours." The Director lets this sink in. "If you desert your route within that time and abandon your mission, your kill switch won't go off. But Javier's will."

My vision swims as I stare up at Javier, glowering at Erik. Erik is smiling at him triumphantly.

"... You wouldn't."

"Try me."

The call cuts off, and I lean my head on my fists, my whole body turned to lead.

"What did he say?"

"It's Dennis. They killed Dennis. They killed him and it's my fault."

A stunned beat, then Erik shakes his head. "No. No no no. There's no way. He's too valuable. Maybe I can still get in touch with him." He holds out his hand. "I need to borrow your car. Just for an hour, so I can go find him online. I *promise you*, Signal, he's alive!"

"What the hell are you even doing here?" Javier yells at Erik.

Erik ignores Javier and focuses on me. "I know how to reach him, Signal. There's still a chance he could be free."

With a guilty look at Javier, I hand Erik the keys. "We need it back by dark."

"I'll have it back," Erik promises, his eyes darting between me and Javier as he opens the driver's side door. "Maybe use that time to, uh, have a little talk?"

Javier turns to me as the car pulls away. I wait for him to say something, anything, horribly conscious that my lips are swollen, almost bruised by the kiss he just witnessed.

"Before you ran out on me," Javier says, his chin high, his neck tensed, "you said being my girlfriend was the best thing that ever happened to you, correct?!"

"Can I just try and explain—"

"There's nothing to explain." Javier shakes his head. "You're a cheater and a liar. Got it. Great."

"Javier, come on!"

"It kills me that I was so wrong about you." He turns and strides back up the path to our motel bungalow. I chase him back into our room, then freeze in my tracks.

Who the hell is this dude?

A tall, muscled man leans next to the window. He has a short beard, a black bandanna tied around his bald head, and a tear tattoo beside his eye just like Javier's.

"Ray, this is Jenny. Jenny, this is Ray," Javier says in clipped tones.

Oh right. The leader of the Death Heads.

"The famous Jenny!" Ray says, voice low and even. "This one's been praising you all day. You got him pretty whipped."

"Right." I clear my throat nervously. "Javier, can I just talk to you outside for like five minutes?"

"We need to focus on this right now," Javier says coolly. "They're expecting us over at Owl's Nest for dinner."

"Six o'clock," Ray adds. "We should head over pretty soon."

My stomach flips over. "My friend borrowed our car—"

"Can't use it anyway, they don't let strange cars in the compound. No outside phones come in either. I rode my bike up here. My buddy rode another bike up for you two to take." He looks at me, not smiling, just assessing. "We gotta keep our eye on this one, Javi," he says at last. "She's just Angel's type."

"That's the idea. We need her to bat her lashes at Angel, get him alone, get him to make a move so I can take him out. Think you can handle that, 'Jenny'?" Javier's face is stiff. "Think you can trick a guy into believing you're into him, so someone else can come put a knife in his back?" He tilts his head back. "Yeah, I bet you can handle that all right."

"*Javier,*" I say through clenched teeth. "Do you even care what this afternoon has been like for me?"

"Do you even care what this afternoon been like for *me?!*" Javier yells, his scarred fist landing so hard on the oak dresser beside him that a framed picture jumps forward and falls flat. "I spent the last hour telling the Director that you were right in front of me, asleep! I didn't even know what I was covering you for! I didn't know if you'd run away or if you were lying dead in a ditch! And then you finally come back *with Erik?!*" His mouth contracts, like it makes him sick just to say the name. "The same guy I've had to watch you flirt with every day—"

"Flirt with Erik?!" I sputter. "I *never* flirted with Erik!—"

"That's why you were kissing him, right?"

"*Enough!*" Ray barks.

He takes two strides over to Javier and grabs his ear, forcing him to lock eyes. "Tonight is no joke. We're about to go into a fortress. God knows I owe you, but I'm not taking you in there unless you go in like a soldier." He looks at me, hard. "Both of you: soldiers. Angel is *crazy*, you get it? I'm talking mad-dog insane. And so is his little hippy army. So you settle this stupid high school drama, or I call this whole thing off right now."

"Got it," Javier breathes, his hands still in fists.

"Good." Ray glares at me again. "We ride in fifteen. I'll be out front when you two grow up." He strides outside, shaking his head, slamming the door behind him.

Javier opens his backpack and pulls out a change of clothes, turning his back on me.

"So where were you anyway?" he says at last.

"I was investigating Rose's murderer. And to do that, I had to get Dennis to turn off my kill switch."

Javier turns around, his face stricken. "You *what?! He did what?!*"

"He turned it off, remotely. But they caught him hacking it, and now he's . . . he might be dead because of me." He might. There's still a chance he might be alive. I have to believe Erik is right: they can't kill Dennis. *They can't.*

A vein flutters wildly in Javier's throat. "Why didn't you tell me?!"

"I didn't know if it would work."

"And if it didn't, then what? You'd have been killed? Like Troy?!" The panic is hitting him after the fact, hard. "Why didn't you tell me?"

"I thought you'd try to stop me."

"Hell yes, I would've stopped you! Someone should have stopped you! I can't believe Dennis went along with it!"

"We thought if it worked, he could disable everyone's kill switch."

"Signal . . . ," Javier sighs. *"You should have told me."*

I wrestle clothes out of my backpack, not answering him.

"So what, you told Erik to meet you there?" Javier asks, pulling off his own shirt.

"No, he just knew about this guy, and wanted to help me figure out what happened to Rose. And because of him, I think I finally know. And that's . . ." My voice breaks and I have to clear my throat. "That's the most important thing for me, okay? Figuring out what happened to Rose. Don't you understand, to finally know what happened, what that means? I was so grateful—"

"So grateful you let him kiss you?"

"No! No, it had nothing to do with being *grateful*. We fought the whole drive back, but when he said goodbye, I thought I wasn't going to see him again and . . . I don't know, we kissed! I don't know what else to say."

Javier stands in front of me, his expression soft. His bare chest is carved out of the pink dying light of late afternoon, his shirt clutched in one scarred hand. I can actually see him shake a little, like his heart is beating that hard. I have hurt him so terribly and all he has ever done is protect me. I reach out, wanting to comfort him, but he grabs my wrists to prevent me.

"This isn't just about you making out with Erik, Signal—though, trust me, it's burned into my head for life," he says furiously. "It's also the fact that you didn't tell me what was going on with you. I told you *everything*, and you still held this back from me?"

"I'm sorry." I mean it. "But I knew you'd try to stop me."

"So what, you'd rather be with someone who doesn't care what happens to you?" He stares down at me, restraining me from holding him and yet still keeping me close. "You think *Erik* cares about you?"

His expression is almost pitying as he releases me.

"We should finish getting dressed." He turns away. "We'll talk about it on the ride back."

As if there's any chance of getting a ride back.

* * *

Standing in the small shower under the hot water, I watch the line of my dandelion fading, though I try to keep it out of the stream. I inhale the smell of the soap, the steam from the water, trying to anchor myself to the present instead of going crazy with fear.

How have I managed to mess everything up so badly? Dennis could be dead and we're next. Javier hates me now, I have no idea where Erik is, and I'm crying in the shower in what is possibly the last hour of my life. All this time I've feared an instantaneous death triggered by my kill switch. This afternoon, for a few brief hours I thought I'd escaped that dread. I'd seen years stretching ahead of me, a future as blank as a check. Now we're back on course for certain death—the target's, or our own.

I'd comforted myself when we looked at the maps of the compound that I'd never have to actually go in. That if I died trying to escape, at least I wouldn't have to go into the compound of a murderous cult, to do the unthinkable.

And now I'm on the floor of the shower, rocking back and forth, and the moaning I hear is my own, echoing up the tiles. If I could just cling to this moment, if I could stay in it a little bit longer and hide from the future. But the water drains, and Javier knocks on the bathroom door, and the future has come for me.

Shaking, I pull on high-waisted jean shorts and slim plimsolls, then position my knife sheath along the inside of my belt, tucking it into my shorts and pulling a tight tank top over to cinch it closer. I choose a loose blue cotton peasant blouse to help conceal the bulge at the small of my back. I line my eyes the way Jada showed me, stain and gloss my lips, pull my fingers through my dyed bronze hair, and practice looking normal in the mirror. But all I see in the mirror is fear.

I step out into the living room and Javier's eyes flicker at the sight of me.

"He'll want to talk to you, all right," he says coldly. And then it's time to go.

* * *

"We're going to keep this simple," Ray says before he gets on his bike, standing out in front of the motel. "I'll ask the girls if you two can crash there tonight. Angel will come by to check you out. At some point during dinner, I'll go walk one of the bikes to the back fence for you guys, and unlock it from the inside. I'll come back in to say goodbye so you know that's all set, then act like I'm taking off. But instead I'll loop around and wait for you two to come through.

"That's all I need to know, and that's all I want to hear," Ray says, stomping out the tail end of a cigarillo.

"Thank you," Javier says, and he turns to me. "When you get the chance to talk to Angel, try and get him alone and keep him with you. I'll be watching. As soon as you get him away from the main crowd, I'll come find you. I should only be a few minutes. After," he swallows quickly, "we hide his body as best we can. Then we go to the back fence and get the hell out of there."

I nod as confidently as I can. "Seems straightforward to me."

"Everything depends on you getting him alone."

I nod again, dully. Dread collects in the pit of my stomach like a knot of cold, slithering snakes.

"All right." Ray mounts his bike. "We seriously need to go."

Javier gets on the bike, and I clamber up behind him, and we're off.

The sun is setting as our bikes climb up the winding hill toward the Owl's Nest compound. A wood rail fence runs alongside us, but otherwise the only thing for miles are rolling gold hills, with clusters of black, bent-sideways trees, trailing shadows of violet.

Ray turns at an old billboard with "CIDER" printed on it in rust-red block letters, his bike disappearing down the sloping hillside, and Javier follows after him. The sycamore trees close around the single lane, their upraised branches the color of bleached bones.

The red of Ray's taillight glows brighter. I watch it over Javier's shoulder to keep my nerves calm as we take the long switchbacks, veering left and right, left and right, winding along curves that leave me almost seasick. The asphalt goes from smooth to rough and patchy as we hit dirt roads, gritty blue clouds blooming from Ray's back tire. The trees flatten into one dark shape, one endless void we're flying into.

And at last, straight ahead, there's a rusted-out car in front of a tall wood fence, silhouetted by a motion light. Pasted on the fence are about a thousand glow-in-the-dark star stickers, and a handwritten sign that reads:

PRIVATE PROPERTY
TRESPASSERS WILL BE SHOT

Ray's motorcycle slows to a stop. Javier's engine rumbles and chokes as he cuts it, hanging back as Ray waves at the car.

"Ray! Hey, man!"

"We didn't miss dinner, did we?"

"Nah, they're just getting started." A lanky barefoot kid unfolds himself from the passenger seat, a cloud of weed following him out of the car as he flicks on a walkie-talkie. Another motion light snaps on above us, illuminating the other side of the tall wood fence.

"Three guests for dinner. Ray and uh . . ." He looks up at me.

"Hector and Jenny," Ray says gruffly.

"Hey Hector, hey Jenny. I'm Cygnus." He holds out an empty coffee can. "I'll take your phones, thanks," he says pleasantly.

Ray shakes his head. "I told 'em no phones."

"That's easy, then," Cygnus says, eyes swooping over us. I'm so sure he'll pat us down I almost step back. But instead he speaks quietly into his walkie-talkie, which beeps in response.

Then comes a heavy creak of the metal fence. It cracks open and two girls step out into the road. "Ray! Long time no see!" A girl with long dark hair and a threadbare yellow sundress throws her arm around him, but she's scanning me and Javier with cool wariness. "These are the guests you wanted to bring to dinner? Nice to meet you both! I'm Compass."

"I'm Starbrite, and I'm a *hugger*," the other, in a long blue sundress says; she hugs me like we're long-lost sisters. Her hands graze just inches above my sheathed knife. She smells like hay and something earthy I don't quite recognize.

"We should head up to the Big Sky Barn." Compass brings her hands together under her chin. "Dinner is supposed to start soon. Cygnus, we'll bring you down a plate after, okay?"

Cygnus gives her a thumbs-up, folding himself back into the smoky car.

We follow them into the compound, the fence closing heavily behind us.

"Watch for crossing chickens!" Compass laughs, then points out where the guys can park the bikes, alongside a row of VW vans. The motion lights pinned up in the trees cast strange shadows on the dirt path that winds up the lawn. The trees are all strung with clothesline, from which hang not just drying clothes but bundles of herbs and flowers, knotted ribbons, and shell wind chimes. It makes a sort of web around the path that shields our surroundings from direct view.

"What's for dinner?" Ray asks.

"We've been bringing in our vegetable harvest this last week. It's incredible this year." Compass plucks a dried flower from one of the clotheslines and tucks it behind Javier's ear, then turns to me, smiling. "So you two are road-tripping?"

"Yeah. On our way to San Francisco."

"Taking me to meet the family," Javier adds.

"Oh, so you're college students!" Starbrite grins at me. "What school? What are you studying?"

"USC. I'm an English major," I lie quickly.

"That was my major too!" She grins at me, her lanky tan arm threading through mine. She's so close I can see the brush strokes of the teeny-tiny gold triangles painted on her forehead and neck and around her bright blue eyes. Compass has them too, like they've been doodling on themselves with a gold paint pen.

"Cool!" I stutter. "But now you're not in school?"

"Nope! I'm a dropout." She rolls her eyes and chuckles. "I gave up classes and trying for some corporate career to live the simple life. I want to do chores on a farm with my friends instead."

"Sounds fun?" I manage.

"It *is*," she says earnestly. "It's the most fun I've ever had. Didn't you feel a sense of relief and lightness just walking through the fence?"

"Uh . . ."

I'm thankful Ray's voice cuts through our conversation. "Angel will be at dinner, right? These two need a place to crash. I wanted to ask him if that'd be cool."

"Oh, of course, of course." Compass nods serenely. "He likes for us all to eat as a family. Everyone stops their chores, no matter how much work they have left to do, and comes together for dinner." She gestures toward the huge, old-fashioned red barn a hundred feet ahead of us, its first-story windows glowing orange.

Smiling girls dressed like Compass and Starbrite carry platters of food, jugs of water, or sheaves of flowers toward the barn.

"Compass! There you are—" A girl hurries over.

"You be copilot for a second?" Compass calls to Starbrite, who nods seriously.

"Copilot?" Ray asks.

"All first-time visitors need a copilot while they're here," Starbrite says, moving slightly in front of us so we can't go farther up the path.

"That's new." Ray lights up his cigarillo.

"Don't think you're not welcome! We *love* visitors." Starbrite bites her lip. "It's just been necessary the last few months. We're trying to put in some root cellars ahead of winter so we're digging pits, and not everybody is great about roping those areas off."

Compass jogs back to us, several giggling girls waving at us as they stream in through the open double doors. "*Sorry* about that. We've been trying to make our own bandages and everybody's digging, so it's blisters, blisters, blisters, and we're running out!" She laughs, wearily.

"No kidding," Javier says. "How many people live here?"

"About a hundred," Compass says proudly.

Our information had said fifty. Javier and I trade a nervous glance, then join the crowd streaming into the barn.

Inside is quite pretty, like an extremely rustic, DIY wedding reception. There's one low, continuous table made from old doors laid flat on stacks of bricks and cement blocks. It's set up in a giant U-shape that encircles the room, snaking around the tall wooden support beams of the barn, laden with mismatched china and silverware. There's lots of glass milk bottles stuffed with wildflowers, and the air is heavy with the heat-ripened scent of the petals. But there's another smell I can't quite identify, earthier, almost animal. Rancid. The hay at our feet is matted and unclean. The glass of the oil lamps that hang from the beams is the color of popcorn butter. Are they burning grease?

The girls add to the wedding reception vibe with their long, flowing hair, ankle-length vintage dresses, and blissed-out smiles. But much like the barn, behind the initial impression of loveliness is an underlying filth. They're all bones-jutting-out thin and some degree of sunburnt, their hands covered in blood-filled blisters and split nails.

As we walk in through the wide-open barn doors, they all turn to us, eyes wide, and start rubbing their palms together in a circular motion. This makes a soft whispering sound not unlike light, falling rain. Then they start chanting something, softly, all in unison, words I can't understand.

I'm stunned until Starbrite takes my shoulder and forcefully spins me around to face the small, muscled figure walking just behind us.

This is the person they're *actually* welcoming: Angel Childs.

He's been walking behind us, *right behind me*, and I didn't even realize it.

The chant grows louder as he walks to the middle of the room, a broad smile on his tan face, and the chant rises to meet him: "Heaven is coming! Heaven is coming!"

Chapter
Twenty-Three

The Target

❧

Angel reaches out his arms as far as he can.

"HEAVEN IS COMING! HEAVEN IS COMING!"

His arms are heavily muscled under his thin linen shirt, his feet bare, and he wears worn buckskin pants that are fringed along the sides.

The invisible rain is louder. It sounds like a storm is trapped in the barn with us, because of all the people now clapping and snapping and rubbing their hands.

"HEAVEN IS COMING! HEAVEN IS COMING!"

Angel lets his head fall back, like he's overcome. The cheering is deafening, the smiling faces around me dotted with pinpricks of sweat, possessed with joy.

And then the noise stops as Angel brings his fists into his chest, and the barn falls eerily quiet, quieter than a crowd this big should ever be.

In the jarring silence, Angel strides over to the wall where a pristine high-end guitar is leaning in a chrome stand, throws the embroidered strap over his shoulder, and breaks into the first bars of One Direction's "You Don't Know You're Beautiful."

There's knowing laughter, distant whistles, and appreciative snaps as Angel picks his way through the crowd, girls darting up to hand him flowers or kiss him shyly on the cheek.

"We don't start eating until Angel does," Compass whispers as she pulls us down to the ground beside the table. Not that I'd want to:

balanced on a bamboo bowl in front of me is a full rack of charred, mangled ribs. I've never seen meat butchered like this, the rib cage left almost intact, the bones hacked unevenly and the meat half raw, half charred, from being cooked on open flames.

Angel makes his way through the crowd to the large wicker peacock chair presiding over the table, the only chair in the room. He leans down and picks up a wheat roll off the top of a pile, takes a bite and hands the rest to the girl at his feet. Immediately hands swarm the tables, the other girls finally allowing themselves to eat. The girls' faces, turned away from Angel and to the business of splitting up the food, become intensely focused and stern.

"Okay, let's go say hi!" Starbrite says. We follow her through the feeding crowd.

Angel sits noodling on his guitar, his bare feet crossed at the ankles, their soles black and calloused. At our approach he looks up and calls out, loud enough to draw the attention of the room: "Starbrite! You feeling it?"

"You know it!" she cries back.

"*What* do you feel?"

"Well, if you want to know, I feel like . . ." She smiles at the room. ". . . Like I'm glowing!"

"I see it." Angel nods. "Don't you all see it? How she's *glowing?*"

Scattered whistles and claps from the crowd seated on the floor.

"That glowing when you *know* you belong in Heaven!" He points upward. "All my Stars have fallen here from Heaven. And Heaven wants you all back, desperately."

Starbrite's hand pulls me down beside her to the ground, to squat in the matted hay with the others. Compass is doing the same with Javier and Ray, behind us. I lean in toward her.

"Aren't we going to say hi?"

"Shhh. Angel's teaching," she whispers back, her words clipped.

"But Heaven can't have you yet!" Angel booms. "Earth is a lesson some of us still have to learn. Though, as we all know, we're way off the curriculum. Yeah, this classroom has fallen into the hands of some bad teachers, hasn't it?"

There are scattered groans of agreement.

"Ray here looks surprised," Angel chuckles. "You never heard me teach before, have you, brother?"

Ray shakes his head.

"I promise, I'm not high right now," Angel says, and all the girls laugh. "I'm lower, actually, than I've ever been." He winks, and points skyward, and they cheer.

"I got some stuff in my bag for you, Angel," Ray calls, jerking his thumb back down the path.

"Get what you need, brother!" Angel smiles and goes back to strumming. Ray slips away without an escort. Relief washes over me, we've gotten to the first step as planned: Ray can go move the bikes.

Now all I have to do is get Angel alone.

Almost as I'm thinking this, Angel's eyes connect with mine. He puts out a finger and crooks it.

"He wants to say hi," Starbrite practically chokes and pulls me and Javier to our feet.

"Just the little stranger girl," Angel adds in the same light, friendly tone. Compass's arm flashes up and grabs Javier's hand, gently but unmistakably restraining him.

Starbrite whispers in my ear, her voice trembling: "Go on. He's *asked* for you."

I walk toward Angel Childs, his hand reaching for mine over the table where his emaciated followers are wolfing down food. His grip is hard, but his hands are smooth, the nails clean and even.

"You here for some teaching?" he asks.

"I don't know, um . . . it sounds a little over my head," I say diplomatically.

"You mean it sounds like a bunch of bull crap." He laughs, a sharp, shrewd look in his eyes that catches me off guard. "That's okay. Probably took a while for you to learn reading, writing, and 'rithmetic too. Only way to find out what I'm really teaching is to learn it! So. Why're you here, little girl?"

"My boyfriend and I were hoping to crash here tonight. We'd heard Owl's Nest was like, um, kind of a scene?" I stammer.

He nods. "That it is, and we'd love to have you . . . long as you don't spend all night telling us we'd be better off at the old college thought factory, USC girl!"

He waits for me to react—whether to the fact he was eavesdropping or just his opinions on getting a degree, I don't know.

"Well, I mean . . . nothing wrong with getting an education, right?"

"Learning's the most important thing in the world." He nods seriously. "But school's no good for learning anymore, and that's a fact. You want to learn something, little girl?"

". . . Okay."

"Then why don't you come sit by me." Angel brushes idly at the hair of the girl sitting on the ground closest to his feet. "Lightbeam, sweetheart, where's that old piany stool?"

Lightbeam hops up to fetch it, and then Angel, with a courtly flourish, gestures for me to take his seat. It's surreal that I've progressed this fast. The surrounding girls can't seem to believe it either; they openly gawk as I step over the low table and perch on the rough wicker edge of Angel's throne. Urgent whispering spreads through the crowd, and Javier's eyes connect with mine.

He nods slightly: *so far so good.*

"That your boyfriend?" Angel's voice cuts in as he settles onto a tall piano stool beside me.

"Yeah. Are these your girlfriends?" I indicate the crowded barn.

"What? No, no, no. You got that one all wrong. This is my *Constellation.*" Angel grins. "All of us burning with our own unique fire. But only when we're together can our meaning be seen."

I force what I hope sounds like sincerity into my voice: "That's really beautiful. So you believe everyone is like, a star?"

"Not *everyone,*" Lightbeam interjects from below us. "What we have been raised to call stars are actually *angels,* looking down on us."

"Easy now!" Angel cuts her off. "Let's get to know her a little, huh?" He rests his chin on his hand and looks deep in my eyes. "You're a USC girl, huh? Funny, you don't seem stuck up like most rich girls. How'd you run into Ray?"

"H-Hector and Ray are friends," I say, remembering Javier's fake name just in time. Speaking of Ray, why isn't he back yet from putting up the bikes?

"And where'd you meet Hector?" Angel glances at Javier again, eyes twinkling.

"School."

Angel's focus shifts back to me, his face tense. "Is that a fact?"

He holds my gaze for an uncomfortably long time, like we're in a staring contest. I suppress a nervous urge to laugh.

"So you want to stay with us for a while, little girl?"

"Yeah, I mean, if it's okay, we'd like to crash for the night."

"No hotel with daddy's credit card?"

"Hotels are so . . ." I swallow, my throat dry. "Sterile."

He nods, seriously, as though cleanliness is a real bummer. "Compass?" he calls.

"Yes?" she says eagerly, sitting up straight.

"Would you get Hector all set up in the guest house?" He smiles at her, then turns to me, his voice dropping. "We're a little full up in the barn at the moment, so Hector might have to sleep with some of the angels in the guest house tonight. I hope you don't mind."

The girls down on the floor around Javier are introducing themselves, throwing their arms around him in a series of quick hugs and tucking flowers into his hair.

"Whatever works. It's your place."

Compass gets up and after another moment Javier stands, staring at me with obvious concern; he doesn't want to leave. I don't want him to either. But I have to get Angel alone, and right now things seem headed in that direction.

I nod to Javier: *I'm fine, I promise.*

He slowly turns and takes Compass's outstretched hand, and the two of them move through the seated crowd toward the wide-open barn doors and the dark night beyond.

Then, just at the threshold, Javier turns and calls back to me: "You'll be okay?"

Angel answers for me: "She's never been more okay! Isn't that right, uh . . . what's your name?" Angel laughs, one of his hands resting heavily on my shoulder.

"Jenny."

"That's not your name." Angel smiles, and my throat goes dry. "Come on, now. You know that's not your name."

Does he know!? How would he know?!

"Ce-les-tial." He draws out the word. "That's your name." He leans toward me until his forehead touches mine, his hand moving to the nape of my neck and clinging there, hot and intimate under my hair, pushing my forehead closer to his. I can feel my kill switch scar itch under his sweaty palm.

"Y-yes," I say quickly. "Sure. Call me Celestial."

He leans back, releasing me, and laughs, long and loud.

"Everyone!" Angel stands up as Compass leads Javier out of the range of the lamplight. "Meet Celestial!"

The girls rub their hands together, and I hear the name passed in whispers all the way to the far corners of the barn: *Celestial! Celestial!*

"Celestial is staying here for the night." He turns to me, cocking his head slightly. "Actually, Celestial, that was a lie. That was a lie, wasn't it?" He turns to them, with an air of a teacher announcing a holiday. "She's not going to be here just for the night. She's going to be here forever! Can't you feel it?"

"I FEEL IT!" Starbrite cries out, arms shooting over her head.

Angel takes my hand, and pulls me in for a long hug, then rears back and looks at me with that shrewd air of appraisal that's so completely at odds with everything he says.

"I feel you are a part of this Constellation. *Do you feel it, Celestial?*"

The crowd leans in to hear my answer.

"I feel it!" I cry feebly, not feeling it at all.

"All right, then! We feel it too!" Angel drops my hand, steps over the table, and smiles down at his followers, extending his hands to them.

Once he's in the middle of the crowd he turns and points at me, his eyes hard and glinting.

"Tonight we do a Star-Making for Celestial!"

A gasp goes through the barn. "Already?!" I hear someone whisper. Lightbeam is already on her feet, wrapping me in a constraining hug, and I see Starbrite over her shoulder, her lips curling back in a desperate smile that's more like a snarl.

"I had a feeling about you, Celestial, right from the start!" Starbrite weeps.

A knot of lanky girls knit themselves around me on all sides, wide-eyed and smiling, yet they don't seem to make eye contact with me as they congratulate me on entering The Constellation.

I just need to get in a room with Angel alone. That's all I need. Not whatever this is.

"Love Loft! Let's go, Brides!" Lightbeam cries, and with frantic, trembling pressure a dozen whippet-thin arms steer me toward a narrow back staircase hidden in the shadowy recesses of the barn.

I look over my shoulder, confused, to see Angel with his guitar hanging from his shoulder at the barn doors. He swings first one and then the other closed, then slides a heavy piece of lumber through the handles, bolting them shut.

*   *   *

The walls and ceiling of the hayloft have been painted black, and wild constellations of glow-in-the-dark star stickers are pasted everywhere. There are thousands of them, all the way up to the ceiling, covering even the support beams that span the width of the room almost ten feet over-head. I can just make out the dim green glow of stars on the vaulted ceiling, twinkling down at us from almost twenty feet above.

A half pyramid of hay bales takes up most of the room, the blocks of hay stacked into massive steps that climb into darkness. Sheets and blankets cover most of them, suggesting this is where dozens of "angels" sleep.

Cut out high in the opposite wall from the haystack is one giant square window. Wide enough to drive a truck through, with no screen, no glass, just an unfiltered view of the actual stars, and a baffled moon peering in. The moonlight is the only light in the room, a bright square of blue stamped across the broad wood planks of the floor.

"I've *never* seen Angel declare a Star-Making so fast," one of the girls mutters to Lightbeam, the trap door clapping closed behind her.

"I know," another agrees. "She just got here. How is she going to find the Sky Path—"

"Hey!" Starbrite snaps. "Let's not have any of that Earthly negativity. It's not our job to judge her. It's our job to get her ready for Angel." She turns and smiles at me again. "This is your night. Now take off your clothes."

"What?!" I shriek.

There's a scraping sound, and two of the Heavenly Brides drag a galvanized washtub in front of me, while another two girls strain to hold up and tilt the kind of five-gallon blue water container you usually see upside down in an office cooler. Water splashes heavily into the tub and a girl holding a bunch of dried herbs rips them into shreds and casts them into the water.

"You need your bath," Starbrite says, plucking at my peasant blouse. "Before you join with Angel."

"What is a Star-Making, exactly?" I stall desperately.

"Well . . ." Starbrite bites her lip. "The Constellation is one big relationship. We all relate to Angel emotionally, spiritually, and physically. We're not possessive, we're not into jealousy or ownership, but . . ." She tilts her head back and forth, eyes wide. "When someone new relates to him, we like to be involved. So we get you ready for the Star-Making, we witness your commitment with a family ritual, and then you have until dawn with Angel to be consummated as a Star."

"Consummated?"

The girls giggle.

"What, while all you of lie around and w-watch?!"

Starbrite shushes me like she's calming a skittish horse. "We want to hold your hand through it and be part of the experience."

"Um, no. No way." I shake my head. "I want us to . . . consummate or whatever *alone*. Just me and Angel. Please."

"That's never been done before," one of the girls mutters unhappily.

"There's a first time for everything," I snap.

"I can ask him, if you're sure that's what you want," Starbrite says disapprovingly.

"I'm sure."

She disappears back down the stairs. Without warning, Lightbeam jerks me toward the tub. I stumble forward, the metal edge biting into my bare shins. The water smells like mothy sweaters and rotted sage, the surface scattered with spiky weeds.

"Before we start with the bath, maybe I should break it to my boyfriend Hector that I'm a Star Bride now?" I suggest, as one of the girls sinks to my feet and wrestles off my shoes.

Lightbeam shakes her head. "He's with Compass, and Compass really shouldn't be told about the Star-Making until after it happens. Compass thinks enough Stars have been made."

"I'll bet," I mutter, then almost fall backward as the girl kneeling at my feet grabs my ankle and knee and forcibly plunges my leg into the washtub. The icy water has a heavy sheen to it, some kind of essential oil? To keep my balance I quickly step in with my other foot, and the other girls kneel around the tub, splashing water up past my knees and sponging my arms as I wince.

Another girl is fetching something from the top of the hay bales. She runs back down with something gauzy and white in her hands, then unfurls it in front of me.

"Ta-da!"

It's an old wedding dress from the '70s, with long sleeves and a flowing skirt and a thin, lacy bodice that narrows at the waist. There's no way I'll be able to fit it over my sheath without ripping the fabric. My best hope is to roll my sheath into my shorts as I take them off, ball the knife up in the thick denim and stow it away in the hay, where I can retrieve it later if I have to.

I really hope I don't have to.

But I'll have to manage this while they all watch me.

She holds it out to me, and I throw it over my head so the skirt covers the top half of me like a white organza tent. Very carefully, I tuck the sheath into the denim as I roll down my shorts. Despite the icy water, the small of my back is slick with sweat. I wriggle one leg from my shorts, then the other, then ball my blouse and tank top around them.

The girls help pull the bodice down and button up the back. I protectively wad the shorts up under my arm.

"I'll take the old clothes." Lightbeam snatches them from under my arm before I can jerk away.

CLACK-CLACK-CLACK!

With a clatter as loud as a hammer, my knife travels end over end across the wood floor and skids to a stop, spinning round and round in the full light of the window.

No one says anything for a long moment. Then Lightbeam walks over, picks it up, and turns it over in her hands, inspecting it calmly.

"Nice knife," she smiles at last. "But you need something to hold it better. Like this." She bends down and lifts her long cotton skirt, revealing a much larger knife tied just above her bony knee with a strap of leather.

No no no no.

"Anyway, you won't be needing it now." Lightbeam tucks it under her arm. "So I'll just hang onto it, okay?"

The other girls close in wordlessly. They grip my elbows, my shoulders, standing so close I can smell their unwashed hair, the half-raw meat on their breath. None of them are smiling anymore.

As they steer me out of the tub, the girl who was muttering before gets right in front of me. Her front two teeth overlap slightly. What are they going to do now? I can't move, they have my arms pinned to my sides. The others hold me tight as she pulls something from her pocket, a glint of metal flashing in the moonlight.

I wince back and swallow a scream as she holds up a tube of silver body paint.

"The finishing touch," she says. "Don't blink."

She grabs my chin, hard, and starts to line my eyes with her fingertip, daubed in the silver. I'm utterly defenseless. She's painting my face, but she could just as easily be slashing it, and there is nothing I could do to stop her.

BANG!

The door in the floor falls open again and Starbrite climbs back up. I can hear the sound of chanting floating up through the gaps between the broad old planks of the hayloft floor.

"Angel says *of course* you can have your Star-Making alone!" She takes both my hands in hers.

"Will Hector come?" I plead.

"No." Starbrite shakes her head, her grip tightening on my hands. "He's sleeping now. He said he needed to go to sleep."

Don't panic. Don't panic. Javier told them he needed to sleep so he could loop back to the barn. He's probably sneaking in right now, waiting for me to get Angel alone. He's fine. Everything is going to be fine. We have a plan. Just stick to the plan.

I hear the creak of many feet on the wooden stairs, the chanting from below growing louder and closer. The sound is truly terrifying, the atonal, mindless chanting a reminder of how many people Angel has at his command.

"Heaven is coming! Heaven is coming!"

Five girls come up the stairs, each holding something in their hands—some kind of bowls? They climb the stairs and form a circle under the hayloft window, in the glowing square of moonlight that slants across the floor.

Angel comes up the stairs last, wearing the exact same getup as before, except now there's a gold circle painted on his forehead. He grins at me and takes my hands from Starbrite, then leads me into the center of their circle, nodding, laughing a little, his eyes crinkling at the corners. Then he makes his hands into fists, brings them into his chest, and the chanting cuts off.

"I knew tonight was going to be *pretty cool*," he addresses the Heavenly Brides. "Didn't I tell you? Something good was headed our way!" He takes my hand and spins me around and all the girls laugh and whistle, like we're two prom dates getting our photos taken, not a man in his thirties getting ready to have sex with a teenage girl.

Starbrite takes something from the girls and brings it over to Angel, bowing as he takes it from her hands and lifts it toward the moon.

"A toast to the eternity of space," Angel says. "To seal our forever."

As the creamy moonlight bathes the bowl, I realize it's no bowl at all.

It's a skull.

An upside-down skull, the eyeholes blocked in, the jaw ripped off at the hinge.

As he hands it to me, the eerie green glow of the thousands and thousands of stickers on the walls seems to press closer, swirling around the edges of my vision in slow, queasy circles.

The skull's dry irregular surface fills the hollow of my hands. The joints under my thumbs are threaded with the vestiges of something now dried that was once juicy and strong. The sweet rotten smell I've been trying to place since I got here is at its strongest in the depths of the bowl, the skull, the thing I hold that used to be a human head.

"*Drink!*" someone calls from the back.

"Taste eternity!"

"You first," I tell Angel through clenched teeth. There's an awkward beat as he stares back at me. Then, grinning, he takes the skull and gulps from it, aggressively holding my gaze.

He hands it back to me and I pretend to drink, careful not to let any of the chemical-smelling liquid seep into my mouth. I hand it back and he passes it off to one of the girls, his eyes sparkling with mischief, not even close to fooled. Then he takes my hand tightly, pulling me closer, and turns to the room.

"Celestial has asked for the Star-Making to be private. I guess she's a little shy!" He pats my hand and giggles, and they all laugh along. "You guys go back to your tasks. I'll be down soon."

As they troop down the stairs a chill travels up my spine, but I shake it off. I've done the impossible. We are alone, at last, in the cavernous Love Loft, me and the target.

"So . . . ," I say weakly. "What now?"

Angel grins down at me, taking both my hands in his.

"How about a little talk?" He smiles. "Tell me, how are Kate and Dave doing these days?"

Chapter Twenty-Four

The Wedding Night

❧

I snatch my hands away as tumbler after tumbler of memories release and fit into place in my head:

The previous campers were all kicked out of camp when they were in their thirties.

"We won't go quiet."

Dog Mask had help, a beautiful device made by someone else, someone who wanted to kill us. Someone like Dennis's target, the paranoid genius hidden away in a compound?

Erik and Jada's target knew they were coming for her.

Starbrite said Angel had insisted on new visitors having copilots in the last few months.

That knowing look in Angel's eyes, his palm clamped over my kill switch scar: *That's not your name.*

There was only one way our targets could have known we were coming. We'd been sent out to kill the previous campers. The generation who trained before us.

"You went to camp, didn't you?" I fight to keep my voice calm. "You're a Class A too."

"We didn't have fancy names for it back then." Angel's smile deepens. "They just called us psycho killers. Not very politically correct! But then, they didn't have all that nasty technology either." He pats the back of his neck. "We just have scannable microchips, same as you'd put in a dog. You guys get the fancy names but you also gotta deal with those neat-o kill switches. So I'd say *you* got the short end of the stick."

"So all that 'teaching' about stars and angels is just . . ." I think of the girls downstairs, slavishly hanging on his every word. "Some *act?*"

"I needed an army." He looks at me seriously. "We knew you little kiddies were coming because we killed the class ahead of us. New class kills old class. That's the job interview. Back then, they seemed so old . . ." He laughs and shakes his head. "Some of us decided to prepare. Some of us had no intention of going quiet."

"Like the guy in the Dog Mask?"

"Mutt. Yes. Came through about a month ago, asked me if I wanted to come help him take you all out. How'd he go? Did Dave do it?"

"*We* killed him." I lift my chin.

"Well, *good for you*," Angel says sarcastically. "Guess what that wins you? A full-time job killing and cuttin' up some of the nastiest, dirtiest rats on this earth's surface. Five, six of 'em a year. You survive fifteen, sixteen, seventeen years of butcherin', then you'll wind up right in my shoes, with some little pissant showing up to take you out without even a first thought to why you should die."

He shakes his head, then leans heavily on his knees. "Hey, it was an honest question before: how *are* Kate and Dave?" His tone is casual but his stance is not relaxed. I shift my weight to my back foot.

"They're good."

"They always were a pair of suck-ups," he says flatly. "Worst campers in the place."

I shake my head, stunned by the thought. "Dave and Kate were campers?"

"Little goody two-shoes, the pair of 'em. Just about broke their arms clappin' themselves on the back when they got picked to stay behind and train the new recruits. Still. That's rough that Kate had to see Mutt taken out, they had, uh . . ." He wiggles his eyebrows. "Had quite *a thing* going for a while. Lots of hookups at camp! It was some wild times, man . . ." Angel leans forward then, his grin faltering.

"Speaking of which . . . you sure look like that one . . . don't tell me, Deer something . . . the one who killed Nene's little girl?"

". . . *What?*"

"Nene's little girl, who got her head cut off?" Angel says impatiently. I'm going to be sick.

I remember the sheet Dennis showed us. The one entry who had been pardoned. He means Nene like Janeane. Janeane who came from a powerful family, and had gotten pregnant when she was sixteen.

"Janeane got pregnant . . . at camp?"

"Oh yeah," Angel says with a dark smile. "Nene's fancy family got her out for the baby's sake. When she and the kid popped up in the news, well, we were *all* following that case."

The newspapers about Rose's murder that I found in the pantry, I'd assumed they were saved because they were about me. But they were saved because they were about *Janeane*.

"'Specially Dave, I'm sure," Angel says. "Seeing as how the little girl was his kid."

Dave's face, the first day he met me, the way he'd spilled out the crime scene photos and jeered that I didn't feel remorse. The way he'd saved me the bleeder that looked like Rose, and pushed me harder than anyone else. Because Rose was his . . . daughter?

Impossible. But my head starts spinning. Rose's grandparents had put aside a trust for her that couldn't be touched until she turned eighteen. Why not just give it to Janeane? Or have her move back in? They wanted to keep their distance from Janeane. Because she was a teen killer.

Rose had said her mom was always snooping around her room. The message board had said Janeane had found the pentagram necklace that linked Rose to Jaw.

I had thought Erik was saying that Tom, Rose's stepdad, had killed Rose. That Tom was obsessed with controlling Rose, and could have followed Jaw to the shed. But the killer had drugged the thermos, that was one of Erik's three main points. How would Tom know about the thermos in the floor? That was a detail only someone close to Jaw would know. And if Jaw was taking Janeane to his hookup spot, then they were . . . hooking up?

That would explain why Mr. Moody was such a secret. Jaw couldn't risk his ex, Janeane, finding out he was with *her daughter*, Rose. Maybe he sensed how disturbed she was. Rose had known a long time. I just hadn't taken her seriously.

From Janeane's point of view, Rose was about to get her "rightful" inheritance in a month. Then she found the necklace, and realized Rose had taken Jaw as well. *She* drugged the thermos, intending to kill Rose and frame Jaw if they ever met in the shed. To punish them both. The burning smell from my dream. The skinny nightmare creature. That was my drugged memory of Janeane clearing the scene with bleach, just like they trained her to at camp.

"Good times, good times," Angel says, shifting his weight forward. "So you and the guy you're with, you're together too, huh?"

"You can ask him," I say coolly. "When he gets here."

Angel's eyebrows go up. "Is that what you're waiting for? I wouldn't hold my breath. He's where Compass put him now."

"And where's that?"

"Root cellar," Angel says, rising to his feet in one powerful gesture. "I call it the 'guest house' when I want someone shut up in there."

No no no no.

"She either cut him or drugged him—probably she drugged him. Compass doesn't like blood. That's why she doesn't come to Star-Makings." He cracks his knuckles and then his neck. "She likes the Heavenly Weddings all right, but she has a hard time watching me, uh, 'release an angel back into a star.'"

It's important I do not flinch. I must not show fear. I must not show weakness. I force myself to grin.

"So that's what you've been doing out here?"

He imitates my smile, a mocking gesture, and then drops it.

"You're no good at bravado, little girl. I'd say you're shaking in your shoes, but I always have them remove the shoes. In case I got a kicker on my hands." We circle each other. His arm is angled so his hand hovers at his hip. He grows still. Too still. Like a bowstring pulled back before it's let go. What is he waiting for? *Why not just attack me?*

"Alright. Show me what you got," he snaps.

Of course: he's waiting for me to make the first move. He wants to see what they're teaching us at camp these days.

"Your girls took my knife."

"So what, you want me to give you a weapon to kill me with?"

"Unless you're afraid of a fair fight."

He laughs again. "Nothing fair about this. You know how many targets I've taken out in the last fifteen years? I could break you with my bare hands."

"So let me have a knife then." I lift my chin. "Unless you're afraid."

"You're the one backing away," he says, and there's a flash at his hip as he unsheathes the bowie knife.

Then he sets it on the floor and kicks it my way.

He holds out his arms. "Come and get it."

I move to pick up the knife, but I am quick, or too relieved. Something betrays me, because as I snatch it up his tongue flashes out of his mouth and licks his lips in animal anticipation.

He knows I'm prey.

Run.

I feint right, and then as he lunges left toward the trap door I turn around and run in the other direction, toward the hay bales, racing up the tall stacks as he rages after me.

"What the hell is this?! You can't even hold the thing right!"

I scrabble up the scratchy hay, slipping on the blankets and dirty sheets, clutching the knife in my hands with the blade stuck out to the side. If I can make it to the beam, I can climb up and out of reach. Get across the beam to the open window, climb down—

A hand closes on my ankle, and he swings me by my leg, throwing me sideways down the stack of hay bales. I go end over end and feel my skin crushed between my bones and the floor, my breath knocked out of me by the impact.

Before I can roll to my side he's above me, the black sole of his bare foot across my throat. He stares down at me, not even winded. I hold the knife with both hands against my own chest, which rises and falls, rises and falls, faster and faster.

"I had a feeling Nene did it." He bends down, peering into my eyes. "Not a lot of maternal instinct in that one." He shakes his head. "So you didn't even kill anyone, huh, little girl? Man, that's tough."

His foot is so hard against my neck I can't answer. I can't breathe, there's only a thin thread of air getting through, it's not enough. My heart is trying to punch through my straining chest.

"Man, that's got to be the worst luck I ever heard." My vision swims, I can only hear his voice. "A *zero* gets sent to camp for killing the counselor's kid!" The floor feels strangely hot under my back, and the stars swirl above me, looping down and around and evaporating in front of my eyes.

"And then you get assigned *to kill me?!* To kill *me*. You! Oh man!!"

Angel releases his foot from my neck and air rushes back into my lungs. It tastes unmistakably of smoke. I sit up, gulping it anyway, my vision clearing as he sits down on the hay bale across from me, throws his head back, and laughs.

I hoist myself up to my feet, the knife still in my hand. The smell of smoke is getting stronger.

"Hey—" He stretches out his arms, grinning at me. "Come here. Come give me a stab."

I stand there panting and cupping my sore throat, gritty from the sole of his foot.

"Come on!" He beckons with one hand. "Come on, little girl! Come stab me! Clear shot, right to the heart, have at it."

I roll the handle of the bowie knife in my hands, holding it properly, and take a wary step toward him. His eyes are sparkling.

"It's not a trick!" he sings out merrily. "I just know you're too chicken to stab someone. I know that *for a fact*."

I stumble toward him, gritting my teeth. Javier is in a cellar. Even if by some miracle he's okay, and I don't kill this guy, we'll both be dead.

This man is *evil*. He preys on girls. He brainwashes them. He's built up a personal army of ruined lives.

Angel tips his head back, eyes closed, arms outstretched, a dopey smile on his face. It could be the drugs are making him act erratic. Or it could be complete contempt.

I grip the knife with both hands and raise it level with my face. I'm right over him. One down stroke and the knife goes into his heart. I stand there, trembling so hard my teeth chatter.

He peeks open one eye and starts hooting again.

"What stops you?" he asks, flabbergasted. "What in the world stops you?"

Nothing. Nothing will stop me. I have to do this. I have to do this. I have to do this.

I have to do this!

I bring the knife down through the air with all my strength, yelling out loud as the blade breaks his skin and buries itself in flesh, and then I spring away, unable to bear the sensations any longer.

I've buried the knife maybe three inches in his right shoulder. Because I couldn't go for the heart.

Because I'm not a killer. I never was, I never will be. No matter what the Wylie-Stanton diagnosed me as. I am not the Girl From Hell. My fate is mine to choose. My knees buckle and I burst into tears of relief as the nightmare fears of a year release me at last.

And then Angel swings out and seizes me, his laughter echoing through the loft. His fingers tear at my flesh as he wrenches me toward him, the fabric of my sleeve ripping from the force.

"You poor little *idiot*." He laughs, the knife still quivering in his shoulder.

He reaches up and takes the knife out of his shoulder with a swift jerk. Barely a flesh wound. He lays the blade flat against the fine hairs of my cheek, and slowly wipes his blood off on my skin. First one side, then the other, smearing stripes of blood across my face, his laughter in my ears as I try to twist my head away.

"Aww, are those tears? Were you *crying* at the thought of killing me?" he howls. "What could make *anyone* that *stupid?* That *weak?*"

My head falls back, and that's when I see it. A dark shape silhouetted by the neon stars overhead. A shape like a shoulder, on a figure lying prone on the beam just above us.

Angel looks up, following my gaze, and as he does the figure drops, like a leopard leaping down on its prey from a tree.

I scramble back as they sprawl across the floor. Hot, orange light streams in through the space between the floorboards, and glowing curls of smoke drift around Erik's face—Erik's beautiful, focused face—as he knocks Angel to the floor, grabs Angel's head with both hands and jerks hard to one side.

It takes both hands pressed to my mouth to keep from screaming as Angel rolls away, clearly shaken, his hands reaching for his neck.

Erik, all in black, waits for him to get up.

Standing but unsteady, Angel turns on Erik with a roar. Erik is ready for him, both arms out, his teen idol smile spreading across his face.

They circle each other the way we circled each other a moment before, but there's no taunting or laughter from Angel now. An animal silence hangs between them, and Angel's jerky feints forward, his quick, clumsy lunges, seem desperate across from Erik's self-possessed calm. When he pretends to pounce, Erik doesn't even flinch.

"Look, kid—" Angel starts in, and that's when Erik strikes. He grabs Angel's hand holding the knife and snaps Angel's fingers backward while sinking his teeth—*actually sinking his teeth*—into the wound I made in Angel's shoulder.

Angel lets out an agonized yell, and the knife clatters to the floor.

Everything happens very fast: Erik punches him, once, twice, three times hard in the gut, and while Angel struggles to get his breath back, Erik snatches up the knife and they grapple, Angel howling and snapping his teeth, Erik's face utterly blank.

The smoke billows up from the first story, a gray veil rising between us just as Erik twists Angel on his back, and stray pieces of chaff light up as the hay behind me rips into flame. I spin around to see tongues of fire zipping up to the tall ceiling, then turn back to where they were fighting a moment before.

It's just a wall of black smoke.

"Erik?!"

A figure all in black comes through the smoke, and I see his red, bloody mouth and, more horrible, the look in his eyes, and know he's won.

"Signal!"

The flames roar behind us as more of the hay catches, and Erik reaches out his hand. The tendons stand out strangely in his wrist and neck, and down at his side he's flicking the tightly held knife again and again on his pants, compulsively, and I understand that he is not yet done.

"Come here," he says through gritted teeth.

The smoke from the fire sends my gauzy skirt rising in a white cloud around us as I step forward and take his hand. He spins me around, my back almost bouncing off his chest, and says something I can barely make out over the flames.

"I'm sorry—this is the only way—"

"Erik, what are you doing?!"

"Setting you free," he answers, his mouth right against my ear, his arm crossing over my chest.

And with those words his knife slides into my neck.

Chapter
Twenty-Five
Wound Assessment

❧

As the blade cuts through my flesh I kick backward. *Go for his knee, his outer thigh. Remember what Javier told you, dig in with your elbows—stomach, instep, go!*

In a fury of embarrassed rage, I stomp on his instep, dig my elbows backward, but he grips me tighter, the knife ripping deeper as I struggle, hot blood pouring down my shoulder.

"Signal, stop, I'm trying to help—"

Another stomp on his instep and I'm loose, running through the smoke, toward the window. And then, impossibly, Javier appears above me; he straddles the windowsill, lit up by the inferno below.

Javier twists the end of a rope to some kind of fastening under the tall square windowsill, then rappels down the wall, onto the steaming floor of the burning hayloft, lifting the collar of his shirt up over his mouth to screen the smoke.

"What took you so long?!" Erik calls to him. "Could you hold her, please?"

Javier's expression is hidden behind his shirt as he grabs my arms and grips me like a vice. "Javier, NO!" I plead, choking on the burning air. He grabs my hair, yanks it into a tail and pulls my head to one side as Erik steps behind me.

"You got her?"

Javier's voice, muffled: "Just hurry, all right?"

Erik's fingers dig into the wound, right above my kill switch scar. My scream is lost in the sound of fire and something else, a knocking, a beating like a drum. Javier is saying something over and over I can't make out, and the drum-like beating grows louder and fiercer.

"It's out!" Erik bellows. "Take her and go! GO!"

Just as suddenly as he grabbed me, Javier releases me, and I turn to see Erik holding a chrome pill blinking like a firefly. He drops it between the broad planks of the floor, letting it fall into the fire below.

He's cut out my kill switch.

I grab Erik's arms, the fire behind him so bright I can't make out his face.

"Signal, GO." He yells before I can say anything, pushing me toward Javier.

CRACK!

The trap door flies open and the Heavenly Brides, faces streaked with ash, start pulling themselves up from the floor.

Javier's hand closes around my arm and he pulls me toward the rope still swinging from the hayloft window.

"Erik! Come on!" I scream.

Javier pulls me up after him, up the rough timbers of the inside of the barn. I clutch at the rope, the gash in my neck still streaming as I climb. I get one arm over the windowsill and turn back around, wringing the blood from my open wound. I don't care, I have to make sure he's behind us.

"ERIK?!"

Below us the crowd of Angel's followers have circled the end of the rope, their faces twisted masks of rage, their hands clawing out toward me, their shrieking at a fever pitch.

"Hell demon! Murderer!"

They want to pull me down and rip me to pieces, but they can't, because Erik is crouched in a battle stance, knife out, ready to take them all on.

"ERIK!" I cry down to him. "Come on!"

But he doesn't turn around. He doesn't take his eyes off them. What is he doing?! Even if he could fight them all, the room is a hell of fire and heat. I scream to Erik again, but Javier, who is now side-saddle on the windowsill, grabs me up and pulls me tight against his chest.

"NO!" I fight against him. *"ERIK!"* I need to climb back down, but Javier tilts forward and we fall into the night, but then somehow fly out and across at an angle, shooting over the ground in a low swoop that ends with us sprawling across cold grass far from the barn.

Javier had fastened the rope to a post fifty yards from the hayloft window, and used that as a zip line away from the burning building. The few cult members outside don't notice us. They're too busy trying to save the barn and members inside with a pathetic makeshift fire brigade. Javier tries to lead me toward the fence, but I tear myself away.

Panting and coughing, I hurl myself toward the barn, or what used to be the barn and is now just a raging red fire caged in black timbers.

"ERIK!" I sprint toward the barn, my voice breaking into a hoarse wheeze. *"ERIK, PLEASE!"* I try to yell, but it comes out like a seagull cry.

With a thunder crack the loft falls in on the first story, its timbers crumbling into piles of molten red jewels, a pillar of smoke soaring up through the night sky, flames roaring with a sound like applause as they swallow the barn.

"NO!" I scream, sobbing, fighting to free myself from Javier's grasp. I bend in half over his arm, trying desperately to get loose.

"We have to go!" Javier coughs, dragging me away. "Signal, we have to go!"

Javier impatiently throws me over his shoulder and starts running for the back fence. I try to yell for Erik again but my voice is gone, it's all gone.

Just outside the fence Ray is waiting, not with the bikes, but idling in the Volvo. Javier gets us into the back seat and before he's even slammed the door shut Ray guns the motor and we fly across the moonlit field, the car bucking and jouncing over brush and clots of earth. Sobbing, I turn to stare at the column of smoke we've left behind.

"We have to go back!" I rasp.

"The cops are going to be here soon," Ray yells. "Trust me, Jenny, you don't want to stick around!"

"There's no way we can help him now," Javier says softly, rocking me in his lap. "This is what he wanted. He wanted you out."

Javier gently lifts my blood-drenched hair from the back of my neck and I hear him suck his breath in through his teeth.

"Oh hell, man, what happened to her?!" Ray yells. "She needs stitches, man! We gotta get her to a hospital!"

"We'll handle it in the room." Javier carefully rips my torn sleeve off, balling it up and pressing it to the back of my neck.

Their voices seem far away. I keep seeing Erik, knife out, holding back the crowd so we could escape. I keep hearing the crack as the barn sank in on itself, the horrible red heat. I can't bear to think of him in there. I can't bear it.

* * *

Ray hands me a flask as I sit on the floor of the motel room, my white dress half scarlet from my blood.

"You'll need it for the pain," he says quietly.

I take the bottle from his hand, unscrew the top and tilt my head back. The alcohol sears my raw throat on the way down.

"What happened?" I wince. Javier threads a needle from a small hotel sewing kit and Ray peels off his bandanna, which is stiff with sweat, and lets out a heavy sigh.

"When I went out to get my bike, your friend Erik appeared out of nowhere. And I mean *nowhere*. I thought he was one of Angel's followers at first, but he said he was with you guys and had your car parked down the road, and how could he help. I told him to give me the keys and I'd take the car around the back fence—it'd be an easier getaway than the bikes—and that you both were in the barn. He threw me the keys and took off. I walked the bikes past the fence, parked the car out back, and took a nap for a while. Still gotta go get those bikes," he says pointedly to Javier. "After you get her sewn up, you can drive me and my buddy out."

Javier, who has been holding the needle in the flame of Ray's lighter all this time, pulls it away and shakes it, then hands the lighter back to him.

"Soon as I get this done,"

"Well." Ray takes the lighter and stands, looking down on me uneasily. "I need a smoke." He walks out, and Javier gently pinches the flesh together at the back of my neck.

"This is going to hurt."

He tilts the flask over the wound and the burning makes me ball my fists, but it's welcome. I absorb all of it but it's still not enough to distract me.

"What happened with you?" I wheeze.

Javier's needle breaks through first one and then the other side of my wound, and there is the itchy pull of thread dragging through skin as Javier explains.

"When I went out with Compass, she led me out to some cellar and called three guys over. They were trying to wrestle me down the stairs, and they probably would have, except Erik came out of nowhere. We ended up locking the four of them in there instead."

He lets out a sigh and begins the second stitch.

"Erik told me then he'd driven out to an internet station to check in on some chat thread he had with Dennis, and they messaged back and forth. So the good news is, Dennis is still alive."

"Oh, thank God!" I gasp. "Where is he? Is he safe?"

"Erik said after Dennis turned off your switch, he turned off his own and Nobody's. But HQ caught on and started locking everything down, so he and Nobody cut their switches out, ditched their phones, and drove to LA. But the Director rerouted Jada and Kurt to go after them."

Rage heats my face. Javier's needle bites through my skin for the third time, and I feel the pinch as he gently pulls the stitch through.

"How could Jada and Kurt do that?" I wince.

"They didn't have a choice," Javier sighs. "It was either bring Dennis in or get their kill switches tripped. Dennis didn't have time to turn off all of ours."

He hands me the flask. "Have some more of this, you're shaking too much."

I choke down more. When I set it down it falls on its side, empty, and the room rocks gently around me.

"So then what? Go on."

"Jada and Kurt are currently escorting Nobody and Dennis back to camp, but they agreed to look the other way while Dennis got online and explained what went down to Erik. They figured Erik needed to know, since Kate was getting the switches back online and would have them all up and running again in a few hours. So Erik cut his out, and came back to get yours."

"What? Erik cut out his kill switch?" I'm so confused. "How? Dennis never turned off Erik's kill switch."

"Yes he did, yesterday, before we got to Ojai," Javier says quietly. "When Dennis told him you'd volunteered your kill switch, Erik insisted Dennis do his first. In case something went wrong."

It's like a punch to the gut. I cup both hands over my mouth.

"Hold still, hold still," Javier says.

Erik volunteered his kill switch in my place. And I'd told him he didn't understand real strength. That he didn't know what it was to really help someone.

And he hadn't said a word.

"Back at Owl's Nest," Javier goes on, "after the cellar, I filled him in on our plan. We snuck back around to the barn and heard you were upstairs. I knew I'd need a rope to get us out of the hayloft, since all the cult members were waiting for Angel to get done with you. I went to fix up the zipline while Erik tried to find a way in." He swallows, hard. "You know the rest."

It's a while before I can speak.

"And the fire?"

Javier shakes his head. "When I was looking for rope around the barn, someone saw me. I knocked over one of the lanterns to distract them." He snips the thread, and then there's a sigh as he sits back against the bed. "It was my fault."

I turn, very carefully, to stare at him.

"I thought they'd be able to put it out," Javier says, not looking in my eyes. "I didn't realize how fast everything . . . the hay and everything, you know, I didn't know . . ."

"You didn't mean to . . ."

"Of course not!" Javier cries angrily. I close my eyes, the room rolling around me. It's tempting to just push it all on Javier. To absolve myself that way. It would be easier to pretend Javier caused Erik's death than to that it's all my fault.

Both our phones go off, and Javier picks his up. I reach for mine but he knocks it away.

"Hello? Director? Yes, it's safe to talk. I'm fine but Signal . . . Signal is dead. Yes, that's her phone. We left them in the room before going into the compound."

He puts my phone down. It continues to ring beside me.

"Yes, Erik too. He came to help us out, I guess . . . In a fire, yes. I saw it myself. I can give a full, uh, debriefing or whatever when I get back. Okay. Really? Okay. Thank you, sir. We'll speak again tomorrow."

He clicks off the call and looks at me, his eyes flat.

And just like that, I'm just another in the body count for the Teen Killers Club.

* * *

Is this a nightmare? My eyes open from a hazy half sleep. I could swear I hear Erik moving around under the bed. But it's just a dream. I sit up, fighting to catch my breath, when I hear banging at the window. Nobody? No.

My eyes open, I wake up again. *That* was the nightmare, this is real. But who is that standing at the end of the bed? Is it the Director? His hand is extended, my switch is back in my neck somehow, it's about to go off—

I wake up again, blankets pulled over my head. They're so heavy, I can't pull them off, they're suffocating me.

With a strangled, soundless scream I lurch out of the bed, awake at last, and throw myself out into the first light of dawn, gulping the open air of the parking lot. I stumble to the car, the same car where Erik kissed me not even a day before, curl up in the front seat, and sob, a pathetic wheezing sob, because my voice is gone.

A tap on the glass beside my head. I turn on the engine and roll the window down.

"Come on," Javier says gruffly, face thick with sleep. "I'll drive you to the bus station, get in the passenger seat."

"My stuff?" I croak.

"I packed it all up." Javier moves to the back of the car and throws open the trunk so he can toss my stuff inside. The driver's side door dings in measured alarm as I get out, wobble around the back, and slide into the passenger seat.

"Camp can't track you anymore," Javier says once we've pulled out of the parking lot, "But if someone sees you and recognizes you, and camp finds out you're still alive—"

"I won't let that happen."

"They'll debrief me. I might slip up. So you need to go as far and as fast as you can. Mexico maybe."

"And you?" I ask dully. "And Jada? And Troy, and Nobody, and Dennis? What's going to happen to you?"

"We'll see you in seventeen years or so."

"Javier," I wheeze. "It's a lie, you don't get retired, Angel told me—"

"*Don't*," he cuts me off, his voice so sharp it surprises me, and his bloodshot gaze cuts from the road to meet mine. "Please. Don't."

"You don't want the truth?!"

"If the truth is I'm doomed, then no," Javier says quietly.

The drive to the bus depot is quiet. We spot a police car in the lot, so Javier parks on the street and carries my backpack and bedroll for me as I get a ticket on the first bus headed out of town, departing in twenty minutes.

"You're not doomed," I promise. "I'm going to find a way to get you guys out of camp."

He looks so exasperated for a moment, then he says slowly and with great intention: "That's not what Erik wanted. He did what he did because you deserve to be free."

My hands cover my face and his arms go around me, he holds me so tight. His head pulls back, and his mouth is so close. Just twenty-four hours ago it would have been natural to kiss him. Now it's unthinkable. And then his arms slide away, a tide receding from a hostile shore.

The bus's lights go on, the doors sigh open, and I move toward them, when Javier's hand catches my elbow.

"See?" he says, and in a last moment of contact, his finger drags on the inside of my arm, the blank spot where the dandelion used to be. "It was fun while it lasted." Javier smiles sadly. "Bye, gorgeous."

And he walks away without looking back.

*   *   *

I sit in the very back of the bus. The seats begin to fill, but it's like everyone knows to leave me alone. Maybe it's because my face is swollen from crying. Or because I smell like smoke. Or because I'm about to cry again, watching Javier's car slip into the flow of traffic.

When he gets to camp, will everyone be circled round the fire with s'mores, ready to embrace him? Or will they have all changed from the people I knew? Are they scarred from their encounters with the hardened assassins who graduated camp? And if they aren't, how long will it take? Another target, another two targets? How long before everything human in them is chipped away, kill by kill, until they're all just like Dog Mask?

No. I won't stand for it. I will go back to Ledmonton. I have the safety deposit box key Erik found. I will figure out where it fits. I will clear my name, and then expose camp for what it is. I will end the program, I will save my friends, and that is what all of this will have been for.

But when I consider what has been lost: his mind, his voice, his smile. It's not enough. Nothing will ever be enough again.

I knit my hands over my mouth and curl over with a sob as someone sinks heavily into the seat next to me.

"Well, well, well," he croaks.

I whip around as though I've been slapped.

He's singed, his eyes riddled with red veins making them the green-est they've ever been. His hair must have burnt because he never would have cut it that short otherwise.

"Didn't even need three weeks." The slow, wolfish grin lights up his face as he leans, wincing a little, back in his seat. "All it took was one night thinking I was gone."

Erik. My Erik. Alive and well.

"Admit it, Signal." Erik smiles. "You love me."

I could kill him.

Acknowledgments

This book would not have been possible without the enthusiasm and faith of my literary agent, Stacia Decker. My sincere thanks to Matt Martz for bringing this story out into the world, and to Ashley Di Dio, Sylvan Creekmore and Melissa Rechter at Crooked Lane Books, for making this literary process so deeply rewarding.

I am grateful to my parents Richard and Barbara Sparks for always valuing creativity and imagination, and to my sisters Cinnamon and Allison for their love, excitement, and being the world's best baby-sitters! Personal thanks are due to Darren Herczeg, who told me to share this manuscript with the pros. Thank you to Jason Micallef, who's taught me so much about telling stories. And thank you to the coolest senior in the world, Price Peterson, without whom my writing/life would be dark indeed.

But most importantly I want to thank my husband Ryan Sandoval for believing in my dreams. And for filling so many days of Lovey's first year with magic, while mom went off and typed.